AF470521

GOD IN THE MACHINE

COLE MARTYN

MESSIER PUBLISHING

First published in Great Britain in 2020 by Messier Publishing

A CIP catalogue record of this book is available from the British Library

ISBN 978-1-8384-0610-3

First Edition

www.godinthemachine.co.uk

For my boys,
Per Aspera Ad Astra

1

———————

RESISTANCE

"Rage. The legacy of our forefathers. To rage against a dying planet. A world in ruin, our species on the path to oblivion. But from the ashes, rose a new dawn."

Autarch Vicentine paused and looked down at the scores of people gathered beneath his gold-plated podium. Thousands of wide-eyes stared back at him in anticipation, desperate to hear his every word. A stout man with a scarred, bald head, the high collar of his black military overcoat extenuated his pale, sunken features.

"When the governments of the world failed to act, left you stranded and exposed to face nature at its most deadly, who rose to your defence? The Republic?" Vicentine let the silence linger long enough for the crowd below to stir.

"No…it was the Sovereign." He raised his hand to quieten the crowd as they erupted into wild applause, hollering and screaming his name.

"When our planet turned against us, my men built the great walls that shelter us from the elements, those walls still shield you to this day. We bleed for our common goals, striving forward for the glory of the Sovereign." Vicentine hammered his fist against the podium.

"When the cowards in the Republic begged us for help, we did not turn our backs like those before us. We did not walk away from the challenge and leave mankind to fade into extinction. Democracy they cried, the sycophants in their ivory towers. Demanding saviour while the world around them crumbled into dust. The Republic led us into oblivion. But in humanity's darkest hour, an opportunity arose, for a new world. Not led by cowardice and weakness, but by strength, and power…" Vicentine stepped back and took in a deep breath.

"Power over nature!" He roared, raising his clenched fist high into the air, saluting the masses.

"Today, until the end of days, the Sovereign shall stand as the last bastion of mankind." His words rang out as the enormous projection screens displaying his speech cut to images of the crowds packed into the city square.

"Children of the Citadel, on this sacred day I promise you. We will destroy those dogs that call themselves 'The Army of Shadows'. Freedom fighters…dissidents…terrorists," Vicentine accentuated every word.

"Call them what you want, the consequence will be the same; complete and utter extermination. There shall be no mercy for the enemies of the Sovereign. For too long this resistance has threatened our way of life, our very existence is at stake. If we do not defeat this scourge, this affront to our beliefs, they will drag us back to the dark ages, living like scavengers in reliance upon this pitiful planet."

Vicentine spat out the words with such vitriol the veins around his throat bulged to prominence. A twisted smile broke across his face as he carefully straightened the red armband he wore over his uniform. The Sovereign flags adorning his palace fluttered in the evening breeze as a sense of excitement gripped the crowd. Vicentine snapped his heels to attention and raised the Sovereign salute, beating his fist against his chest before lifting it high into the air.

"Our future is bright, out there amongst the stars lies the hope of a better world, a planet of unlimited resources. Our leading scientists are working tirelessly to identify and locate a new planet which will be humanity's home for generations to come. We shall break free from the shackles that tie us to this husk and finally, take back control of our own fate. Soon… very soon…I shall reveal our plans for humanity's next great leap. But at this crucial point, we must pull together. Unite in the face of adversity. Therefore, to ensure we can maintain good order and public safety, with immediate effect, I will be authorising new emergency powers to the Senate. Now more than ever, we need the tools required to hunt down and destroy our enemies."

The crowd below began to grow restless, and people started to struggle against the cordon, trying to push past the guards. Somebody snuck through the barriers leading up to Vicentine's palace while the guards dealt with a scuffle that had broken out nearby. The man leapt up the steps, taking them two at a time, his gaze fixated on Vicentine. A metal baton smashed against his shins, causing him to crash into the concrete steps, cracking his head against the floor.

A soldier wearing a carbon-fibre exoskeleton pointed to the man with his baton. Two police officers dressed in riot gear came running over, they hauled up the man and dragged his limp body back towards the crowd.

"It is on this day we gather here to celebrate the technology that saved us from nature's destructive force. We honour the sacrifices of those that went before us as we once again resurrect the Iron Lung!" Vicentine pointed to a colossal cannon in the distance, the tip of its giant steel barrel barely visible over the towering buildings of the city skyline.

"From this day until the end of days, power over nature!" Vicentine's hand, still raised in the air, slowly lowered as the city trembled under the thunderous roar of the cannons.

The sky was set ablaze with a radiant blue fire that hung from the clouds above, shimmering brilliantly. Vicentine stepped away from his podium and walked out to the edge of his platform. He waved to the people below and then snapped his heels together to give the Sovereign salute one final time. The crowds shrieked as they struggled to catch a glimpse of Vicentine before he disappeared from view, returning to the safety of his palace. A vast stone fortress with a glass dome at its heart that overlooked the city square.

The drones hovering overhead swooped down to the surging crowds below, focussing their cameras on the people screaming in adulation and waving Sovereign banners high into the air. The massive projection screens situated throughout the city cut to the images of riot police storming out of the palace and making their way down the stone steps. The heavily armed police tussled with the baying crowd, striking them with the butts of their assault rifles and shoving them back. People scrambled to escape the violence as the police marched forward.

"Can we go yet Dash?" Benoît said as he shook his head and looked away from the screen. "I don't think I can take much more of this."

"Yeah, we've seen enough," Dash said as the few people gathered around it began to disperse.

"What do you think he means by emergency powers?"

"Tiberius got some intel before we left, he didn't share the details with me, but it didn't sound good."

They turned away from the giant screen, and their shadows stretched across the run-down city square. In Sam's Town, no one had time for the Sovereign, they had lived through enough propaganda to know the truth. The Earth was dead, and Vicentine would never find the planet he had been promising. In the slums, you didn't think about the future you tried to survive the day.

"Things can't get much worse in this city, can they?" Benoît grumbled.

"Don't underestimate the Sovereign," Dash said as he stared up at the fiery blue clouds.

Another thunderous barrage of artillery fire sounded off in the distance. The noise from the colossal ion cannons was deafening. Part of the Sovereign's early forays into geo-engineering. The cannons maintained a manageable climate within the Citadel by creating a synthetic ozone layer above it, every year they blasted the air with a barrage of sulphur dioxide particles to block out the sun's rays. Dash and Benoît stood for a few moments marvelling at the grotesque sight above them.

"You think we can win this war?" Benoît asked as he shook his head in disgust.

"Against an enemy who would do this?" Dash replied, not

looking away from the sapphire storm growing overhead. "We don't have a choice."

Dash's mind drifted home. He longed to return to Albion, to be reunited with his family. He had already missed so much of his son's life. The days turning into months, the months into years. Before he knew it, his baby boy was a stubborn ten-year-old he hardly even recognised. He promised his wife before he left, this would be his last deployment to the Citadel. She almost believed him this time. But how could he ever walk away from this fight? If they didn't stop the Sovereign, his son wouldn't have a home to grow up in.

"Come on, we better get moving; Maelstrom should be arriving soon. We can't afford to be late." He pointed down a dimly lit side street separating two dilapidated buildings.

Dash caught a glimpse of himself in the window of a tech supply store on the edge of the square; his features illuminated by the bright neon sign hanging above. He'd lost weight, six weeks beyond the wire gathering intel for the Shadows had taken its toll. His skin was pale and tired from a lack of sleep. Moving at night had been easy for a while, but now he looked exhausted. He swept his hair back; his thick brown mane had grown long and unkempt since he entered the Citadel, it made him look like a local, and that was exactly what he wanted.

Dash and Benoît hurried down the alleyway and made their way towards a market up ahead. Staying in one place for too long was a bad idea. The cameras situated throughout the city tracked the movements of everyone, but in Sam's Town, most of them had been destroyed in the riots. The police came in sporadically to repair them, but they couldn't keep up with the rate of destruction. Every time they installed a new camera, it got taken down by another enraged citizen. That was how the Shadows liked it, operating off the Sovereign's radar.

"So how do we know we aren't walking into a trap?" Benoît asked.

"We don't," Dash said flatly. "But the stakes are too high, we have to meet him."

"How will we know it's him? Do you even know what he looks like?"

"Don't worry about that. That's my problem, you're here to provide security, okay." Dash said as he jabbed his finger into Benoît's chest.

"Doesn't mean I have to like it," Benoît muttered to himself as he patted the pistol concealed under his jacket.

Sam's Town was not a pleasant place to be at the best of times, but at night it took a turn for the worse. They walked into a small clearing, a few flickering street lamps created a light hue, illuminating the burnt-out vehicles and crumbling buildings surrounding them. They hurried across the clearing, avoiding eye contact with a group of hooded figures deep in discussion around the smouldering wreck of a car.

As Dash and Benoît headed out of the clearing, they spotted an enormous power station in the distance, wherever you went in Sam's Town its shadow loomed over you. The old brick buildings looked tiny next to the gigantic circular fortress that was the SYCO power station. A monstrous maze of metal and thick, char stained concrete, its towering metallic vents pumped out a constant stream of thick black smoke.

They came to the end of the clearing and walked down some steps into a bustling marketplace. A flash of flame drew Dash's gaze, he turned and saw a street vendor cooking something in a large pan. Dash looked at the street stall; a small neon sign hung above with something written in a language he didn't understand. Several people sat on stools along the outskirts of a small corrugated steel hut, leaning against the bar as they ate out of bowls.

Making their way through the crowds, they passed several market stall owners selling raw food produce, most of which appeared to be well past its best. Benoît was so busy looking at the items on offer he walked straight into the back of a police officer patrolling the market. Benoît took a step back and looked at the officer and his partner; both wore matching black body armour, their faces hidden behind a reflective helmet. The officer lowered the assault rifle he was carrying.

"Watch where you're going, punk." The officer said sternly, Benoît stood his ground, staring at his reflection in the helmet.

"Sorry officer," Dash smiled as he grabbed Benoît by the shoulder and tried to pull him away.

Benoît glared at the police officer, who's reflective helmet retracted to reveal his face. He looked tired and grizzled, his left eye had been replaced with an augmentation; an ocular impact that glowed a deep shade of red as it focused in on Benoît.

"What you staring at boy?" The officer poked Benoît in the chest with his mechanical finger.

"My buddy here, he's had a bit too much to drink." Dash joked as he pulled him away.

"Well, you better keep your dog on a leash. Otherwise, we've got a problem." The officer said as he walked off, his reflective helmet snapping shut as he turned away.

"What are you doing?" Dash whispered into Benoît's ear as he dragged him down the street, melting back into the sea of misfits that surrounded them.

"Damn SPF, I hate them" Benoît spat as he looked back at the police officers meandering through the market.

"Listen. You've got to grip this, we aren't here for them." Dash dragged Benoît roughly through the crowd.

Benoît muttered something under his breath as he shrugged off Dash.

"Look you know why we are here, just do your job, and we both might make it back to Albion," Dash said as he hurried beside Benoît.

They walked past a few bars offering virtual reality experiences; several patrons sat in their private booths whiling away the night; pretending to be manning a mech during the great war or riding a hoverbike through the city in an illegal street race. Benoît winked and smiled at the scantily dressed hosts as they fought for his attention.

"Sorry boys, we've got somewhere to be tonight," said Benoît, turning to stroke the side of the host's face. Dash laughed as he dragged Benoît by the elbow down a dreary side street.

"Come on, no more distractions. We are nearly there."

They stepped out from the side street and discreetly went their separate ways. Benoît hurried over to a run-down old bar across the road. Dash watched him as he ordered a drink before shuffling through the crowd and securing a window seat looking out onto the restaurant Dash's meeting was scheduled to take place in.

Their entire route to the restaurant had been meticulously planned to identify if anyone was following them. Dash had even included a tactical stop off at a local viewing platform to watch Vicentine's latest speech to try and flush out any would-be followers. Dash was confident he had been clear, no one was following him.

But for some reason as he approached the entrance, Dash stopped, his fingers gripped around the cold steel door handle.

He didn't know what it was, but something didn't feel right. He swallowed the urge to turn back and stepped inside.

The place was empty, just like it had been every time Dash had visited it. The restaurant had a bad reputation for two good reasons; the food was lousy, and it was located right beside a power plant. Dash had been visiting the restaurant on the same day, every week since he arrived in the Citadel. Tiberius and Munro had been clear with their instructions before he left. Adagio Restaurant; get a window seat with a view of SYCO and wait. When Maelstrom thought it was safe to proceed, he would provide a signal from within the facility; at 2200 the lights on the tenth floor would go off for five seconds.

"Good evening Sir," the waiter said stiffly as he escorted Dash through the restaurant. "Your usual table?"

"Yes please," Dash nodded as he took off his trench coat and sat down by the window. He pulled out a small red tablet and placed it next to the digital menu on his table, ordering his food via the touchscreen before staring out of the grimy window.

By the time his food arrived, Dash had already been in the restaurant for half an hour. Every passing minute seemed to go on forever. His heart stopped whenever he heard the distinctive chime of the doorbell, expecting at any minute the SPF to burst in and drag him away.

Eating was excoriating, he struggled to choke down every disgusting morsel. Masking his grimace with a smile every time the waiter jerkily approached his table. Could an android ever know how bad the food tasted in here, Dash thought as he swallowed the last mouthful. It was getting close to 2200 and Dash was starting to grow restless. He pushed his plate to one side and watched the tenth floor out of the window.

Then the lights went out.

One, two, three, four, five seconds.

At first, he wasn't sure what he had seen. He replayed the image over in his head. Was his mind playing tricks on him after all this time?

No, he was sure.

The lights had gone off. The meeting was on.

Maelstrom was coming.

2

____

THE JUNGLE

Elias stumbled through the darkness. Lost yet unafraid, he walked blindly until he spotted a single ray of light in the distance. A narrow beam, piercing through the black that surrounded him. He noticed something standing in the light; a tree. A thick, brown, grizzled trunk branching out into a glorious arch of vibrant green leaves. Elias had never seen anything like it, trees had long since perished in his world, but somehow he felt strangely comforted by its presence.

He started to run, racing towards it when suddenly he tripped and fell flat on his face. As he hit the ground, a shockwave reverberated from underneath him, it spiralled out and smashed into the tree. The tree jolted and groaned, slowly tipping backwards, its roots violently tearing from the ground. Elias fixated on the tree, unable to look away as it crumpled back onto itself. He winced as the tree crashed to the floor underneath a halo of broken branches.

The ground shuddered beneath Elias as he dragged himself back to his feet. The tremors tore open a crack between his legs, widening until it stretched all the way to the tree. He tried to scramble away as the world collapsed around him. Rays of dazzling light shot up from the crevices, illuminating the darkness. He covered his eyes as the ground split in two, sending him plummeting into a blinding chasm.

Elias awoke abruptly, his body jolting him from his sleep. He sat up in his grubby sleeping bag and rubbed the sweat from his brow. The vision had come again, only this time it went further than ever before. The falling tree didn't frighten him any more; instead, he was gripped by a sense of sorrow as it crashed to the ground. The visions had haunted his dreams for over a year, sometimes coming once a month or once a week, but they were becoming more frequent now. Every day this week, the same scenes played out in his head, only now they were more vivid, more visceral. He felt in control of and connected to the events but for some reason, unable to alter them.

Elias unzipped his sleeping bag and stretched out his skinny, pale legs, it was freezing in his shelter, but once again he was covered in sweat. He waved his tousled brown hair out of his face; it was matted with a thick layer of grease and looked like he had not washed it in several weeks. Elias stared down at the brightly coloured sleeping bag next to him to see if he had woken his younger brother. Somehow, Leo was still asleep, apparently unperturbed by Elias's latest nightmare. He never planned on telling Leo about his dreams, he didn't want him to think he was going crazy, but Leo had overheard him mumbling in his sleep one night.

Elias couldn't remember speaking to anyone, but Leo told him that he was screaming and trying to stop something from falling. He was quietly relieved when Leo raised his dreams. He hated keeping secrets from him, and even though his brother was only ten years old, Leo was wise beyond his years. Talking to him always helped alleviate the pressure building up inside his head. Elias had finally started to feel in control of his dreams again when suddenly the ground split in half beneath him. That was new, and he didn't like it one bit.

Elias freed his legs and pulled on some tattered overalls; he had a solid frame but was skinny for his age. Twelve years living outside the city walls had taken its toll on him. People often thought he was far older than he was, never guessing his actual age of eighteen. He slipped on some heavy brown work boots and threw on an ill-fitting navy overcoat which hung loosely off his shoulders. He looked around the tent; all his possessions stacked neatly in the opposite corner, a small gas stove, a lamp and a spare pair of clothes. That was the entirety of his life.

Elias tiptoed over Leo, inching closer to the entrance before carefully unzipping the tent. He looked back at his brother; his tiny body still curled up tightly. He hated this part of the day. Leaving his brother behind in the Jungle was never easy. Elias's heart sank when he thought of how Leo would spend his day; scavenging with the other Ronin children in the Sovereign waste pits. He couldn't stand watching his little brother while away his childhood sifting through the scraps of other peoples lives; apparitions from a world he would never be part of. Leo spent hours there, trying to discover something that he could repair, anything they might be able to trade.

When he first took Leo to the pits, Elias tried to make a game out of it, telling his brother they were searching for some long-lost treasure. Something that would turn their lives around, their ticket out of the Jungle. Leo was old enough now to know what that place really was, but he would still go.

Everyday.

Not once did he ever complain, whenever Elias arrived home, he would always greet him with the same smile that would light up his heart and give him the strength to keep going. Leo's world still had colour in it, because it was viewed through the eyes of a child. He still believed their life would get better. Elias held no such illusions. His world was grey and bitter. All pain and hardship, the world wasn't fair; it was brutal.

Elias clumsily knocked over a small pile of electrical junk as he tried to sneak out of the tent. Leo had scavenged it all over the last few weeks, his brother had a real knack with electronics. It amazed Elias how he could forage items from the pits and turn them into some device that Elias had never heard of. Many a time Leo saved the day, trading in his latest invention for a much-needed hot meal.

The benefit of Elias's sleepless nights meant he could get a head start on the daily plasma roundups. He would always be one of the first in line when the Citadel's black marketeers would arrive to drain the Jungle's youth of their blood. A single specimen of plasma paid enough to feed him and Leo for a week. In their quest for eternal youth, the rich and famous within the Citadel developed a technology to extend their own lives by infusing the blood of the young.

The procedure cost a fortune and was reserved for the Citadel's elite, but that was where the black marketeers stepped in. Realising that they could harvest the blood of the poor and the desperate in the Jungle and serve it to the masses in the Citadel for a fraction of the cost. Overnight a new underground economy was established. Elias dreaded the procedure, he would leave the extraction labs feeling like his insides had been ripped out through his skin, but in a place like the Jungle, it was the quickest way to earn a living.

Elias took one last look at Leo and stepped out into the Jungle. What began as a makeshift refugee camp outside the Citadel had developed into a city of its own. In the vast undulating desert wastelands beyond the walls, a spiralling shanty town made up of shabbily built corrugated iron shelters, and grimy, smoke-stained tents had appeared. It was a cruel, harsh, unforgiving place that swallowed up hope and spat out despair. Elias despised every last inch of it. He vowed to himself that if he only achieved one thing in his life; it would be to give Leo a home, a real home away from this place. Elias stared back at his pitiful tent and shook his head as the cold north wind hit, chilling his bones.

He pulled his overcoat around him and started to make his way through the rows of rundown shelters; the arid desert floor cracked beneath his feet. It was the smell of the Jungle that Elias loathed the most, an unavoidable stench that flooded your lungs. A potent mix of burning garbage, human waste and the fumes that bellowed out from the Citadel night and day. Every breath felt like he was drowning in a sea of smog.

Elias was a Ronin, like all those who lived in the Jungle, the lucky few who survived the fall of Roninhya and threw themselves at the mercy of their conquerors. The last remnants of a shattered civilisation defeated in the great war. Life outside the city walls was harsh; freezing temperatures at night were followed by the scorching heat of the day. The dense clouds that hung over the Citadel stretched for miles, creating a layer of humid air in the Jungle. The heat was stifling, the Ronin would build crude shelters to try and stay cool, but it was useless. The searing temperatures were relentless, forcing the Ronin to hide in the shade for the majority of the day.

Elias gazed up at the sky; the ash-like clouds glowed blue as a magnificent fluorescent storm brewed within. He noticed the bore of one of the colossal ion cannons jutting out above the city walls. The Ronin lived in the shadows of the last city on Earth, forever trapped under a man-made sky.

He looped around the back of the Jungle and made his ways through row after row of grimy, sand-encrusted tents and dusty, corrugated iron shacks. He continued down the winding streets, passing the charred husks of several burnt-out vehicles. He eventually came to a clearing with a roaring fire at its heart, several rough-looking Ronin wearing chunky shawls stood around the barrel, their arms draped over the flames.

Elias tucked his face into his overcoat, as another blast of sand whipped through the clearing. He walked over to an open-fronted shack with a handwritten sign hung above it. There was already a queue of people waiting, Elias did a quick number count; twelve. That should guarantee him a place, he thought.

The transporters usually took at least a twenty-five people to the lab, a small covert facility hidden away in the depths of the wastelands. The donors were paid thirty creds for every packet of plasma they provided. That was less than the cost of one food pill in the city, but in the Jungle, it was enough to buy supplies for a week. Elias made his way over to the back of the line.

"Got any change kid?" Elias stared down at his arm; a crude mechanical hand had latched around his elbow. He peered down at the owner, a skinny, haggard man wearing a tattered track top. The man looked up from his stool as a pair of ill-fitting optical implants focussed in on Elias.

"No, I don't have anything on me," Elias lied as he tried to free himself from the man's grip, the metal fingers dug into Elias's flesh as they tightened around his wrist.

"Come on man, help a brother out." The man demanded as he tried to pull Elias towards him.

"I said, no!" Elias shouted as he hooked his hands together and yanked his arm out of the man's grip. Elias pulled away with such force that he detached the mechanical arm from its host, its grip loosening instantly. The arm hit the ground with a dull thud.

"Oh man, good for nuthin piece of junk." The man muttered as he knelt down and reached for his detached limb.

The Ronin gathered around the flaming barrel turned their gaze from the glowing fire and watched as Elias ran over to the shack, quickly joining the back of the queue. The watchful eyes followed him before losing interest and returning to their conversations. Elias rubbed his wrist where the man had grabbed him, he lifted up his sleeve to reveal a shining silver tattoo; three shimmering silver rectangles carved deeply into his skin. He detested it, the symbol that marked him as a refugee; someone who didn't belong in the Citadel. It wasn't so much a tattoo as a branding seared on everyone in the Jungle; it also served a purpose. It contained a small strip of circuitry made of silver leaf that contained the bio-data and vital statistics of its host. It allowed the Sovereign to monitor population growth in the Jungle.

As Elias waited for the plasma transporters to arrive, the queue swelled, and soon there were scores of Ronin lined around the square. He peered behind him to see who else would be donating; he saw the same, familiar, worn-out faces queued up behind him. Elias spotted more cheap augmentations or 'augs' as people called them. Ronin who had been able to buy cheap cybernetic implants that were no longer good enough for the people of the Citadel. Once again, the black market saw another opportunity to exploit the Ronin.

He saw a small child, maybe five or six. He was never very good at guessing ages. The child had aug implants on his lower half, a hulking pair of silver callipers hugged his spindly legs and a tight band wrapped around his waist. The child walked along the queue sluggishly dragging his legs with his hands as he asked for loose change. Elias avoided his gaze as he passed by, he hated situations like this. He wanted to help, but he barely had enough creds to keep him and Leo going, let alone help anyone else.

He shuffled awkwardly on the spot, pushing back against the surging crowd behind him. Then he heard it, the deafening noise as the plasma transporter blared its horn. The Ronin scattered to either side as a bulky six-wheeled vehicle rolled into the centre of the clearing flanked either side by a small 4x4 jeep; each mounted with a 0.50 calibre machine gun cannon on its rear. It came to a sharp stop by the side of the shack, and its doors slid open.

Several heavily armed mercenaries jumped out of the jeeps and pushed the Ronin back, creating a gap around the door. A thin-looking man stepped out from the vehicle; he had a long narrow face that was severely disfigured and had a tattoo of a dragon that twisted around his neck. He wore a transparent air filter over the lower half of his face. He was a mercenary working for the Shenmue, the criminal underworld of the Citadel who owned the black market on plasma.

"Disgusting," the disfigured Merc said to himself as he fixated on the thin layer of dust covering his boots.

"Right, we are having issues on site today. Therefore we only have ten spaces. No more, no less!" He shouted before turning around, waving his hand dismissively and stepping back on the transporter.

"Make it quick," he said to a bearded giant standing by the door.

As soon as he disappeared from view, Elias felt the crowd surge behind him as the queuing Ronin struggled to get to the front. A fight broke out beside him, and someone threw a punch that knocked Elias off his feet. He flailed on the ground as the crowd relentlessly marched over him. He fought to catch his breath, crawling through the sand as people trampled on him. He inched forward until he was able to push through a small gap and break free.

"Right, that's ten," the bearded giant shouted as he dragged Elias by the scruff of the neck.

Elias looked up at the giant Merc, and a cruel, twisted face hidden behind a wild brown beard glared back at him. He spun Elias around and shoved him into the side of the transporter, he grabbed Elias by the arm and pulled up his sleeve. Another Merc came over and scanned Elias's tattoo with a bizarre-looking device.

"He's clean," The Merc with the device declared as he bundled Elias onboard.

The Merc's fired their weapons into the air as the crowd started to push forward, they retreated back onboard the transporter and hastily closed the doors behind them.

"God, I hate this place," the giant said as he rested his assault rifle on an empty seat.

Elias sat slumped on the steps.

"You!" The Merc caught Elias in his sight, "Up! Your seats are at the back," he shouted, pointing to some benches at the back of the transporter.

"Okay, okay, sorry," Elias said as he jumped to his feet, dusting himself down as he walked over to the benches and took an empty seat by a small window. Most of the spaces were already taken with other bruised and battered Ronin, the lucky few who made it on board before him.

Once the transporter navigated its way out of the winding streets of the Jungle, they picked up speed, thundering across the desert. It would be a good couple of hours before they arrived, the lab was situated well away from any prying eyes, in the deep of the Wildlands. Elias craned his neck to peer out of the filthy window, watching as they cleared the last ramshackle huts and the camp faded away into the distance. He leaned back, stretched out his legs and breathed a huge sigh of relief.

He'd made it.

3

MAELSTROM

Dash sat impatiently in his seat and drummed his fingers on the glass table; his heart was pounding. A thick stream of sweat ran down his neck, causing his shirt to stick to his back.

The chime of the door went off again as it swung open.

He could hear somebody talking to the waiter. Their voices were muffled, so it was difficult to understand what was being said. He tried to catch a glimpse of the new arrival through the reflection in the window, but before he had the chance, the footsteps were heading his way.

Dash looked up and saw a small, hooked nosed man in a long black over-coat, shuffling rigidly beside the waiter. The hooked nose man glanced at him as he walked past before quickly looking away, he took the table behind Dash. He listened intently as the man spoke to the waiter, he sounded nervous.

Was that him? He doesn't look like a hero of the resistance Dash thought. He shuffled in his seat and craned his neck straining for a better view at the reflection in the window.

"Do not turn around." The man snapped in a hushed voice.

Dash jolted back into his seat and looked dead ahead.

"The food in here is lousy, but the view is fantastic," The man added.

The validation phrase. Maelstrom.

"You should try the Vaults of Highgate, the views are breathtaking," Dash added.

The second half of the code.

"Is this your first meet?" Maelstrom asked, this time returning to his hushed tone.

"No,"

"Then why do you look so nervous?"

"I'm sorry, it's been a long time since we received your message. I was starting to think the meeting might not happen. Your signal took me a little by surprise."

"I should be the one apologising. When I sent my message, I didn't think it would take me this long to identify a suitable opportunity for us to meet,"

"How long have you been here for?"

"Tomorrow will be my seventh week," said Dash.

"So you must have been dispatched the day after my message arrived?"

"The same night, been sleeping rough ever since trying to keep a low profile. We were warned not to make contact with any other assets while in the Citadel, in case they were being monitored by the Sovereign."

"Are you sure you weren't followed?" Maelstrom asked urgently.

"Yeah, our route took over two hours before we came here. I'm clean."

"And you've been doing this every time?"

"Every time. Different routes. Disguises. Stop-offs. The lot."

"Well, thank you. I appreciate your tireless efforts. Most wouldn't have persevered for seven weeks in the Citadel with no access to a support network."

"Like I said. It's not my first time."

"Then why so worried?"

"I have known Tiberius for over fifteen years, fought by his side during the great war, and I've never seen him look more troubled than the night he received your message. Which means whatever information you have, must be of vital importance to our cause." Dash drummed his fingers on the tablet in front of him.

"Indeed. I have secured that which Tiberius asked of me many years ago." Maelstrom removed a small memory card from his breast pocket and slyly handed it to Dash round the side of the booth. "Here, take it."

Dash snatched the memory card and slid it into a small opening covertly hidden within the back of his tablet.

"That my friend is a complete schematic of the SYCO facility. I think we both know what Tiberius intends to do with the information."

The SYCO power facility had been a target of the Shadows for years. They'd had some limited success in disrupting the flow of raw materials by hitting the supply convoys, but it was too fortified to ever consider a full-scale assault. But maybe, a small commando unit who knew precisely where to strike would stand a chance. It would be a suicide mission, but they might be able to pull it off. This could turn the tide of the war.

"I'll get it to Tiberius straight away," Dash took out his payment card and tapped it on the digital menu.

"Wait. There is something else. Something of grave importance to the resistance...those plans were not the reason I requested an urgent meeting."

"What, what is it?" Dash sat back down into his seat.

"I...I have heard...they are only whispers, hear-say, fragments of conversations about a covert research project..."

"Right," Dash leant forward trying to focus his hearing.

"Our management is putting unprecedented demands on our facility. We've been instructed to increase our energy input by twenty percent to meet the demands of this new project."

Dash sensed the frustration in his voice.

"I told them it's impossible, it can't be done. But our superiors told us Vicentine himself had authorised the project, and he wants daily updates on our progress."

"Vicentine's authorised it himself," Dash pondered aloud. "But why would he be overseeing a research project? It doesn't make any sense."

"That is the question I've been asking myself. If they want to syphon off enough energy to power fifty city blocks whatever they are working on must be big..." Maelstrom said ominously. "Real big."

Dash lent back into the booth and rubbed his chin; he checked his watch. Almost an hour had passed since he arrived; time to go. It wasn't a good idea to stay in one place for too long in the city.

"Is there anything else you picked up about this?"

"Only one thing, they are calling it Project Icarus."

Dash could not remember the last time he had heard those words. The Shadows had only learnt about Project Icarus after they experienced the tremors reverberating from the explosion that destroyed the Sovereign's covert drill site. For years they had heard whispers about something the Sovereign was working on, but even in their worst nightmares, they couldn't have dreamt up what was actually going on there.

The traitor Voltaire, Vicentine's guardian, drunk on his own hubris thought he was powerful enough to tame the power of the Earth's core. He disappeared after the accident, never to be seen again. The explosion had decimated everything within fifteen square miles, to this day, ten years after the incident, the Icarus fires still burned.

Surely without Voltaire, by his side, Vicentine wouldn't be stupid enough to reignite Project Icarus.

He had to get back to Albion.

Now.

"It's time to go," Dash said abruptly. "If you hear anything, anything at all about Icarus you must get word to us."

"Okay,"

"The Shadows need to know about this,"

"You must go now. Tell Tiberius and Munro I miss them, and by the grace of Gaia, I hope I will see Albion again one day soon. Now go!"

Dash shot to his feet, pulled on his trench coat and placed the tablet into his inside breast pocket. The waiter scurried over to him and ushered him to the exit, holding open the door as he left.

"Thanks again Kayto," Dash saluted the waiter as he headed out. He heard the chime of the bell as the door closed behind him. It was raining now, the thick clouds that hung over the Citadel would often open up, releasing monsoon-like rainfall over the city.

"Great," Dash said to himself as he pulled up the collar of his coat.

Dash looked across the street, Benoît was still sitting in the window of the bar opposite, he tried to cross the road, dodging in and out of the hover cars and scooters as they darted past. Dash had a clearer view of Benoît now; he appeared to be arguing with someone.

"What's he playing at," Dash muttered to himself. "So much for keeping a low profile."

A series of bright flashes lit up the bar as somebody opened fire on Benoît. He jolted backwards and crashed into the table behind him, his lifeless body slumping to the floor. Dash stood in the rain and watched in horror as two Sovereign soldiers, dressed in matching black exoskeletons marched over to Benoît and started searching his body.

Dash remained rooted to the spot; he tried to stop his hands from trembling in his pockets. One of the soldiers flipped Benoît over and pulled out the pistol holstered to his chest. He looked up and locked his sight on Dash who was still stood motionless in the street outside as the rain beat down on him, staring through the window at the distinctive t-shaped visor of the soldier's helmet.

He turned away and hurried across the road, narrowly avoiding a speeding car, its driver beeping angrily at him. Dash looked back over his shoulder and saw the soldier pointing his comrades in his direction. Dash started to sprint and bolted down the street, working his way through the sea of umbrellas in front of him. He glanced back again and caught sight of several soldiers pushing their way through the crowd in pursuit.

"Damn it." Dash cursed as he came to a pedestrian crossing, dozens of people, all packed in tightly, waiting for the signal to cross the junction.

Dash eased his way to the front and stood by the side of the road, the speed of the vehicles threw him off balance as they whizzed passed at a blistering pace. The noise from the passing traffic instantly died down as a hologram of a man projected into the middle of the road, advising the pedestrians it was safe to cross.

The vehicles came to an abrupt halt inches away from the hologram. At the front of the queue, Dash spotted a crimson red hover-bike; a single large turbine housed underneath a sleek, streamlined chassis. Its owner was dressed in black leathers and wore a matching helmet; he was resting back on the seat as the bike floated a few inches off the ground.

"I'm sorry about this," Dash said as he reached into his jacket pocket and pulled out his pistol. In one fluid motion, he smashed the butt into the side of the biker's helmet, knocking them into the middle of the road. He jumped on the hover-bike and pressed a few buttons on the touch-screen in the centre of the handlebars.

"CAUTION!" The bike screeched in a loud mechanical voice.

"YOU ARE NOT AUTHORISED TO DISABLE AUTOPILOT ON THIS VEHICLE!" It blurted out as the touch-screen began flashing red.

"This is why I hate technology," Dash said to himself as he fired two shots at the screen. The noise was deafening. People scattered in all directions, rushing access the road in a blind panic at the sound of gunfire. The soldiers raised their rifles at Dash and opened fire as he desperately kicked down on the accelerator pedal.

The engine ignited, and he struggled to control the bike as its instant torque kicked in, accelerating from zero to one hundred miles per hour in under three seconds. He lurched forward as the last of the pedestrians jumped out of his way. Dash leaned in and hugged the bike with his body, grasping the handlebars with both hands. He heard several shots ring about behind him as he sped up, then in the blink of an eye he was gone.

Dash raced through the city at a breathtaking speed, narrowly avoiding the oncoming vehicles as he weaved in and out of the passing traffic. He had spent so long in this part of the Citadel he was familiar with the roads. Unlike most of its citizens who sat back in their seats blindly being driven around by their autonomous vehicles, Dash had been taking everything in. Every turn, every street light, every sign. Memorising them all for a moment like this.

The traffic became a blur as he swept alongside the vehicles, in his digital rearview mirror, he caught sight of a flashing red and blue light. He cursed himself as he focused in on his mirror, a passing SPF car had spotted him and moved out from a line of traffic as he sped by. The black and white police car floated a few inches off the ground; a mohawk of red and blue lights ran along the centre of its roof. It glided effortlessly out of the traffic and burst forward, speeding up instantly.

The noise of the sirens closed in on him as he veered off sharply, taking an exit that led to an auto-way; the home of the Citadel's ultra fast-moving vehicles. The noise was deafening as Dash's tiny hover-bike was swamped by a convoy of platooning lorries, following so closely behind each other there was barely enough room for Dash to slide into. He drifted into the narrow gap between two of the lorries and matched their speed. The police car stalked Dash down the exit and joined the same platoon, a few vehicles after him. The distinctive flash of emergency lights lit up his mirror again as the police car inched closer, passing one lorry after another. He spotted the police car out the corner of his eye as it moved out, closing in behind him.

Dash slid one of his hands into his jacket and drew his pistol, without taking his eyes off the road he pointed the gun behind his back and fired wildly. The police car braked suddenly, swerving from side to side as it desperately tried to avoid the incoming fire. One of the lorries thumped into the back of the police car, shattering its windows and crushing it into a shape beyond recognition. Dash heard the screech of brakes as the lorries automated pilots brought their vehicles to a stop. He slowed his bike down and came off at the next exit, following the road around a tight bend that led to a darkened street running parallel beneath the auto-way.

He cruised along the darkened streets, passing one flickering street lamp after another; this part of the city was a lot quieter than Sam's Town. There weren't many people still awake at this time, only a few noop heads stumbling through the night shouting abuse at Dash as he noisily drove past. He cruised through the streets, sweeping the path ahead until he finally spotted what he had been searching for, the abandoned factory.

He parked the hover-bike by the side of a wire fence surrounding the dilapidated building. As he tried to climb off the seat, his legs buckled underneath him and he tumbled to the ground. He struggled back to his feet and felt a sharp pain stabbing in his lower back. He reached inside his jacket and felt a strange warmth, he pulled out his hand, and it was slick with blood. He gripped his wound tightly and limped off down an alleyway running alongside the factory. The blood seeped through his fingers and trickled down the inside of his jacket, dripping off the hem and leaving a small trail of blood behind him. He staggered forwards, pushing himself through a narrow gate that blocked his path.

Dash grimaced as he crouched down to his knees beside a

manhole cover. He struggled for a few moments trying to free the slab of steel from its place. Eventually, he managed to prize it open, revealing a narrow ladder leading into the darkness below. He pulled out a torch and clenched it between his teeth as he started to climb inside, sliding the cover back into place after him. The ladder led down to the depths of the Citadel's sewage system. Thousands of miles of concrete tunnels responsible for ensuring the waste of a billion people made its way safely out of the city limits.

The stench was overwhelming, a nauseating mix of faeces and urine, Dash tried not to gag as he climbed down. He winced with every step, the pain in his back starting to spread into his legs. Suddenly, his back spasmed and his legs gave way, he grasped for the ladder and felt the torch fall from his mouth. He lost his footing, trying to catch it and watched agonisingly as it slipped through his fingers, plunging into the abyss below. He fell backwards and crashed into the side of the shaft as he plummeted downwards. He reached out frantically and caught hold of a rung of the ladder; his arm yanking out of its socket as he struggled to hold on.

"Gaia guide me," he whispered, carefully regaining his footing and resting his head on the ladder. He looked down and saw his torch bobbing up and down in a shallow pool of water not far beneath him.

Dash steadily made his way down and dropped into the murky water, he collected his torch and shone it around the chamber, twelve circular tunnels ran off in a clockwork design. After a few moments, he spotted what he was searching for; a small arrow, etched into the concrete, pointing down one of the tunnels. He wandered through the dark for what felt like hours, following the etchings that marked the way.

Finally, up ahead, he spotted a glimmer of light piercing

through a grate. He imagined the warm rays of the sun on his skin and broke out into a smile, it had been so long since he last saw the sun, the memory of its radiance lifted his spirits. He slumped into the grate that blocked off the sewer, gasping for fresh air and reaching out at the light.

After a few moments, he readied himself and with a concerted effort, pushed with all his might against the dead iron weight in front of him. Slowly, inch by inch, it crept open, creating just enough space for him to slip through before slamming shut behind him with a crash. He fell to his knees, clawing at the dry, dusty ground. He laid there for several minutes sobbing uncontrollably as he played with the sand between his fingers, his sense of relief palpable.

Dash dragged himself back to his feet and staggered through the desert. He walked for so long he lost all sense of time. Dehydrated and exhausted. He stumbled on, his body growing weaker with every step. He could feel himself fading. Then he noticed something up ahead and his heart leapt. At first, he thought it was a mirage, his faltering mind playing a cruel trick on him. But as it came into view, his emotions overwhelmed him. The tears cutting a path through his dirt-encrusted face; never in all his life did he think he would be so happy to see the Jungle.

4

GHOSTS

Leo rolled over and let out a sigh as he patted the empty sleeping bag next to him. It hurt to know where his brother was heading; he hated the thought of those monsters bleeding the life out of him. Time after time he begged Elias not to go, he would rather starve than allow him to go back to that awful place. But Elias never listened, he'd crawl back to their tent, like his spirit had been shattered into a thousand pieces, and Leo would spend the next week nursing him back to health.

He sat up and rubbed his strikingly green eyes, catching his knuckle on a deep scar that ran over his left brow. One of his eyelids had a permanent droop to it, the result of a blow to the head that had never healed properly. He loosened a bandana tied around his wrist and slipped it over his forehead, tying back his long, greasy, brown hair. After spending several minutes tinkering with a pile of rusted electrical components, he crawled out of his sleeping bag and unzipped the tent.

Wearing all the clothes he owned, a vibrant green vest and a pair of ill-fitting cargo shorts he slipped on some oversized boots and stepped out into the searing heat of the Jungle. After grabbing a crumpled drawstring bag from inside, he zipped up their tent and headed down the narrow rows of shelters zig-zagging through the Jungle. Stopping outside a small tin shack not far away, he gently knocked on the makeshift door.

Inside somebody coughed uncontrollably.

"Who is it?" A voice said weakly.

"It's me, Leo."

"Oh, come in my love."

Leo let himself in and closed the door behind him, he glanced around the darkened room and noticed a grey-haired woman, covered in shawls and blankets lying on a camp bed at the back of the shack. She started coughing again as Leo approached her.

Perching beside her on the camp bed, he pulled his bag onto his lap.

"How you holding up today?"

"Not good little one. Not good at all. I barely slept a wink last night. This blasted cough is keeping me up all hours," she groaned, bursting out into another vicious coughing fit. Leo gently stroked her back, trying to soothe her.

"I'm sorry Maz, it sounds really bad. I traded some stuff I repaired last week for this," Leo said quietly as he rummaged through his bag and pulled out a small metallic inhaler.

"Oh, Leo." Her eyes started to well up. "I don't know what I'd do without you."

"Took me a while to track down a supplier I could trust." Leo declared proudly. "But this is the best on the market apparently, should sort your cough out in no time," he wrapped Maz's hand around the inhaler.

"Thank you," she gripped it tightly in her grasp as if it was her most treasured possession.

"I can't stay long, there is a new shipment arriving soon, and I want first dibs on it."

"Okay, my dear. You better be off then. Thank you so much for this, I don't know how I can ever repay you." Maz smiled as she shook the inhaler in the air. "I am lucky to have you in my life."

"Don't worry about it." Leo blushed. "I'll try and pop by tomorrow to see how you are getting on with it," he said, closing the door behind him.

The waste pits were on the outskirts of the Jungle, lurking ominously over the top of the shantytown. Positioned far enough from the Citadel, so the wind didn't carry the stench back to the city. Somehow, the Ronin had grown accustomed to the foul odours that filled their streets. Fifteen square miles and over a billion tons of garbage, the waste pits were a man-made mountain range of trash. Towering dunes over a thousand feet high, growing taller every day as the Citadel's refuse transporters piled more and more rubbish on to the site.

Leo cut through the Jungle, weaving in and out of the maze of narrow streets, coming to the muster point where his brother would have queued a few hours ago, waiting patiently for the agony that awaited him in the desert. The area was deserted now, except for a few stray Ronin who had set up camp nearby. Two men danced with each other as several others sat in beat-up old deck chairs passing a bottle of swill around.

Leo laughed as the men linked arms and merrily jigged in front of the others. A familiar folk tune blared out from a pair of muffled speakers. It didn't make much sense to Leo as he didn't speak the old tongue, but he enjoyed the rhythmic beats. The music of the Jungle was one of the few things he actually liked about the place, despite the Sovereign's efforts to snuff out Ronin culture, somehow their music survived. Passed on to the next generation by the few alive old enough to remember their home.

The men broke out into a toothy grin and tipped their caps to Leo as he stopped and linked arms with them, briefly joining in with their dance. The old boys let out a cheer and raised their bottle to him as he broke away and playfully bowed in return. A myriad of twisting streets led to the edge of town where he stopped and climbed up the remnants of a burnt-out Sovereign tank. Balancing on the barrel, he carefully walked up it and plonked himself down in the turret to wait for his friends.

After a short while, he pulled out some battered old goggles from his bag and stretched them over his head. He looked out through the cracked lenses and spotted them; Mungo, Oskar and Derrick. Oskar was the first to notice Leo; he began to wave frantically at Leo who was now hanging upside down from the tank's muzzle. Oskar was a short, portly boy with no neck; his round head appeared to be connected directly to his shoulders. Leo could never quite understand how considering he lived in a refugee camp, Oskar had gotten so fat. He wore an ill-fitted pair of shorts and t-shirt that rose up as he walked.

"Be careful up there," Oskar shrieked, fiddling with his glasses as he approached.

"Yeah, you don't want to hurt yourself!" Derrick replied as he ran and jumped up on top of the tank's turret. Derrick was the youngest of the group, a black boy with neatly clipped hair. He wore a baggy vest that hung loosely off his skinny frame.

"Come on you two, we don't want to miss the drop. The transporters should be arriving soon," Mungo said, waving Leo and Derrick down as he walked straight past them.

Mungo had several augmentations, an accident that occurred when he was a baby had left him paralysed from the waist down.

Somehow his parents had scraped together enough creds to pay for some second-hand augs on the black market. His legs had been replaced with a mechanical prosthesis, ultra-thin blades that curved beneath the knee. Mungo wore an oversized pair of cut off dungarees, exposing his aluminium legs. Leo and Derrick jumped off the tank and rolled on to the dusty ground. They sprinted to catch up with Oskar and Mungo, jumping on their backs as they reached them.

"Oi, stop it," Oskar mumbled as he toppled forward with Derrick straddling him.

The journey to the waste pits did not take long, and they soon arrived at the opening to the mountain range. Mungo led them along a wide track that ran through the middle of the site, the makeshift road used by the Sovereign's vehicles. Soon they spotted what they were looking for, one of the giant Sovereign waste transporters depositing its load. The boys noticed several other Ronin on the horizon; their massive netted sacks hung over their shoulders. Just like the boys, they must have heard about the shipment and were ready and waiting to scavenge through the latest offerings from the Citadel.

The boys watched as the transporter's hydraulic pumps methodically lifted its giant cargo container into the air, emptying out its contents with a groan. Another ton of rubbish came tumbling out. They pointed out various items to each other; Mungo had seen a battery pack, and Oskar was convinced he had spotted some medical supplies.

After several minutes the transporter had finished unloading, and its container lowered back into position. A plume of black smoke spiralled from its exhausts stacks as it roared out of the waste pits. When the fumes had dissipated, the boys surveyed the newly created dune before launching themselves at it. Leo clambered up it as fast as he could, he had seen the distinctive green and gold flash of a motherboard and was keen to scoop it up before anyone else did. His feet sunk into the waste, the sinking sludge seemed to morph around his ankles with every step he took.

He reached the peak of the dune and started to rummage through the debris, trying to locate what caught his eye during the drop-off. Then he saw it. Glistening like an emerald in a sea of garbage, a computer motherboard. A small square of green plastic with several strips of gold running down to a large, black lump at its heart. Leo cleaned the motherboard down and held it up for a better view, he twisted and turned it in his hands, examining every detail. He couldn't see any chips or dents, everything seemed in working order.

"Perfect," Leo muttered to himself as he slipped it into his bag. The boys spent several hours in the sweltering midday heat scouring the mounds for any further hidden treasures. Leo lifted his hand to his brow, surveying the terrain ahead, as he scanned the hills, he noticed something below, near the edge of the waste pits. It looked like a body.

"Hey guys, come check this out," Leo clamoured, waving the others over. Mungo scrambled up first, followed by Derrick and Oskar who arrived soon after, huffing and puffing.

"This better be worth it," Oskar grumbled as he wiped the sweat from his face, he pulled his t-shirt down which had ridden up over his belly again.

"Look down there," Leo pointed at the shape in the distance.

"Is that a body?" Mungo said, cupping his eyes for a better view.

"That's what I thought," Leo said.

"Yeah looks that way to me," Derrick chipped in.

"Where are you guys looking?" Oskar tugged on Derrick's sleeve.

"Let's go check it out," Leo said as started to make his way downwards.

"I don't know, Leo," Mungo grumbled.

"Come on, they might need our help," Leo shouted as he sprinted down the hill.

Derrick glanced over at Mungo and Oskar, who had a worried expression on their faces.

"Oh, come on, you two! We can't let him go down there on his own," he said, chasing after Leo.

"This is a bad idea," Mungo muttered to himself as started to canter down after them.

"Oh boy, I don't like this. I don't like this one bit." Oskar mumbled to himself as he carefully navigated his way down the slope, the others had already made it to the bottom while Oskar ambled down after them, one careful step at a time.

Leo was the first to arrive at the body; he tiptoed forward, not wanting to disturb it. Derrick came running up from behind and crashed into him as he tried to stop, they both nearly fell on top of the body as they struggled to regain their balance. Leo pushed him away and delicately manoeuvred his way around the body, taking care not to touch it.

He lent down and saw it was a man wearing a tattered black trench coat, his clothes covered in dried blood. His gaunt, pale face was bruised and battered. Leo glanced up at the others and saw Oskar chattering away. Leo shushed him, and Oskar's gaze drifted down abashed as he stood in between Mungo and Derrick.

Leo reached down and picked up a long stick, he slowly fed it under the man's trench coat and pulled it back, he could see now the wound on the man's back must have killed him. His entire shirt was soaked with dark red blood. Leo scanned down the man's body and caught a glimpse of something tucked into his belt; it looked like a gun.

Leo inched closer and bent over, measuring out his every step. He carefully hunched over and grasped the butt of the gun which was secured in a holster fastened to the man's belt. Leo unclipped it, releasing the weapon. It was much heavier than he was expecting and he had to tug at it several times before it came away. He crouched there marvelling at the gun as the others crowded around him for a closer look.

Leo sprang up as something grabbed his wrist; he let go of the gun, and it dropped to the ground with a clatter. Staring down in horror, the bloodied body dragged itself up, still grasping his wrist. He tried with all his might to prise his arm away, but the man was too strong. He heard the cries of his friends as they clambered back up the slope, sending cascades of debris tumbling down after them. The body wearily rose to its feet and staggered forward, leaning on Leo for balance as he frantically tried to wrestle his arm from the man's grip.

5

PLASMA

Elias jumped up from his seat as the transporter juddered to a stop.

"Are we here?" Elias asked groggily.

"I think..." the Ronin to his left said when one of the Mercs came rushing into their cabin.

"Right, you lazy good for nothin' runts, up! We are here!" the giant screamed as he grabbed Elias by the shoulder, dragging him up from his stupor and pushing him along the carriage.

The giant rounded up the others and shunted them off the transporter. Elias fell out of the door, and a small plume of dust exploded as he collapsed on the sand. He tried to wipe the dirt from his mouth when an immense weight came crashing down on his shoulders. Elias crawled on the ground and turned his head to see the remaining Ronin being shoved off the transporter on top of him. He found himself pinned down under several flailing bodies, arms and legs sticking out every angle.

"Get off-" he gasped as he tried to wriggle his way to freedom, struggling to breathe as the weight pushed down on him.

After a few minutes trying to escape the human pyramid, he stopped fighting against it and focussed on his breath when suddenly he was released. He scrambled back to his feet and dusted himself off. Someone nudged him in the side, and he glanced up to see the face of a Ronin nodding ahead. He straightened up and stared at the entrance of the Shenmue facility, a series of beige trailers laid out in an L-shape. A thin layer of desert camouflage netting covered the entire building, blending it into the surroundings.

The Mercs pulled the rest of the Ronin back to their feet and started shunting them forward, hitting them in the backs with their rifles. Elias's feet didn't touch the floor as he was carried by the momentum of those behind him. As they approached the entrance, the steel doors slid open, and two female lab assistants dressed in fitted white uniforms greeted them.

"It's okay gentlemen, we can take it from here," one of the women said as she welcomed them inside. The giant lifted his rifle and used it to shove a Ronin, causing him to stumble over his own feet.

"Please, that is not necessary," the woman said sternly, as she stepped between the giant and the beaten man, ushering him inside to safety.

"Make it quick." he snarled, standing face-to-face with the woman. She calmly moved aside and called over to the disfigured Merc who was leaning on the side of the transporter.

"Zee, can you please get your...-" she stared up at the giant. "Dogs under control. I can't work with these poor men if they are unconscious."

Zee's scarred face widened into a broken smile, he

unfolded his arms and let out a loud whistle. "You heard the lady," he yelled, climbing back into the cockpit of the transporter.

The giant spat on the ground and grunted as he turned away from the lab assistant, his rifle slung casually over his shoulder as he sauntered back to the transporter.

"I am sorry about that," she said, turning back to face the Ronin who were cowering around the entrance trying to shield themselves from rest of the Mercs.

"My name is Dr Monroe, I run the facility here. I recognise a few of your faces," she said, smiling at Elias.

"So, most of you will be familiar with the procedure but don't worry, we'll have you in and out in no time. Right, let's get started", she said, clapping her hands together assertively.

Dr Monroe cut through the Ronin and escorted them down a series of grimy, dimly lit corridors until they reached a set of mechanical glass doors. She presented a key card to a reader next to the entrance, and the doors made a distinctive whooshing sound as they slid open. Elias had to cover his eyes from the glaring lights as he entered the laboratory, the room was dank and grubby, a once state of the art facility well past its best. The walls were covered with flat-screen monitors displaying various charts and graphs. In the centre stood several battered old medical pods, the whole place felt cold and hostile.

"We aren't running at capacity today I'm afraid, so we will have to process you in small groups," Dr Monroe said as she pointed them over to some fold-down chairs at the rear of the lab. Elias shuffled through the Ronin and took a chair at the back.

"Okay, you, you, and you," Dr Monroe said, pointing at three young-looking Ronin.

"And you two." She directed them over to the medical pods and helped them clamber inside as she explained the process.

Elias fidgeted in his chair as he waited for his turn, the screams that rang out every time the procedure started, made the wait even more agonising. It didn't take long for the nurses to process the Ronin, but they were meticulous in cleaning out the pods after every use, ensuring there was no risk of cross-contamination between donors.

Having watched the first round of limp and weary Ronin being dragged out of the laboratory, Elias's time had arrived. Dr Monroe called over his group. He had done this more times than he could remember, but he still dreaded what was about to come next. He cautiously walked over to the lab assistants who were preparing his pod.

"Please, remove your clothes," one of them spoke, their mouth hidden behind a white surgical mask.

Elias quickly stripped down to his underwear and discarded his clothes in a loose pile on the floor. One of the lab assistants scurried over and with a disapproving shake of her head folded up his things and placed them next to his pod.

"Now lie on the bed,"

Elias tentatively climbed up into the pod; the stiff plastic cushions squeaked underneath him as he laid down on the bed. Elias glared at the lab assistants as they hurried around him and tightened several straps, securing his arms, legs and torso in place.

"Have you done this before?" The assistant asked, her voice was clinical and uncaring, she didn't even make eye contact with him as she hurriedly tightened the straps. Elias nodded as the thick brown leather squeezed around his bare skin.

"Okay, well you will be familiar with the procedure then. In a moment we will seal the pod and begin the extraction, now please take this, it will help regulate your breathing." The assistant pulled down a small oxygen mask and attached it snuggly over his head. Instantly his lungs filled with cold, fresh air that had a peculiar minty taste to it.

"As you know well enough, there may be a slight burning sensation during the transfer process." She said, lowering the glass lid of the medical pod and sealing him inside.

He remembered back to his first time; it felt like someone had shoved a red-hot poker underneath his skin and was trying to drag the veins out of his body one at a time. When he got home that day he was haunted by the thought he had left a piece of himself behind, a sense that stayed with him for weeks afterwards; like somehow, he wasn't whole anymore.

As soon as the lid sealed shut a misty gas filled the pod, it was supposed to act as a mild anaesthetic during the procedure, but it didn't come close to masking the pain. Once the gas had cleared, hundreds of microscopic needles shot out from the pod. Elias flinched and gritted his teeth as the needles penetrated every inch of his body.

He could hear the lab assistants talking, and he knew the transfer was about to begin, this was the worst part of the whole experience. He started to panic; he could feel the sweat running down his back as he breathed in the cold air. He tried to wriggle about and make himself more comfortable, but doing so caused the needles to dig even deeper into his flesh. Then the searing hot pain hit him, flooding his senses like a tidal wave as the blood started to drain away from his body.

He let out a primal scream as the agony consumed him. He watched as the multitude of tubes leading from his pod filled with a dark, red liquid that flowed down into a small centrifuge. There, his blood was spun around at such a rapid rate, the plasma was separated. Elias tried to hold back his tears over the oxygen mask as he lay there, helplessly watching his blood being flushed away; an unwanted by-product. A tiny vile of glimmering white liquid sat beside the now empty tubes, a few millilitres of plasma that would go for thousands of creds in the Citadel. The whole procedure lasted around thirty minutes, but when cocooned within the suffocating embrace of the medical pod it seemed like a lifetime. Elias had been grimacing so much he struggled to open his eyes when they told him it was over. Three of them had to haul him up; his entire body felt hollow.

The lab assistants roughly redressed Elias, forcing his limp limbs through his clothes as he wearily staggered on the spot. He winced with pain as he felt the clothes drag against his bruised skin. Two of the lab assistants lifted Elias between them; his arms hanging limply over their shoulders as they carried him through the laboratory and back on to the transporter. His feet dragged along the floor behind him like a dead weight. His vision was fuzzy, and his hearing was muffled, it sounded like he was being held underwater.

A surge of pain coursed through his body as they dropped him on to an empty chair, the hundreds of needle holes burning again. He let out a muted groan as he pulled up his legs to his chest and curled up into a ball on the seat next to him. He dried his eyes on the back of his sleeve, but they were still blurry, he glanced out the dirty window, he could see that the sun was starting to set behind the clouds, a blazing red skyline bleeding over the horizon. He struggled to focus, and his eyes grew heavier as the familiar feeling of the transporter lurching from side to side, lulled him to sleep.

6

TIME TO LEAVE

"Easy, easy, I ain't gonna hurt you kid," the man spoke groggily as his grip on Leo's wrist relaxed.

Leo backed away, trying to create some distance between him and the bloodied figure. He stared at the gun lying on the ground between them; it was unlike anything he had ever seen before. Somehow different, sleeker and shinier than the firearms the Sovereign used.

"Why do you have that?" Leo asked, nodding at the gun.

"For protection. Not that it did me a lot of good." The man grumbled as he bent down and scooped it up, he wobbled backwards grimacing as he slipped it into his holster.

"What happened to you?"

"Let's just say I had a run-in with the Sovereign," the man nodded to the walls of the Citadel, barely visible over the waste pits.

"In the Citadel?" Leo asked excitedly "Have you come from the city? How did you end up out here?"

"You ask a lot of questions," the man sat down, easing himself on to an overturned barrel. "What's your name?"

"Leonidas, but…my friends call me Leo for short."

"You from the Jungle, Leo?"

"Yeah, me and my brother live on the other side of town."

"Well, pleased to meet you, Leo. My name is Dash."

"So you did come from the Citadel?"

"Sort of," Dash scratched at his face "I take it you and your brother aren't supporters of the Sovereign?" He said, breaking out into a smile.

"Are you…" Leo paused as he inched closer to Dash. "Are you from the Army of Shadows?" He whispered.

"You haven't been branded. How did you manage that?" Dash nodded, noticing Leo's uncovered wrists.

"My brother, he hid me when the Sovereign came to the Jungle. They never found me," Leo said proudly. "So you are from the resistance, what are you doing all the way out here?"

"Look, you seem like a good kid, and I don't want to lie to you but trust me, the less you know, the better."

"I always wanted to join the Shadows when I was growing up," Leo said gazing at Dash.

"I need a place to lay low for a while until I can figure a way out of here," Dash said, speaking over Leo.

"So you are a Shadow." Leo tried to conceal the excitement in his voice.

"I didn't say that. Anyway, your friends. The ones that left you here with a gun-toting corpse, they are getting help for you, right?" Dash nodded over at Leo's companions as they noisily made their way back up the mound of rubbish.

Leo stared up at his friends and paused for a few moments before chuckling to himself.

"Well, I hope so."

Dash laughed.

"Then I need to make a move, it won't be long before the Sovereign gets word of my arrival in the Jungle," He pushed himself off the barrel and turned away from Leo. "Good to meet you Leonidas, take care of yourself."

Leo stood there watching Dash limp through the waste pits when a strange sensation came over him. A voice, deep inside of him, telling him he had to help Dash, whether he was a Shadow or not it was the right thing to do. Leo broke into a sprint and chased after him.

"Dash, Dash," he said, skidding to a stop. "I know a place where you can stay, it's not much, but you'll be safe, and no one will find you. I promise."

"Why are you helping me?" said Dash, staring at Leo with an incredulous look on his face.

Leo looked down, avoiding Dash's gaze and kicked a can by his foot.

"Well, it's the right the thing to do. I always say to my brother, the world won't ever become a better place if no one helps each other."

Dash shook his head in astonishment and smiled.

"Why are you looking at me like that?" Leo asked, noticing a peculiar expression creeping over Dash's face.

"It's just…you remind me of someone I know." Dash said sadly, "You sure you want to help me?"

"Of course, I can hardly leave you out here now can I, and… I know you're a Shadow really." Leo's face burst into a broad smile.

The journey back to the Jungle took some time. Dash struggled to traverse the rugged, uneven landscape, every step appeared to pain him more than the last. Leo carefully led him by the hand through the trickier parts. He told Dash all about his life in the Jungle and how Elias was saving up to smuggle themselves into the Citadel.

"So it's just you and brother now then?" Dash asked.

"Yeah, my mum and dad died when I was a baby. Never even met them." Leo said flippantly.

Dash grimaced at his words.

"It's fine though, it's just the two of us, but we like it that way," Leo added quickly.

Dash smiled awkwardly. "So where is he now?"

Leo paused and pulled a concerned expression.

"Sorry, I didn't mean to pry." Dash added quickly.

"No, it's okay. It's just…" Leo hesitated. "He's at the plasma banks."

Dash stopped in his tracks.

"With the Shenmue?"

Leo nodded.

"How many times has he donated?"

"About fifteen."

Dash scrunched up his face at the thought. "My god."

"I hate it when he goes there," Leo blurted out.

"I'm sorry, Leo. I've seen their facilities; they are not pleasant places. Your brother must be made of iron to keep going back there."

"He thinks it's the only way we can make ends meet, but I keep telling him I can find more stuff out here, things I can repair. But sometimes he sneaks out before I can stop him." Leo blurted out the words as his eyes started to well up.

Dash patted him on the shoulder. "I forget sometimes, how hard life is out here."

"It's not too bad," Leo said quickly, drying his eyes with the palm of his hand, he pointed up to another steep hill. "Not far now, it's just over here."

"Great." Dash sighed as he wearily started to clamber up. Leo doubled back and grabbed his arm, helping steady him as he slowly crawled to the top. They passed several Ronin scavenging through the pits, their giant sacks now stuffed so full with precious loot, it dwarfed their emaciated bodies. Leo greeted every one of them as they walked by.

"Is there anyone in the Jungle you don't know?"

Leo laughed. "Yeah, it's a big place, there are thousands of us here. But not many people come to the pits, so you kind of get to know everyone and it's nice to say hello to people. Everyone here is in the same boat I am. Trying to find something that will make their life a little bit better."

"You speak a lot of sense." Dash smiled. "You come here a lot?"

"Everyday."

Dash stopped and shook his head. He sighed and looked down at Leo, wrinkling his nose as if trying to hold back tears.

"I'm sorry, Leo."

"What for?" Leo asked, staring up at Dash in bemusement.

"For everything. The Sovereign, the war, the Jungle. That you and your brother have to live like this. Everything. This is no place for a child to grow up in…" Dash trailed off as he watched some more Ronin shuffling past them, struggling under the weight of their hauls.

"It's not so bad," Leo added quickly, sensing Dash's unease. "It's the only home I've ever known."

Dash nodded without saying another word.

"Right, this is the last hill!" Leo declared, trying to lighten the mood.

By the time they eventually reached the summit, the sun had started its slow descent into the clouds behind them.

"What's that?" Leo said, pointing to several fast-moving black objects approaching the Jungle.

Dash pulled a strange-looking device out of his jacket pocket and held it up to his eye. It was a small, silver tube with a concave lens attached to the end.

"The Sovereign." Dash muttered as he passed the monocular to Leo who imitated Dash and stared down into it. He was greeted with a crisp, zoomed-in image of the ground below, so close it was like he was stood right there.

Leo could see clearly now that the black objects were dozens of Sovereign rhinos; armoured personnel carriers. Their thick tank tracks kicked up a massive plume of dust that trailed behind them as they approached the Jungle at speed, their machine gun turrets scanning the path ahead. The rhinos came to an abrupt stop by the main entrance to the Jungle, the turrets that sat atop the vehicles swivelled and faced several stray Ronin who had started to drift in their direction. Then in an instant, they opened fire, flashes of light exploded as they shot thousands of rounds into the crowd.

"No!" Leo screamed as he watched the bodies of the Ronin evaporate under the heavy turret fire. He staggered backwards in a state of shock as his eyes started to well up.

"Why? Why are they doing that!"

Dash shook his head. "They are looking for me. We need to go."

Leo looked back down at the Jungle and could see more flashes of light as the rhinos made their way through the camp firing indiscriminately in all directions.

"I...I...I need to go back. My brother..." Leo said stammering; his heart was pounding so hard in his chest; he thought it would explode. His head was spinning; he had no idea what was going on.

"I'm sorry Leo, but you can't go back, you won't last five minutes down there." Dash said, pointing to the Jungle.

The rhinos had stopped and lowered their rear ramps - dozens of heavily armoured soldiers with bulky canisters strapped to their backs and long rods in their hands filed out. A flash of bright orange erupted as the scorch troopers fired up their flamethrowers and started torching everything around them.

Leo watched in horror as the flames ripped through the Jungle like a whirlwind, engulfing the whole camp within minutes. Thick black smoke filled the air as the shantytown exploded into a blazing inferno.

"We've got to go. Now!' Dash shouted.

"I...I can't. I need to find Eli; he'll need me," Leo muttered as he threw Dash's monocular back to him. He sprinted down the hill leading back to the Jungle, rubbish spiralling down all around him.

"Leo, Leo, LEO!" Dash screamed as he stumbled after him, but Leo was too quick. Before Dash had even made it to the bottom, Leo had disappeared into the smoke-filled streets of the Jungle.

"Damn it!" Dash grunted as he collapsed to his knees and looked out at the raging fire.

7

THE WILDLANDS

Elias awoke abruptly as one of the Mercs kicked his legs.

"Up. Now." The Merc gestured with his hands for him to get up and shoved him through the carriage. Elias stumbled to his feet in a groggy haze, his whole body throbbed; it felt like he had been hit by a train.

"What's going on?" Elias asked as he struggled to peer out of a window; he spotted an orange glow on the horizon, lighting up the night sky.

"The Jungle is on fire. The driver says it's not safe to go any further, so you are walking." The Merc said as he bundled Elias and the other Ronin towards the exit.

"A fire," one of the Ronin said wearily.

"What's happening?" asked another.

"When are we going to get paid?" said a third trying to turn and face the Merc.

Elias froze. Only one thought entered his head.

Leo.

He forced his way through the arguing Ronin and hurried

to the door, someone grabbed him by the elbow and forced up his sleeve, Elias turned back as a Merc scanned his tattoo with a small handheld device. It let out a loud beep to indicate Elias's payment had been transferred.

"Here, take your money and get the hell out of here," the Merc said gruffly.

Elias staggered off the transporter and stepped onto the scorched earth, the smell of burning flesh made him gag, he tried his best to stop himself retching. He could see more clearly now. The Jungle was ablaze.

Towering flames bellowed in all directions as a thick plume of black smoke drifted overhead. Elias's heart began to race; his mouth dried up as he broke out into a sprint, running across the desert. Instantly his body stopped aching as it was flooded with adrenaline. His thoughts focused only on Leo, alone and afraid, he had to find him.

The rest of the Ronin hung back and shrieked at Elias, urging him not to go as he rushed towards the fire. He scrambled on all fours up a dune, the sand dragging him back with every step. As he reached the summit and stared down at the Jungle, he raked the back of his neck in frustration, scratching deep into his skin. The roaring flames now blanketed the entire shantytown. Scores of Ronin were running in panic through the twisting streets, desperately trying to find their way through the veil of smoke. Others clutched hold of their children, trying to shield their eyes from the horror unfolding around them.

Elias frantically searched for a clear path, but their home was on the other side of the camp. He clawed at his face; he didn't know what to do.

"What'ya doin?" said a bloodied Ronin clambering up the dune. "You can't go down there. They're torching the place, trying to drive us out!" his face was caked in black soot, his wiry beard singed and still smouldering.

"Who is? What happened?" Elias clamoured as he grabbed the man's overcoat.

"The Sovereign, a load of soldiers turned up and started to burn the place down. Never seen anything like it…the women, the children…" the man said as he drifted off, staring blankly into the distance. Elias released his grip, and the man wandered off aimlessly, shaking his head in disbelief.

Elias threw his overcoat on the floor and set off down the dune at speed, pushing past the Ronin as they tried to escape. He forced his way through the tide of people, but the heat was ferocious. Beads of sweat ran down his neck as he ventured deeper into the blaze.

"LEO!" Elias screamed over and over again as he worked his way through the smoke, ducking in and out of the flames as they tried to ensnare him in their fiery embrace.

He reached the outskirts of town and headed straight for their tent; he counted down the streets. Every row was crumbling in on itself as the raging inferno devoured everything in its path. The smoke started to disorient him, and he became lost in the haze. He desperately clutched at passers-by and asked if they had seen his brother, everyone shrugged him off, telling him they couldn't help as they tried to escape the fire.

Elias made his way down one street after the other, trying to break through the fire. Each time being forced back by the towering flames, ravaging everything in their path. Just when he thought he had broken through, he caught sight of Sovereign Scorch Troopers rampaging through the streets and had to double back on himself. Elias stumbled into an alleyway exhausted; he bent over coughing uncontrollably as he tried to catch his breath.

The heat was unbearable now and was starting to overpower him. *Where was he?* All he wanted was to hear Leo's voice again, to hold him, to let him know everything would be okay. To promise him that they would find a way out of this hell. He had to keep going, he knew Leo would be in there, somewhere, searching for him too. He took a deep breath, pulled his shirt over his face and pushed on around another corner, running headfirst into a Scorch Trooper. He was wearing a bulky backpack containing two enormous fuel canisters and carried a long flamethrower which he swung at Elias.

"Die Ronin scum!" he roared, pulling the trigger on his flamethrower, sending a burst of blazing fire exploding in his direction. Elias fell backwards, trying to avoid the flames.

He rolled on his side and frantically crawled away, the trooper marched after him, swinging the wall of fire at him once again. Elias clambered back to his feet and ran down a side street, the flames licking at his heels as he flung himself around the corner. As he did, he tumbled into someone running in the other direction. They both crashed onto the ground together, and Elias ended up on top of them.

"Quick, we've got to-" Elias paused. He couldn't believe his eyes. His heart stopped.

Leo.

"Elias!" Leo cried. "The Sovereign, they're killing everyone. The Shadows they-" before he had a chance to finish, Elias had leapt up and pulled Leo by the arm back to his feet.

"I know, we can't go back that way," Elias said, nodding back at the alleyway he had escaped from.

"This way!" Leo shouted, dragging his brother by the arm down another side-street as he spotted the Scorch Trooper marching around the corner. Leo rushed ahead of Elias, pulling his brother down a series of winding corridors until he stumbled out into a clearing. Leo immediately froze and let go of Elias's hand, shoving him back into the alleyway.

"You there!" a voice called out.

Leo went rigid. Elias peered out around the wall and saw a dozen Scorch Troopers all carrying flamethrowers stood in front of him.

"Go!" Leo whispered out of the side of his mouth. "I love you, Eli." He added, stepping away from the alleyway and holding his hands in the air.

Elias lent back into the wall and clawed at his face again. Letting out a guttural scream in silence as he smashed his fists into the wall. He wouldn't let Leo's life be snuffed out, not like this. The only thing he ever wanted was for his little brother to escape this place.

"We don't have time for this." He heard one of them shout.

All they had in this world was each other.

"Dispose of him," instructed another as he pointed to Leo.

He would never give up on his brother. Never.

The trooper raised his flamethrower and ignited it.

He wouldn't let him die alone.

Elias heard the roar of the flamethrower as it unleashed its deadly payload. He closed his eyes and leapt out on top of Leo, throwing him to the ground and diving over him. Shielding him as the flamethrower erupted, devouring them both in a flash of wildfire. Elias held Leo more tightly than he had ever held him before, squeezing him with all his might.

"It's okay, Leo. Close your eyes." Elias sobbed as he clutched his brother in his arms, pushing him into the ground. He saw the flames, hissing and spitting all around them. But oddly, it wasn't painful, there was no burning sensation. Nothing at all, in fact, it seemed like the fire was not able to reach him, bending and deflecting away from them. Enveloping the brothers in a circle of flames, but somehow, not consuming them.

"What the…?" the trooper said in astonishment. He squeezed his finger around the trigger again and sent another burst of fire shooting at them. Again the flames danced around Elias. Leaving him there, sprawled over his brother but unharmed. The other troopers turned their attention to Elias and Leo, watching what was unfolding at the end of the street.

"That's impossible!" one of them yelled.

"What are you playing at? Finish them off!" shouted another.

A deafening sound reverberated through the street. Several shots flew over Elias's head, slamming into the helmet of a Scorch Trooper, shattering it into dozen pieces. The trooper toppled back on himself, still clutching his weapon. The flames set alight to the gas canisters on his back, causing it to explode in a bright flash that scattered the other scorchers across the clearing.

Several more shots rang out and struck the remaining Scorch Troopers as they struggled back to their feet. Elias lifted his head to see what was going on, a bedraggled man in a trench coat was holding a shining silver pistol and marching forwards firing at the troopers. Leo crawled out from underneath Elias.

"Dash!" he yelled as the man approached them.

"Get out of here!" Dash roared as he helped Elias and Leo back to their feet, shooting rapidly at the troopers who were now taking cover behind some nearby bins.

"But what about you?" Leo cried out over the sound of the gunshots.

"That way is clear, I'll hold them here for as long as I can."

Dash snarled as he shoved Leo away. "Take this." Dash pulled out another smaller gun from behind his back and tossed it to Elias.

Elias caught it in his hands. It was a lot heavier than it appeared and made of black metal. Elias stared at the weapon in front of him.

"Go. NOW!" Dash ordered as the troopers regrouped and started firing back at him.

Leo was standing there, fixated on Dash. Elias grabbed his hand and dragged him away.

"We can't leave him…" Leo pleaded as he tugged and pulled, trying to break free from Elias.

"Leo, you heard what he said, we've got to go."

Elias pulled Leo away and led him down a small passage between several rows of makeshift shelters. They ran as fast as they could, quickly navigating their way through the maze of cramped alleyways; the fires had not reached this part of town yet, but the billowing smoke blanketed the path ahead.

"Eli, stop, please," Leo panted. Elias stopped and watched his brother, who was bent over struggling to breathe.

"I'm sorry, but we can't stay here for long," Elias said softly as he rubbed Leo's back.

"I'll be okay, just give me a minute," Leo said faintly.

Elias, scanning the way ahead for enemies felt the ground beneath him tremble. He looked up as a Sovereign Mech burst through the corrugated iron shelters, crushing the metal huts underneath its giant bipedal legs. A robotic hulk controlled by a Sovereign pilot housed within its torso. The Mech knocked the remains of the hut away with the back of its mechanical arm before lifting it's massive railgun and aiming it at the brothers. They cautiously backed away from the monstrous mechanical beast as it stomped towards them.

Elias raised the gun and fired blindly over his shoulder as he drove Leo forward. Each shot unleashed a thunderous cry that deafened their senses,

"Run!" Elias screamed.

With the sound still ringing in his ears, Elias turned and followed Leo. Chasing him through the rows of abandoned shacks until they finally broke free from the claustrophobic streets of the Jungle, sprinting out into the darkness of the Wildlands.

8

THE FALLING TREE

They ran until their legs couldn't carry them any more. Not stopping until the walls of the Citadel disappeared from view, and the flames of the Jungle fire flickered on the horizon like a dying ember.

"Eli, can we stop now, I'm done." Leo pulled up, panting heavily.

"Okay." Elias bent over and rested his hands on his knees, struggling to breathe.

He straightened up and caught sight of his brother doubled over, trying to catch his breath. They had been running for so long he must be exhausted Elias thought.

"Where are we going?" Leo asked as Elias patted him on the back.

"I don't know," Elias stared out into the darkness. He couldn't see anything; the wastelands were pitch black.

Now he had stopped running, the cold gripped him. His damp, sweaty clothes stuck to his body like a soggy piece of paper, causing him to shiver against the wind.

"We need to find somewhere to stay for the night and decide what we are going to do tomorrow, we won't survive the night if we don't get out of this wind," Elias pulled Leo back to his feet.

"Give me a minute," Leo pushed off Elias's hand, returning to his hunched over position, panting for several minutes before staggering back to his feet. Elias struggled to make out his features against the night.

"Right, we are going to have to head back towards the Citadel at some point. So we'll parallel along the wall until we can be sure we've lost the Sovereign," Elias pointed back to the city. Even from this far out, the lights still shone brightly.

"Hopefully we can find a burnt-out vehicle or something that we can spend the night in,"

"Well, what are we waiting for?" Leo said, marching past his brother.

"You've changed your tune," Elias said, jogging a few steps to catch up with him. "I thought I was gonna lose you back there the way you were wheezing,"

"Not a chance. I've always wanted to explore the Wildlands, but you'd never let me," Leo said defiantly.

"That's true. I never thought we'd end up exploring it like this though…"

"It's not so bad," said Leo "I kind of like it, the desert. Feels more like home than the Jungle ever did."

"What the hell happened back there? I got booted off my transporter, and the whole place was on fire." Elias hung his head. "And who was that guy who saved us?"

"His name is Dash," Leo said solemnly. "He is with the Shadows, I was helping him."

Elias groped in the dark for his brother's arm.

"What do you mean you were helping him?"

"We found him in the waste pits, he was really banged up and needed somewhere to stay. The boys, Mungo, Derick, Oskar..." Leo stopped walking and crouched down.

Elias glanced down and could just about make out Leo's tiny frame shuddering up and down.

"Hey, don't cry Leo," Elias said softly as he sat down next to his brother and cradled him. "I'm sure they made it out, and when it's safe, we can go back to find them."

"They...they...were killing everyone, Eli. Even the babies." Leo sobbed.

"It's okay," Elias said, holding him tightly to his chest.

"The people...they had nowhere to go. The smoke was everywhere. I couldn't breathe. I saw it all from the waste pits, the Sovereign coming, the fire, the killing. Dash wanted me to go with him...but I...I...couldn't leave you." Leo stuttered.

"You came back for me?" Elias squeezed his brother again.

"Yeah," Leo replied, drying his nose on Elias's shirt.

"I love you, bro." Elias kissed the top of his head and held him close to his chest, trying to stop him shivering. They sat there in the dead of night until Leo cried himself out.

"Eli, what happened when you jumped on top of me?"

Elias paused, struggling to find the right words.

"I don't know Leo. I can't explain it."

"Did you control the fire again?" Leo asked. Elias could sense the suspicion in his voice. "Like last time?"

Elias's thoughts drifted to a memory he had tried his best to suppress, but with Leo's question, a vision came searing into his consciousness. His mind flashed back three years ago when the long night came to the Jungle, and an arctic wind dropped the temperature outside the Citadel's walls to sub-zero. Thousands of helpless Ronin lost their lives that night as they battled to survive the bitter cold. Elias and Leo could have easily been another nameless victim, frozen in the wastelands, if it hadn't been for the eternal fire.

He still remembered how it felt that night, so cold it cut to the bone. He sat huddled with Leo, sheltering from the wind, fixated on a burnt out-oil drum in front of him. Trying futilely to numb out the pain of his failing body while he clung to his little brother for dear life. He imagined the drum contained a roaring fire, its gentle heat keeping them warm. Somehow the thought of its heat kept him going.

Then, just as he felt Leo's life ebbing away, his tiny, emaciated body shivering in his grasp, a flash a wildfire exploded in the drum. Elias didn't understand what had happened, but he didn't waste time thinking about it and quickly dragged his brother's limp body towards it. The fire burned all night. Dozens of Ronin drifted towards the flaming beacon, hunkering together to take refuge from the brutal weather. In the Jungle, the long night and the eternal fire became the stuff of legend.

Elias felt his brother shiver by his side, and he snapped back to attention.

"Yeah, I think so. It was different this time, I could still feel the heat, but it didn't hurt me. It was almost as if the flames couldn't come near me. Are you okay?" Elias asked urgently, feeling his brother trembling in his grip.

"I'm cold, Eli." Leo's body began to shake uncontrollably as another gust of wind lashed them. Now the adrenalin that had fuelled their bodies over the last few hours was finally abandoning them they suddenly felt the bitter north wind again.

"I know. We need to go, we'll freeze to death if we don't

find some shelter soon. Can you keep going?" Elias asked as he pulled Leo to his feet.

"I think so."

"Let's crack on. Here, get on my back," Elias said as he stooped down. Leo trudged forward and slumped on top of his brother.

Elias heaved himself upwards with Leo feeling like a lead weight on his back. He plodded onward, one heavy footstep at a time. The pair walked through the wastelands for hours without coming across anything they might be able to use as a refuge. He could feel Leo shivering on his back as the vicious wind whipped against them. The landscape was barren, offering no protection from the elements at all. He started to grow weaker as the aches from the plasma extraction returned, every step becoming a struggle.

"Not much further now, I think I saw something up ahead," he lied. Leo barely mustered a response. Elias could feel his brother's heartbeat growing fainter on his back.

"Leo, Leo, stay with me. Keep those eyes open, okay?" Elias tried to rouse Leo as he drifted off.

"Wha..." Leo muttered in confusion.

"Tell me about Dash," Elias said, racking his brains for something to try and keep Leo talking. "He's with the resistance, right?"

"Yeah...he was a shado…" Leo said weakly, trailing off.

Elias paused in his tracks, and his knees buckled as he felt the ground beneath him begin to shake. A crack started to form between his feet, and he stepped back as the ground crumbled around him. The floor gave way, and he lost his footing, falling into the newly created chasm. Elias panicked as they tumbled down a steep slope, hopelessly trying to grab hold of something, anything, as they bumped and crashed their way down a series of sharp, jagged canyons. Leo slipped off his back, and he desperately reached out for his brother, but it was too late. Leo's hand slipped through his grasp.

"LEO!" he screamed as he tumbled down the canyon.

Elias hit the ground hard, his head smashing into a rock with a sickening thud. He lay there for a few moments in a daze before slipping into unconsciousness.

———

Elias slowly opened his eyes, he blinked several times before realising he was surrounded by complete and utter darkness. He crawled on to his belly, and shakily got back to his feet; his legs trembling as he tried to walk.

"LEO!" Elias's voice echoed all around him.

"ELI!" Leo's voice appeared from nowhere; hidden behind the shadows.

"Where are you?" his voice boomeranged.

"Is that a serious question. I don't know. We're lost." Leo replied.

Elias laughed to himself as he limped forward, his face grimacing with every step. He tried to follow the sound of Leo's voice, but it was hopeless. Their echoes were cascading off into a sonar spiral over his head. His spirits lifted when he noticed something in the distance; a small ray of light piercing through the darkness. A sense of deja vu struck him, the scene was oddly familiar.

"Leo, can you see that light?"

"Yeah, just about."

"Start heading over to it. Let's hope we cross paths," Elias stumbled forward, his hands stretched out, groping the air in front of him. After a few moments, he bumped into something small and squishy.

"Eli, you got me. Get your hand out of my face." Leo laughed as he swatted his hand away.

"You alright?" Elias grabbed hold of Leo's shoulder, the relief evident in his voice.

"Yeah I think so, every part of my body is aching though."

"Right, let's head to the light," Elias said as he guided Leo to the mysterious glow ahead.

The brothers edged their way through a series of narrowing and winding tunnels, getting closer to the faraway light. Eventually, they noticed something silhouetted within it.

"What...is that?" Leo whispered out the side of his mouth.

"No idea, but..." Elias trailed off, he felt stupid even thinking about what he was about to say. "I think I've been here before," he blurted out quickly.

"What are you on about?"

"I've seen this place before...in my dreams."

Elias wandered towards the peculiar shape; fixated on the mysterious wonder before him. He saw it more clearly now, located on a platform just ahead; a tree, covered by a faint layer of mist. Several rays of light penetrated the darkness from different angles, refracting off the moisture to create a stunning, shimmering effect. Elias was drawn to it, something called out to him, beckoning him forwards.

"Eli, watch where you are going," Leo whispered. But before he could get his attention, Elias misplaced his next step and went tumbling over a ledge.

"Eli!" Leo screamed as he stumbled backwards, clinging on to a nearby rock.

Elias tried to regain his balance, but he was travelling too fast and skidded down a steep slope on his back. He picked up speed and felt the ground fall away as he shot off another ledge and crashed in front of the tree, kicking up a thick plume of dust as he landed.

"Urgh," Elias grunted as his head bounced off the floor again; he let out a loud cough as the dust settled around him.

He lay there on his back for a few moments trying to clear his head, the bright light momentarily blinding him. He heard Leo's voice shouting from afar but couldn't make out what he was saying. He rolled onto his front, and groggily looked up, his vision still blurry. Rubbing his eyes, the tree came into view, it was enormous, exactly like the one from his dreams. A vast, brown trunk with myriad twisting branches spreading out in all directions, topped with vibrant green foliage that glistened in the light. Elias had never seen anything so beautiful.

He stared at the tree, astounded by what stood before him. He started to feel the ground beneath him quiver and shake, as a blast of energy shot out from underneath him and smashed into the tree with an almighty crash. The tree creaked and groaned as it was forced out of the ground, its deep roots ripped violently from the soil. Elias gasped in horror as the tree slipped backwards and crumpled on to itself, it seemed to take an age to fall to the floor before crashing with a deafening crunch. Bark exploded as the tree collapsed into a ruined heap. Branches cracked and splintered, jutting out at awkward angles.

Elias wearily rose to his feet, his head still spinning from the fall. Leo's voice rang out all around him, but he couldn't place it. Standing in the light made the darkness seem even darker. It was impossible to find his brother out there.

Hunching over with his hands resting on his knees, the felled tree behind him, he didn't notice as branch by branch, it pulled itself back together as if controlled by an unseen force. First, driving its roots back into the soil and then reattaching the splinters of bark scattered around it.

Elias turned to face the wreckage and jumped back in shock when he saw the tree once again standing proudly before him. As Elias flinched, the tree shivered, its branches shaking wildly. Elias jerked his head back with a confused expression, and the tree appeared to arch back its trunk. He started to pace around it, ducking in and out of the light, as he did the tree swayed calmly from side to side. He paused mid-step and, the tree abruptly stopped quivering and stood motionless.

Elias ran his fingers through his greasy hair, and the tree's branches arched backwards, shaking its leaves vigorously at him. He didn't have a clue what was going on; the tree seemed to be mirroring his every move. He jumped up and down, and the tree swiftly followed, trying to tear its roots up from the soil. Elias reached his hands high into the air and swung them from side to side, once again the tree tried to copy him, its branches rearing upwards and swaying serenely as if waving back at him. Elias smiled to himself and shook his head in disbelief; the top of the tree rustled, and a few leaves dropped off, floating majestically to the ground.

Leo looked on in amazement from the ledge above, he didn't understand what was going on.

"ELI!" Leo shouted again, cupping his hands around his

mouth. He waved frantically at his brother who appeared to be staring straight through him.

Leo was so enthralled by Elias that he didn't notice the figure behind him until it was too late. A hand grabbed Leo by the shoulder, and he froze, slowly turning around he came face-to-face with a grizzled old man.

"What are you doing here?" the bearded figure asked.

9

GENESIS

Elias didn't know how long he had been standing there, mesmerised by the tree. He turned on the spot; trying to catch a glimpse of Leo in the shadows, but it was hopeless.

"Leo, are you okay?" His words echoed around him.

There was no reply.

Something wasn't right. A sudden panic overcame him; they were completely and utterly lost. It would take them weeks to find a way out.

"You're a natural," a voice rang out from the darkness. Elias couldn't see who it belonged to.

"Where...who...who are you? Where is my brother?" Elias shouted, not knowing which question to ask first.

"Your brother is fine, in fact, he is right here. Careful now, mind your step young lad," the voice said calmly. Leo stepped out of the darkness and was immediately bathed in the bright white light.

Elias ran over and gave him a big hug, his arms squeezing so tightly, Leo struggled to breathe. The shadowy figure walked into the light; he wore a long grey cloak, beige fatigues and a clunky set of desert boots. He had a kind, yet weathered face that broke out into a broad grin as he approached the boys.

"My, my, you are indeed something spectacular," he said, smiling down at Elias.

"Who are you? What is this place?" Elias stammered, pointing to the tree behind the grey man.

"I must apologise for startling you. Young Leonidas here was telling me about how you two came across this place. Most fortuitous, but then again, Gaia truly works in mysterious ways. My name is General Orion Tiberius," he spoke with a calm familiar tone like he had known the boys all their lives. He flicked his long grey hair effortlessly off his face as he spoke.

"General? Of what? The Sovereign?" Elias asked as he stepped in front of Leo.

"Oh, dear no, absolutely not. My title is a formality from a life long since lived. I suspect you have never heard of me, the Sovereign has developed quite a skill for erasing people from the annals of history. You may be more familiar with the organisation I now serve; the Army of Shadows." Tiberius said as he hunkered down in front of the boys, carefully crossing his legs. He sat there for a few moments staring at Elias as he stroked his beard.

"Please take a seat Elias, we have much to discuss."

Elias and Leo stared at each other, Elias was lost for words. First, the escape, then the tree and now they stumble across some crazy old fool who thought he was the leader of the resistance.

"Can we have a quick minute?" Leo smiled at Tiberius as he peered around Elias.

"Of course, take as long as you need!" Tiberius replied.

Elias led Leo off a few paces and turned to his brother.

"I like him, I say we hear him out", Leo said quietly.

"How can you like him? You've only just met him!" Elias whispered back angrily.

"I dunno, I've got a good feeling about him."

"Are you serious? He thinks he's a General in the Shadows. I mean, look at him. He looks like he's lived down here for years."

The brothers cautiously turned towards Tiberius to get a clearer view of him. He was still sitting on the ground, cross-legged, beaming at them. They smiled awkwardly back at him.

"How can you not want to hear him out? I bet he's got some cracking stories," Leo said nodding at Tiberius.

"That's my point. They will be stories! Make-believe and gobbledegook from a crazy old fool who lives in a cave! Honestly, what's wrong with you, Leonidas!" Elias snapped.

"Alright, well what's your plan, stumble around in the dark for a few more hours until we fall into another hole?" Leo grumbled. They peered back at Tiberius and waved.

"Won't be a minute," Leo added and Tiberius smiled as he waved his hand for them to continue.

"Okay, okay, we'll listen to what he's got to say. He might know a way out of here, but when I say we need to go. WE NEED TO GO. Okay?" Elias said placing emphasis on his words.

"OK-AY," Leo mouthed the word slowly.

"He might also be able to explain what that was all about," Leo said, pointing over to the tree.

"Did you see that?" Elias asked excitedly.

"Yeah, it was incredible. What is that thing?"

Before Elias could answer Tiberius interjected.

"I am awfully sorry to eavesdrop, but I think I may be of assistance with regards to your last question. That is a tree. A Ginkgo Biloba to be exact, it's the great tree of Albion and more importantly, the last surviving tree on planet Earth."

Elias and Leo stared at Tiberius, then at the tree, then back to Tiberius - who still had a massive grin on his face. Leo pushed Elias out of the way and sat down cross-legged in front of him.

"What's a tree?" Leo asked, gazing at Tiberius.

Elias rolled his eyes and sat down next to Leo, jabbing his brother in the ribs as he sat beside him. He shuffled forward and nodded at Tiberius, who let out a small chuckle.

"Sometimes I forget what it must be like nowadays, to be raised away from Albion," said Tiberius, with a hint of sadness in his voice.

"Trees were once the lungs of the world. In a time long since passed, trees were nature's way of producing the air we breathe and maintaining a climate suitable for us to live in. Not too long ago, when we did not always rely on machines to do this for us. This magnificent specimen here, I am afraid to say, is the last tree in existence."

"Why is it here?" Leo asked inquisitively.

"We planted it here many years ago when we first established our fair city. We hoped one day to sow its seedlings to establish our own forest and, in time, restart the cycle of creation. For a reason we do not know, this tree did not yield any seedlings." Tiberius said sadly, shaking his head. "We tried the most advanced methods of propagation known to man to try and encourage it to reproduce, but despite our best efforts, nothing seemed to work. Its offspring simply will not grow."

"What's with the lights?" Leo interjected again.

"Good question, trees need three things to survive: air,

water and light. Unfortunately, down here, natural light is not an option. Therefore, we needed to create artificial light to ensure our wonderful tree here had everything required to thrive in its subterranean home. As we are very deep underground, we need to refract light from our city into this chamber. And the mist, that is water vapour." Tiberius explained

"And why..." before Leo could finish, Elias found his voice.

"Why does it copy me?"

"Alas, that is the most pertinent question. The answer, I'm pleased to tell you is quite simple. However, the implications of what it means for you, I suspect, will lead to many more questions." Tiberius paused for a few moments, staring at the boys until Leo nodded encouragingly for him to continue.

"Elias. You are a Nihon." he said casually as if his words made perfect sense.

Elias and Leo stared blankly at Tiberius; they had no idea what a Nihon was or why being one meant he would be able to control the tree.

"A nee-on? What's that then?" Leo asked.

"The Nihon are the guardians of Earth, dedicated to protecting our planet and its inhabitants in their darkest hour. The Nihon work in harmony with the world around them, reading and interpreting Gaia's will to guide mankind."

"Who is Gaia?" Leo fired off another question.

"Gaia...she is everything. You, me, the tree, the citizens of the Citadel, the Sovereign, everything and everyone, they all makeup Gaia. She is the very soul of our world, the spirit of humanity and of every species that ever graced our beautiful planet. She guides us, feeds us and protects us."

"So why does it follow me?" Elias interrupted.

"It wasn't following you, Elias, you were controlling it."

Elias and Leo exchanged worried glances.

"What binds of all this together is mana."

"Maa nah," repeated Elias.

"Exactly," Tiberius smiled.

"What's mana?" asked Leo.

"Mana is the life force of Gaia, the blood that runs through her veins, her very essence. Mana is the energy that controls and drives everything on our planet. Elias, as a Nihon you can tap into this invisible channel of energy and use it in ways you cannot even begin to fathom. You can control and influence the world around you like you just did with our tree."

"But I didn't do anything."

"That is the beauty of Gaia, the Nihon are so naturally in sync with the world, Gaia's creations respond instantly to them. The tree is one the purest examples of Gaia's grace, therefore without knowing it, you have complete and utter power over it." Tiberius explained.

Elias looked over at the tree. Did he really have control over it? He sat in stunned silence and shook his head. Out the corner of his eye, he noticed the tree gently shaking its leaves. Elias snapped his gaze back to Tiberius.

"So how many other Nihon are there?" Leo continued his inquisition, unfazed by the revelations.

"Only two - and one is sitting right next to you."

Elias shot up to his feet and walked away, running his fingers through his hair.

"None of this makes sense, how can any of this be true?" Elias said as he paced up and down, not noticing the tree swaying from side to side behind him.

"Gaia works in mysterious ways, Elias. I'm afraid even the Nihon do not have the answers to all of life's questions. They can only seek to interpret the signals around them to the best of their abilities. I have been witness to the immense power of the Nihon, Elias you have no idea the strength that lies within you." Tiberius stopped and stared at Elias, his eyes focusing in on him intently.

"But, like all great power, the gifts Gaia presents to her guardians can corrupt even the noblest of souls. The man we now know as Voltaire was the last Nihon, but he grew thirsty for power and betrayed his people. His actions drove Earth to the brink of destruction, but just when all hope seemed lost. Gaia has led you to us."

Elias stood up. His mind went into overdrive. He had so many questions he needed answers to. How could any of this be true? Him, the chosen one, Earth's guardian - he was just a refugee from the Jungle.

A nobody.

Nothing.

As quickly as the doubts entered his head, they faded away, replaced by memories of all the peculiar events in his life that he could never explain. He'd always had a strange affinity with fire that baffled those around him. The earliest memory from his childhood was as a young boy, sitting and waving his hand over a burning candle. The wail of his mother when she walked in and saw his chubby little fist resting in the flickering flame still haunted him to this day. But when she scooped him up and cradled him in her arms, she fell silent. Staring at his hands in disbelief. Astonished by what she discovered, no burns, no scorched skin, no redness at all.

The night of the eternal fire was another event that had confounded him, even thinking about it made him feel crazy. He knew you couldn't just will a fire into existence, no matter how much you wanted to. But there was no other explanation. The barrel was empty. No fuel, no kindling, nothing. Yet somehow imagining a flame in his mind, transformed a burnt-out oil drum into a voracious fire.

But tonight was the most extraordinary event of all. He had shielded Leo from the Sovereign's flamethrowers and survived without a scratch. The attack had destroyed their home and forced them out into the wilderness, yet somehow they ended up here. In their darkest hour, they had discovered the last tree on Earth.

Throughout his life, Elias had always felt guided by an invisible hand. An intuition that came to the fore when he needed it most, helping him find a way through the fog when he couldn't see a path ahead. As Elias looked back, he realised all of these things had been leading him to this very moment, to this encounter with Tiberius. Suddenly he was not scared anymore; instead, excitement gripped him. He yearned to learn more, to know where this road would lead. To finally understood who he was.

Elias turned back to face Tiberius and Leo.

"So, what now?"

"Now, you take the first step on your journey. Elias, Leo, would you like to visit the home of the resistance?"

Leo smiled and turned to his brother, who let out a laugh.

"What are we waiting for?" he said with a smile.

10

A CITY OF EMBERS

The journey to Albion took longer than expected, Elias and Leo began to wonder if their first impressions of Tiberius were right. Perhaps living underground all these years with a tree for a best friend had gone to his head. Leo started to worry that maybe it was all an elaborate trick he was playing on them.

Tiberius led the boys through a glistening chamber covered in glimmering mineral deposits. The light from his torch refracted off the sparkling roof, sending rays of light dancing all around them. The scenery became more breathtaking as they descended deeper underground. Traversing through a spiralling canyon, encrusted with shimmering silver ice that forked off into the darkness.

Tiberius explained that Albion was housed nearly a mile beneath the surface in a vast, impenetrable cave complex and very few Shadows knew the way in and out. They continued down a series of narrow, dimly lit passageways that led to a long, dusty road that seemed to stretch out forever. At the end stood a massive wooden door built into the side of a rock. The path flanked either side by hanging lanterns, radiating brightly in the darkness.

"I must warn you, I radioed ahead to let the guards know I would be returning with some unexpected guests. I did request they not make any special arrangements for your arrival. Still, I am afraid the residents of Albion can be somewhat..." Tiberius paused for a few moments, struggling to decide what word to use next.

"...excitable," he added eventually.

"What do you mean, excitable?" Elias asked nervously.

"You must understand Elias, the people of Albion are very different from those who live in the Citadel, they yearn for an alternative way of life, based on respect for Gaia. Therefore your role as a Nihon places you in quite an exalted position in their eyes."

"But I've only just found out that I might be a Nihon, they won't expect me to do anything will they?" Elias stopped.

"Oh no, not at all, they hold the Nihon in far too high regard to make any demands of them."

Tiberius reached the gate and tapped on it three times with his knuckles, he took a step back and winked at a security camera perched overhead. The doors opened, creaking and groaning as they revealed a massive crowd that had swelled around the entrance.

"Oh dear," Tiberius turned back and smiled at the boys, both of whom had an expression of horror on their faces. Tiberius stepped over the threshold and entered Albion.

"Hello, Davies. Melasandra, lovely to see you. Please clear a way for our guests," Tiberius greeted the people, nodding to everyone as he forced his way through.

"Come on, follow me," he shouted, peering over the top of several people as he tried to manoeuvre them out of the way.

Elias and Leo shared a worried glance, the same thoughts flying through their heads. What was this place and, who were all these strange-looking people? Their clothes were made of peculiar-looking materials, simple robes and shawls, all in bland colours, unlike anything in the Jungle. There wasn't an Aug insight, it was like a postcard from the past.

People filled the streets for as far as they could see, standing on their tiptoes, craning for a better view, trying to catch a glimpse of them, hundreds of eyes watching their every step. The boys cautiously followed Tiberius as he worked his way through the crowd.

"That's it lads, nothing to be afraid of. The people of Albion have just come out to say hello," Tiberius said, straining to turn his head as he ushered people out of the way.

"Which one do you think he is?" Leo heard a voice ask from the crowd.

"Is he really a Nihon?" said another.

"Never in my lifetime did I think this would happen,"

"Which one is he?"

"He doesn't look like a Nihon!"

What does not a Nihon look like? Leo thought to himself. He glanced at his brother, like Elias apparently.

The crowd watched them with unwavering attention. People were packed several rows back, all squirming and struggling to get sight of the boys. Elias tried to keep his head down and avoid eye contact as he passed by, nodding and smiling politely whenever someone spoke to him. Leo walked closely behind Elias, his mouth wide open.

"Nearly there now, sorry about all of this. As I said, the

people of Albion can be quite excitable." Tiberius said, grinning at the boys.

Excitable, that's an understatement thought Leo. Elias smiled and nodded back at Tiberius.

"I must introduce you to the Council, they will be thrilled to meet you," Tiberius added.

"Who are the Council?" Elias asked.

"They oversee Albion. There are ten councillors who are each responsible for a department that plays a vital role in running the city."

"Like the Sovereigns Senate?" Leo said.

"No, no, nothing like those philanderers. Each councillor is democratically elected by the people and is held accountable to the citizens they serve. If they fail to live up to expectations, they will soon find themselves out of a job." Tiberius chuckled.

"Do they have a leader?" Elias chipped in again.

"Indeed, and you shall soon meet him," Tiberius said as they finally broke free of the throng.

Elias and Leo had been so busy navigating their way through the mass of bodies they completely forgot to take in their new surroundings. They were now at the bottom of a wide stone staircase leading up to a vast palace, the boys had never seen anything like it.

"Wow…" Leo muttered.

The palace was stunning; it was carved out of the rocks that surrounded it. Gigantic stone pillars adorned with elegant carvings held it in place. Set over several levels it had a number of walkways which connected it to different parts of the city. Tiberius escorted Elias and Leo up the stairs and away from the streets below. They noticed some movement at the top as several people started to make their way out of an enormous doorway.

"Here come the Council now," Tiberius whispered out the side of his mouth.

"Tiberius, you said this day would come," a councillor said as he strode out and grabbed Tiberius into a tight hug, patting him roughly on the back. He had a tall, slender frame and his skin was a light brown. His short, well groomed black hair framed his face.

"Truly, Gaia has blessed us. Please, let me introduce you. Boys, this is Commander Benjamin Obasi, leader of the resistance."

"Nice to meet you, sir," said Elias.

"Nice to meet you too." Leo added.

"Welcome to Albion. We are honoured to have you with us," Obasi said as he broke out into a broad smile, he exuded a relaxed confidence . He opened up his arms and pulled both of them into him. "We've got a lot of excited people up there waiting to meet you."

Obasi released his grip and gestured for them to continue up the stairs. Several councillors waited for them at the top of the staircase, the ones at the back peering over their colleague's shoulders for a clearer view. A long, narrow-faced man wearing a tiny pair of spectacles took a step towards them, extending his arm. He was uncomfortably tall and had to stoop over to reach the boys. He was dressed in a high-necked, black cloak and his skin was so pale it was almost translucent.

"Balendin Fallon. This is the architect of Albion, every-thing around us started out as his vision."

"You are too kind Tiberius; it is our pleasure to welcome you both to our fair city." Fallon shook hands with each of them. Leo noticed his very limp handshake as his pale hand slithered through his grip.

"I will keep this brief as I really must be returning to my work." said a pasty-faced councillor, pushing to the front. He had short blonde hair and appeared somewhat dishevelled compared to the rest of the Council, like he was too busy to worry about such trivial things as getting ready in the morning. He awkwardly shook hands with both of the boys before disappearing back down the staircase.

"That's Raleigh Carmichael, he's our resident genius. Don't take it personally, he's always got something more important to be doing. To be honest, you should be quite honoured he even turned up, it's the first time we've got him out of his lab in weeks." Tiberius chortled as he introduced them to the next councillor in line.

"Kibibi Mahiri," a beautiful black woman bowed in front of them, she had a long delicate build with a perfectly bald head that glistened in the light. She wore an extravagant necklace coupled with a simple flowing gown that accentuated her long limbs. The boys blushed and returned Kibibi's bow.

"MacDonald Munro, it's a pleasure to make your acquaintance," said a stiff, well-spoken man. Munro was dressed in an old-fashioned, immaculately pressed military uniform, complete with an abundance of medals and braids. He adjusted his wide, gold-rimmed monocle while looking the boys up and down.

Leo noticed Tiberius drift away and start up a conversation with another councillor; a towering man with a pale, puffy face. A pair of black-rimmed glasses sat in front of some dark, hollow eyes. He had neatly cropped greying hair swooped to one side, and his facial features were oddly out of proportion to the rest of his head. He kept glancing over at them as he spoke with Tiberius, Leo got the suspicion he was talking about them and what he was saying didn't appear altogether positive.

"Glad to have you onboard," a woman with cropped silver hair said as she saluted the boys. She was wearing modern combat fatigues, with a beret held firmly in place under the epaulette on her right shoulder.

"My name is Colonel Mako, I am in charge of the security forces here in Albion. If you encounter any difficulties during your stay, please let me know." Elias snapped to attention and returned her salute. She was quite possibly the tallest woman Leo had ever seen. She towered over her male counterparts and held herself with such poise he thought she might actually be made of iron. He felt a sharp jab in his side from Elias, and his face flushed red when he realised he was still gazing at her. Tiberius waved them over to the puffy-faced councillor.

"Elias, Leo, I'd like to introduce you to councillor Miles Grove."

"Good to meet you," Elias said, shaking hands with Miles.

"Quite," Miles responded curtly as he glanced down at them. He extended his hand to Leo, who just glared at him; he did not like Miles one bit. He swiftly withdrew his hand without shaking Leo's and slid off to join Fallon, his grey cloak dragging along the floor behind him. The remaining members of the Council passed by in a blur and Leo had already forgotten half of their names by the time they were introduced to the last one.

"Come, I will take you over to your new living quarters so you can get settled in," Tiberius said, beckoning over the boys.

"New living quarters?" Elias turned to Tiberius with a bewildered expression on his face. Leo looked up, snapping out of his daydream.

"I am sorry, this must be quite overwhelming for you. We

would be honoured if you would stay with us here in Albion. Elias, you will have all the help you need here to learn the extent of your powers, and in time, reach your full potential as a Nihon. And Leo, you would be more than welcome to start your education here with us. Although I must admit, you might have a bit of catching up to do."

"So are we Shadows now?" Leo asked excitedly.

"If you so wish. For as long as you want, you will have a home here." Tiberius smiled.

"A home?" Leo turned to his brother, "We've never had a home before."

"I know." Elias said, pulling Leo into him, "Maybe this is the home we've been searching for." He whispered to his brother.

"Tiberius, we would be thrilled to stay in Albion with you, well at least until we can figure this out."

"Excellent, well before you go you may wish to turnaround - you can enjoy one of the most stunning views of Albion from our current vantage point." Tiberius pointed behind them.

Elias and Leo turned around and took in the breathtaking scenery of the valley below. Albion was situated in a vast underground cavern, gigantic stalactites drooped down dramatically from the ceiling. Thousands of miniature lanterns dangled overhead, their golden embers floating majestically in the darkness.

The streets tracked the natural flow of the cave and were interspersed with colossal rock formations which the city was built around. The boys were mesmerised by a beautiful, sea green river that cut through the middle of Albion and bled into a lake on the outskirts of the city. The houses of Albion were modest stone buildings from a different age, built-in tight honeycomb formations spread across the valley. They looked nothing like the towering glass and steel structures that made up the Citadel or the ramshackle huts of the Jungle.

"This place is amazing," Elias said to his brother, pulling him in closer as they stood admiring the view.

"I can't believe it. We finally have a home." said Leo.

11
____

A NEW LIFE

Elias laid in his bed, staring up at the ceiling. He had been awake for over an hour tossing and turning, exhausted by the previous day's events, but unable to settle his mind.

He gave up on sleep and sat up, kicking the quilted duvet off his legs in frustration. He rolled out of bed and grimaced, his whole body still ached from the plasma extraction. After fumbling around in the darkness for a few minutes, trying to find the light switch, he was momentarily blinded as his room was illuminated with a brilliant white light. A simple bedroom, with a comfy-looking double bed at its heart, it was sparsely decorated with a thin wooden desk and a floor to ceiling glass wardrobe.

He paced around for a few minutes like a caged animal before flopping back on the bed in defeat. Laying there for a little while longer before giving up and deciding he didn't like it, the mattress felt like a sponge. He slid off the side of the bed, dragging the duvet with him and curled up on the floor; the thick stone tiles felt much more familiar to him.

Elias found it disconcerting not having his little brother asleep next to him. They had spent the last eight years crammed together, in a tent so small they could barely stand. The size of his new room overwhelmed him. Not that he didn't appreciate it, it would just take some getting used to. Tiberius arranged for them to stay in an apartment in the centre of Albion, he told the brothers this was their home for as long as they wanted. Leo's face was a picture when they walked through the door, his mouth almost hit the floor when he saw the size of his bed.

Eventually, Elias gave up on sleep and quietly opened up the door to his bedroom. He was greeted by a spacious open plan living room leading into a kitchen fitted with a variety of machines and appliances he didn't know how to use. He walked through the kitchen and carefully slid open the door to Leo's room, his brother was fast asleep, still fully clothed and spread across the bed like a starfish. From the looks of it, he didn't have any problem adjusting to their new surroundings, Elias thought, quietly closing the door behind him.

He tried laying down on the l-shaped sofa in the middle of the living room but again couldn't settle. A sickening sensation kept coming back to him. Could this all be some cruel joke; a trap by the Sovereign. He stared at the front door to their apartment, expecting at any moment the Sovereign to come bursting in and drag them back to their squalid life in the Jungle. At the sound of his stomach rumbling, he decided to head out to Albion and pick up some food. He had lost all track of time since they arrived and as they were underground, he couldn't tell if it was day or night, but he hoped somewhere would be open whatever time it was.

Elias pulled on his tattered clothes and grabbed a small empty bag that was lying around before heading out. He closed the door behind him, careful not to wake Leo as he left. Tiberius had told him there was a small market located not far from their apartment. Elias climbed down the narrow stone staircase to the street below. The roads were uneven and cobbled with thick rounded yellow stones, rows of small, simple stone cottages lined the streets. He couldn't believe how different this place was to the Jungle.

A few lights flickered through the small panelled windows, but most of the city was asleep. Exquisite glowing lanterns hung overhead and created a warm orange hue that radiated throughout Albion, like a setting sun just out of view. Elias made his way down the street and avoided eye contact with the few people still up. He got a horrible sense that he was being watched.

Elias curled up his hands in his pockets as he suddenly became aware of how different he looked to everyone else. They were all dressed in loosely fitted khaki and brown robes while he was still wearing the sand-encrusted black overcoat that he had escaped the Jungle in. He smelt awful as well, a distinctive stench of smoke and smouldering plastic followed his every step.

He arrived at the market and ducked inside to escape the gazes of the small crowd watching as he entered. He slammed the door shut and slowly turned around, relieved to escape their prying eyes only to discover everyone inside the shop was staring right at him. His heart sank. He took a deep breath and smiled at the unfamiliar faces gawking in his direction. Noticing all the customers carried their shopping in a thin wicker basket, he saw a pile by the door and quickly picked one up.

He awkwardly shuffled through the crowds, nodding and thanking people as he stepped past. They all stood there in awe, mesmerised by his every movement. He hurried through the market, eager to escape as soon as possible. None of the produce for sale looked familiar to him, big brown barrels full of strange and exotic looking ingredients. Odd shapes and colours, bright greens and yellows, he had no idea food could be so vibrant.

Everything they used to eat in the Jungle was always dull and dreary. He grabbed some strange looking yellow sticks and some small, brown, rock shaped things that they felt warm and squidgy as he picked them up. He squeezed past the last of the shoppers and headed over to the counter. One by one, everyone in the queue moved aside and ushered him forward.

"Please take my place," one patron said, smiling as Elias passed by.

"And mine," said another.

"Don't stop there, keep on coming this way," said a third as he patted Elias on the back.

Before he knew it, he was at the front of the queue, where a small, bespectacled, balding man, wearing a bright red apron, stood behind the counter. The man shook open a thick, brown paper bag and placed the items from Elias's basket inside.

"Okay, a dozen bananas and two bread rolls. Is there anything else I can get you, Sir?" the man behind the counter said with a smile.

"No, thank you, that's everything," Elias rolled up his sleeve to reveal his tattoo. "How much is it?"

"I am afraid we don't accept digital currency in Albion." The man said as his smile dropped.

"Oh." Elias went red in the face, flushed with embarrassment as the colour almost burst through his cheeks.

"I'm sorry I don't have anything else. I'll put them back." He said, reaching for the paper bag.

"Oh, don't be silly. They are on us. Consider it a small welcoming gift from the staff at Lock' n'Dam." The man handed Elias the bag, his smile quickly returning.

"Lock' n'Dam?"

"Our store, it's called Lock' n'Dam. It's on the sign outside." The man replied.

"Right, yeah. Of course. Okay, thank you." Elias said woodenly as he headed to the exit, taking one last look behind him

Every single person was waving at him as he left. Elias ran back home without looking back, bounded up the steps two at a time and slammed the door shut behind him as he entered the apartment. He dropped the bag of food on the work surface and sat on the stool beside it.

"What's up?"

Elias jumped up as Leo popped his head out of the bathroom, his hair dripping wet.

"Damn it, Leo," Elias shouted as he slumped back down in his seat, his heart racing. "You scared the life out of me. I didn't think you'd be up yet."

"Sorry. You been out?"

"Yeah, I nipped out to get some food."

"What did you get?"

"I don't know, some ban annas and bred." Elias mouthed the unfamiliar words as he tossed the brown paper bag to Leo.

"Wow, these look amazing," Leo remarked as he pulled out the bananas.

"I think those are the ban annas,"

"What do you do with them?"

"I don't know, eat 'em I guess."

A thunderous knock rattled their front door. The brothers exchanged worried glances before Elias tiptoed over to the door and pressed his ear against the smooth metal. It sounded like two people bickering on the doorstep.

"Who is it?" Elias shouted through the door.

"Good Morning Elias, its Orion," Tiberius shouted back.

Elias relaxed and opened the door to Tiberius, who beamed at him with his broad welcoming smile.

"Morning," Elias replied.

"Slept well I hope?" Tiberius let himself in, brushing past Elias, as he carried two hefty brown paper bags in his arms. A petite, red-haired girl dressed in dirty, oil-stained dungarees and a pair of heavy, brown work boots followed him, she looked about the same age as Leo.

"Morning, Leo," Tiberius said as he dropped the bags on the work surface.

"Boys, please let me introduce you to my daughter. This is young Ginger." Tiberius stood aside and gestured towards the red-haired girl behind him. She placed two more bags on the work surface and smiled at Elias. She turned and stared at Leo with a look of disgust on her face.

"I think you are supposed to peel those before you eat them," she said as she burst out laughing.

Leo peered up at Ginger, his mouth stuffed with banana, skin and all.

"I didn't think it tasted right." He mumbled, struggling to speak with his mouth full.

Ginger was still staring at Leo as he painfully gulped down his mouthful. He suddenly became aware that he had just emerged from the shower and was all but naked except for a well-placed hand towel.

"I'll..., er..., just go put some clothes on," Leo carefully backed across the living room, leaving a trail of sopping wet footprints on the tiled floor. Ginger turned and nodded at Elias confidently.

"Nice to meet you, my dad hasn't shut up about you since he got home."

Elias laughed. Ginger didn't.

"You don't look much like a Nihon." Ginger said accusingly.

Tiberius interjected. "Don't be rude dear, Elias hasn't had the privilege of an upbringing in our wonderful city here. We must do everything we can to support him and young Leonidas during their stay with us."

"Just saying," Ginger said moodily as she shrugged her shoulders and started rifling through the brown bags. She pulled out a strange-looking piece of food and chomped at it aggressively, glaring at Elias as she walked over to the sofa and slumped down into it.

"Don't mind Ginger, she's not best pleased with me this morning as I pulled her away from one of her 'urgent' projects-" Tiberius mimed with his hands.

"I can still hear you!" Ginger shouted across the room.

"Well, I see you've been out exploring our beautiful city already. Excellent." Tiberius said excitedly as he nodded towards Elias's shopping bags "What did you think?"

"Yeah..." Elias paused, not knowing what to say. "It's...er... lovely."

Tiberius's face dropped.

"I mean, it's amazing. Just very different from what we are used to. A lot to take in," Elias added.

"Indeed, it must be. I can only imagine the hardships you both must have faced in your lives so far." Tiberius said darkly, his eyes narrowed off into the distance as if he imagined something terrible. Tiberius visibly shook his head and smiled at Elias once again.

"There are a few things I wanted to discuss with you. I was wondering if you would like to join me for a tour of Albion?" Tiberius asked.

"Would we!" Leo responded enthusiastically, walking back out of his bedroom now fully dressed. "That would be brilliant," he added eagerly.

"Where did you get those from?" Elias nodded at Leo.

"From the wardrobe, you like em?" Leo raised his arms out and turned on the spot.

He was wearing some baggy desert chinos, a sizeable brown sweater and a chunky, chequered shemagh scarf. He looked like a local already thought Elias.

"Excellent, I'm glad they fit," Tiberius clapped his hands together. "I'd made arrangements for some things to be dropped off before you arrived, I thought you might like a change of clothes after your arduous journey. Elias, would you like to shower before breakfast?"

A shower. It had been years since he last had one.

The missionaries used to bring hot water supplies into the Jungle for them to use, but that stopped a long time ago. Bathing used to consist of scavenging any extra water they could and taking turns to wash down by the sewage pipes that flowed out of the Citadel. Elias realised his stench must really stand out in their new surroundings.

"Okay."

"Great, there should be some clothes in your room as well. Hopefully, you will find something that fits. I'll rustle up something for breakfast while we wait. Leo, have you ever tried pancakes?" Tiberius asked, rummaging through one of the brown bags.

Elias retreated from the room, grabbed the clothes out of the wardrobe and dashed over to the bathroom, glancing back at Tiberius, Ginger and Leo who were now busy destroying the kitchen. Elias locked the door behind him and wiped down the mirror which was still covered with condensation from Leo's shower, he stared at his reflection. A pale, gaunt, narrow face looked back. His high cheekbones protruded through his hollow skin, life in the Jungle had indeed taken its toll on him. He had aged badly and looked far older than his eighteen years.

He started to undress, peeling one layer off at a time. It had been a long time since he had seen himself naked. He was lean and underweight, his ribs jutted out unnaturally through his skin. Despite his skinniness, his frame had a naturally athletic build to it; spending his youth toiling in the Jungle crafted a lean and sinewy physique.

He stepped into the shower and let the water pour down over his face, his whole body relaxed instantly. Watching as the filthy water drained off, a sense of lightness drifted over him; like his past was being washed away.

When Elias emerged from the bathroom, he was dressed similarly to Leo and Tiberius, wearing a chunky black hoody and some combat trousers. He took the time to shave as well, removing the dark, black stubble that covered his face, he looked younger now, and fresher. His skin felt alive, clean for the first time in years. Tiberius, Leo and Ginger glanced up from behind the work surface.

"Looking good," Leo laughed.

"Perfect timing, breakfast is ready!" Tiberius announced.

The four of them ate a breakfast of banana pancakes and freshly squeezed fruit juice, Elias and Leo had never tasted anything quite like it. They wolfed down several servings until the ingredients ran out, much to Tiberius's delight. Ginger gawked at the brothers as they continued to shovel in mouthful after mouthful, not wanting to let a single crumb go to waste. Tiberius shot Ginger an angry glance to tell her to stop staring as they served up yet another helping.

While the brothers finished off the remaining pancakes, Tiberius took the time to explain the history of Albion; telling them how the cave complex was discovered by accident as they searched for a suitable place for a bomb shelter before the great war broke out. The caves had been adapted in secret to prepare for a full-scale evacuation of the Citadel if required. Over time, the city had been forgotten about until Tiberius, and Balendin Fallon rediscovered it during the early days of the Sovereign's rule. Fallon's genius crafted the city that stood before them today.

After the fall of Roninhya and the rise of the Sovereign, the Army of Shadows formed and used Albion as the base for their operations. Following the Ronin's arrival at the Citadel's city walls, and the impending human catastrophe unfolding on their doorstep, the Shadows decided to house as many of the refugees as possible in their subterranean city. Thousands of exhausted Ronin made the perilous journey underground and became the first citizens of Albion; scores of men, women and children had been saved from death.

"So all these people are Ronin too?" Elias asked, his eyes starting to well up.

"Yes, almost every citizen of Albion descends from Roninhya. There are a few, myself included, who came from the Citadel, but we are thankfully in the minority. We now have whole generations born and raised in this wonderful city. So this is truly your home, this place belongs more to you than me," Tiberius said with a broad smile as he squeezed Elias on the shoulder.

"But why didn't you come back for the rest of us?"

Leo's question hung in the air as Elias, Ginger and Tiberius all looked at each other uncomfortably. Tiberius sighed heavily.

"That was one of the hardest decisions of my life. It still haunts me to this day that we couldn't save more Ronin from that awful place." He shook his head as if he was trying to block out a painful memory.

"Over the years we rescued many more from the Jungle, but ultimately we could only house so many people here safely. As I will show you, it is a precarious set up we have here, the slightest imbalance could have a devastating impact on our community."

"So we were just unlucky, I guess?" Leo said glancing over at Elias.

"Indeed. But Gaia has seen to guide you here now, and that is the most important thing."

Elias wiped his mouth and kicked Leo discreetly under the table, signalling that he shouldn't ask any more questions.

"Yeah, let's not dwell on the past anymore. I want to have a proper look around this place." Elias said, standing back to his feet.

"Excellent." Tiberius's face erupted into a smile. "There is much to see."

12

ALBION

When Tiberius told them they had much to see he wasn't joking. The tour took over four hours and included everything from the crystal clear freshwater of the Juniper Falls to the endless fields of the Gigafarm; which met the city's demand for electricity. They started by heading through the sea of batteries that made up the Gigafarm; row after row of identical-looking metallic slabs set out in a symmetrical grid format.

"It is a delicate balance to not only power the city but to ensure we keep enough in reserve to see us through an emergency. It is a constant ebb and flow, replacing the old with the new to maintain the status quo." Tiberius explained as they observed some Albion maintenance workers replacing one of the dead battery packs with a new one that had recently arrived, fresh from their geothermal charging station.

Next Tiberius showed them around one of the many subterranean farms that fed the city, a vast semi-circular tunnel stretching out as far as they could see. They made their way through the identical rows of shelves, stacked from floor to ceiling; each containing a variety of hearty looking fruit. Elias shielded his eyes from the glare of thousands of super-bright LED light strips lining the roof.

"There are dozens of farms like this one throughout Albion. These specially designed vaults have highly sophisticated irrigation and ventilation systems that enable us to produce sufficient crops to feed our fair city with minimal energy usage." Tiberius slid out one of the shelves to reveal a tray stacked full of plants each sprouting dozens of delicious-looking red, teardrop-shaped fruit.

"Strawberries." Tiberius picked off a handful of the biggest ones and tossed them to Elias and Leo. They caught the fruit and looked at Tiberius, unsure of what to do next.

"These are one of my favourites, don't tell anyone I have been picking at them again," Tiberius winked at the farmers who stood beside them, dressed in long white lab coats. They smiled and shook their heads in a playful show of disapproval.

Tiberius picked a juicy looking strawberry for himself and bit into it, tearing the fruit from its bright green leaf. Elias and Leo followed his lead and struggled to contain the smiles on their faces as they bit into their strawberries.

Tiberius led the group out of the farm and back to the main pathway that looped around Albion, something caught Elias's eye in the distance, and he froze, anchored to the ground. He tugged on Leo's sleeve as he tried to walk past him.

"What...is...that?" Elias whispered, nodding over to the horrifying sight that caught his attention, Leo's mouth dropped open as he stared in disbelief.

"Oh my go..." Leo mumbled off.

They both stood mesmerised as a massive creature walked straight towards them. Tiberius and Ginger seemed oblivious to its presence. How could they not notice it? The monster was ginormous and stood over eight feet tall, towering above those around it. It had a muscular build and the battle armour it wore, looked to be struggling to contain its hulking frame. Tiberius stopped, noticing Elias and Leo had fallen behind. He turned to face them and saw the concerned expressions on their faces.

"Oh my, you haven't met Maximus yet have you?" Tiberius chuckled to himself. "Please come over and let me introduce you." He beckoned the boys over.

They stepped forward cautiously, holding on to each other. Ginger giggled as Tiberius nudged them towards the creature. Elias turned to face Ginger, who was walking next to him.

"Maximus? He asked nervously.

"Don't worry, he doesn't bite," she laughed before adding "...often."

Elias gulped. As they made their approach, they saw the creature more clearly. Its face had several deep scars carved into it, including one that ran straight over its left eye. The other remaining eye was a dusty sand colour with a thin horizontal slit for a pupil. A magnificent golden mane flowed effortlessly over its shoulders. Elias noticed the creatures whiskers flutter, and its nose twitch as they got closer. It looked half man, half beast.

"Maximus. Please allow me to introduce our guests," Tiberius said, pushing them towards the creature.

"Ugh," Maximus grunted as he peered down at the boys, Elias tried his best to avoid eye contact with it, looking over at Leo who had a massive grin on his face.

"Pleased to meet you. My name is Leo," he said warmly as Maximus's mouth curled into an unwelcoming smile as if the muscles of his face struggled to move to an unfamiliar position. He snorted loudly in response.

"And this is Elias. I'm sure you've heard a lot about him," Tiberius added, patting him on the shoulder.

"Indeed," the creature spoke, it's voice was deep and considered. His long blonde beard tied into a tidy knot a few inches beneath his chin, swayed as he talked.

"Don't let Max fool you, he's a sweetheart really." A well-built black soldier carrying a large assault rifle approached the group. "I'm Diaz, I've been looking forward to meeting you guys."

"This is Captain Diaz, he is the commander of the Deltas and is one of the finest fighters we've got in the resistance,"

"Too kind, General," Diaz said as he pushed Max out of the way, he had a muscular build too but looked tiny next to the beast who towered over him. He had long, thick, black dreadlocks tied behind his back and wore the same battle armour as Max.

"Make sure you swing by the Ops room to meet the rest of the crew, for a lot of them you'll be the first Nihon they've ever met," Diaz added as he smiled at Elias.

"Thanks," Elias said as he thought about having to meet even more people.

"You too, Leo, you're welcome any time," Diaz turned his dazzling smile to Leo.

"Sounds great," Leo added.

"Well, I'll let you guys carry on with your tour. May Gaia guide you," Diaz said as he bowed his head towards them, he patted Max on the shoulder and led him away from the group. They laughed and bumped into each other as they made their way down the street. Elias and Leo looked at each other, then turned to face Tiberius.

"So..." Leo asked. "what…exactly was that?"

"Ah yes, Maximus does take some explaining, doesn't he. He is quite unique." Tiberius stroked his beard.

"He is the result of a particularly nasty series of genetic experiments the Sovereign carried out before the war. In their continuing pursuit of creating the ultimate warriors, they began splicing human DNA with that of some of the fiercest animals that ever roamed the planet. Maximus is what happens when you mix the DNA of a man with that of a lion," Tiberius said gravely. "He was freed from the laboratory where he was created, and he's been with the Shadows ever since."

"What are the Deltas?" Elias asked.

"Excellent question. They are the tip of the spear, so to speak, the resistance's elite soldiers. A small squadron of special forces operators, trained in a vast array of dark arts. Surveillance, covert entry, demolitions, long-range reconnaissance. The usual stuff."

"Wow, they sound amazing," Leo marvelled as he looked back and caught one last glimpse of Diaz and Max as they disappeared from view.

"Yes, they are a spectacular sight to behold when in operation. Now, let's be on our way." Tiberius said gesturing towards a narrow track leading off the main strip.

The journey to the next sight on Tiberius's tour was taken up by the boy's endless questions about Maximus, including what exactly a lion was. Next up, the water treatment facility; a vast circular pool of water housed in a concrete silo. It had a large steel comb in the middle that rotated steadily clockwise around the pool.

Albion had a natural source of water: Juniper Falls. Tiberius explained the river flowed through the heart of the city. But to protect it from contamination and deliver a safe supply of water for their people, they required a state-of-the-art treatment facility. Millions of gallons of contaminated water and sewage entered into it, and freshwater ran out.

"Without this facility, the resistance would fall within a week. Water is the lifeblood of mankind, and we are no different." Tiberius pointed to several other water pools in the distance. "That's why this is one of the most important places in our city. A team of dedicated engineers work around the clock to ensure its survival."

When they left, Tiberius led them back into the centre of Albion, greeting everyone he passed. He appeared to know everybody in the city. It must be exhausting taking the time to acknowledge them all thought Elias.

But he did it, every single time. Greeting them all with his infectious smile and asking about their families, how their children were growing up, what their spouses were up to. Tiberius's memory seemed almost photographic, he had an incredible ability to remember even the most minute detail of their lives. Elias started to grow bored of the awkward stares coming his way. Some were less intrusive, those who caught a quick glance when they thought he wasn't looking while others stood there rooted to the spot gawking at him.

Covering the short distance through the centre of Albion took almost as long as the tour because Tiberius kept stopping to speak to everyone. Elias let out a massive sigh of relief when they finally cleared the last group of pedestrians standing between them and their apartment. Then just before they turned off the high street, Elias spotted a most peculiar-looking person up ahead.

He couldn't tell if it was a man or women at first until he spotted the neatly cropped beard framing his face. He was unusually tall with gangly arms and legs that had a mind of their own as he pranced down the street towards them. Tiberius laughed as the man flicked back his long, waist-length, black hair and pulled Tiberius firmly into a tight hug, kissing him on both cheeks as he did so.

"Octavius, dear friend. It's been too long," Tiberius said sincerely, as he escaped the man's embrace.

"Evidently squire, I have once again been exploring these fair lands, high and low, pontificating the inescapable difficul-ties of our present predicament," Octavius spoke lucidly, his entire body swayed majestically as his words poured out in a verbal torrent.

"And it appears that my absence was entirely unnecessary as you have discovered the answer I've been searching for." He stared intently at Elias and Leo.

"Yes, you are right old boy," Octavius said, turning back to face Tiberius. "Yes, yes, yes,"

He bounced up and down in front of them excitedly before pouncing on Leo, grabbing him by the arms, holding him tightly while looking up and down, inspecting every inch of him.

"Yes, I can sense it. Gaia is strong in this one." He closed his eyes and breathed in deeply as he swung Leo from side to side.

"The mana. It flows deep within him."

Tiberius coughed.

"It is actually young Elias here who is the Nihon that you have heard so much about." Tiberius pointed to Elias, who was stood rooted to the stop with his mouth wide open as he watched his brother being twirled around by Octavius.

"Leonidas here is his brother."

Octavius immediately released his grip on Leo and

snapped his long gangly legs back together, he peered down at Elias, like he couldn't quite bear to look at him.

"Oh, yes. I see my mistake. A Nihon, indeed...right, well a pleasure to meet you both," he said swiftly, his interest dissipating as rapidly as it had been aroused.

"Well, I must be off." He curtsied in front of Elias and danced off down the street. They all stood in quiet amazement, sharing awkward glances at each other until Tiberius broke the silence.

"Octavius is quite...um..." he paused for a moment. "Different. He believes he can communicate with Gaia in many of the same ways that a Nihon can, only he doesn't have any of the natural abilities the Nihon possess. Therefore some within our city are somewhat…sceptical about his claims."

"He's a crackpot," Ginger waved her fingers around her head. "…cuckoo."

"Now, now Ginger, that is unfair. I have always been a firm believer in his gifts. This peculiar incident aside, he usually has an astonishingly accurate trait for detecting Gaia's presence, it is most unlike him to make such a glaring mistake." Tiberius stared off into space for a few moments.

"Oh well, such is life and, to be honest, he hasn't been the same since he returned from his last pilgrimage."

Something about Octavius made Elias feel uneasy, he couldn't put his finger on it but it felt like he held your gaze slightly too long.

"Well, I like him," Leo said.

"You would." Elias laughed as he shoved Leo forward.

"Right you two, I think it's time you headed home, you have quite the day ahead of you tomorrow Elias."

The mood in the group became serious as Tiberius fumbled about trying to retrieve something from his pocket.

"It is time to take the first step in your journey as a Nihon. You must learn how to control your newly discovered gifts. Seek out Hidetoshi Shimada and request his pupilage. He is all that remains of a once-great order that has guarded the Nihon for thousands of years, there is no finer swordsman alive today."

"You'll find him at the temple. Here, I've written down some instructions as its quite a trek from Albion. He's not one for company is old Shimada. He prefers the solitude of the temple, he very rarely ventures beyond its boundaries these days." Tiberius handed Elias a small curled up piece of paper.

Elias opened it up and stared at the scribbled note.

"Thank you," he muttered. "Is he expecting me?"

"Um, not exactly." Tiberius laughed. "Leo, Ginger will pop round in the morning, she is dying to show you her workshop."

"Workshop" Leo repeated, his eyebrows raised. Ginger nodded enthusiastically.

"Anyway, we must be off. Elias, may Gaia guide you," he said, pulling him into a tight hug. "Don't take no for an answer," he whispered into his ear.

"Wha…" Elias went to speak, but before he knew it, Tiberius had ruffled Leo's hair, said his goodbyes and walked away holding Ginger's hand.

Elias and Leo stood for a few moments staring at the piece of paper in Elias's hands.

"What's it say?" Leo said. Elias rolled his eyes before bursting out laughing.

"Very funny, you tell me," Elias said, shoving the note into Leo's chest.

"It's a list of directions on how to get to the temple, it's through one of the canyons. Never-ending steps…" Leo muttered to himself as he scanned down the list of instructions. "Sounds complicated."

"Brilliant. Just what I need."

"Swordsman ey, that sounds fun?" Leo smiled as he raised his eyebrow.

Elias managed a little laugh as they climbed the steps back to their apartment.

13

CROSSING THE THRESHOLD

Elias stood at the bottom of a vast set of stone steps that spiralled around a magnificent waterfall; the Juniper Falls. He stared up in awe, trying to see where the staircase led, but it was impossible. It appeared to reach on forever, at times disappearing behind the cascading water before suddenly remerging on the other side. Elias glanced back down at the crudely drawn map Leo had made for him and nodded.

This was the place.

Despite his attempts to convince Leo he had memorised Tiberius's instructions, his brother still insisted he take it. He knows me well, Elias thought as he folded up the map and slipped it into the side of his rucksack. His journey had started on the outskirts of Albion, a trail made up of hundreds of cobbled steps running alongside the stream that led out of the city. The sound of flowing water slowly faded away as he followed the path into a secluded canyon. Hanging lanterns, dangling from the ceiling, lit the way ahead. Their ropes disappearing into the darkness above. The lanterns became more interspersed as Elias ventured deeper into the cave, forcing him to stumble forwards blindly, vanishing into the shadows until he reached the reassuring glow of the next light.

At the time he thought that was the worst part of the journey, but now gawking up at the vast stone staircase, he knew he was wrong. He begrudgingly started to make his way up the steps but soon lost count as the staircase transformed into a never-ending series of twists and turns, looping around the waterfall. After the first two hundred steps, he stopped at a small alcove hidden behind the rushing water. He ran his fingers through it before dunking his head underneath the ice-cold water. He quickly pulled back, taking a deep breath as he shook off his shaggy, soaking wet hair. He plodded on, one onerous step after the next.

Every time he peered over the side, he always appeared to be right in the middle, never making any progress. Hundreds of steps already taken, yet hundreds left to go. His feet began to throb, and every footstep felt heavier than the last; like his feet were made of lead. With his leg muscles burning, he sunk down to his knees and started to crawl up the steps.

Finally, he felt his hand reach a clearing, the end was in sight. He pulled himself over the last step and slowly raised his eyes, the temple stood before him. It was a simple round structure with a domed roof and appeared to be built from sandstone. It was smaller than he was expecting and looked far older than any of the other buildings in Albion, Elias wondered how long it had stood there for.

He approached the main entrance, a massive stone door adorned with an elegant carving of a strange-looking symbol made up of five intertwined rings. He noticed an exquisite golden knocker in the middle of it. He knocked it softly, but no response came. After waiting a little while, he rattled it again.

Still no answer. Elias hammered the door as hard as he could one final time.

Elias stepped back and looked at the door again with his hands on his hips, huffing in frustration before launching himself at it. He heaved his shoulder into the stone slab and pushed with all his strength, his face turned red as he slowly started to move the deadweight. It gradually swung open, and he stumbled over the threshold. Elias's attention was immediately drawn to the inside of the domed ceiling, struck by its simple elegance.

The reflection from the candles lighting the room flickered against the golden paint on the ceiling, creating a radiant shimmer. The room was sparsely decorated with a polished stone floor, but somehow the emptiness made it even more enchanting. It appeared to be a training ground of some sort, and various weapons hung on the walls. As Elias looked around the temple, he noticed a man kneeling in front of a large shrine at the far end of the room.

"Excuse me," Elias shouted, his voice echoing around him.

The man ignored him; he didn't even turn around to acknowledge Elias's presence. He was kneeling on his arches, with a perfectly straight back staring at the shrine. It was a delicately carved wooden cabinet holding some old scrolls written in a language he had never seen before. In the centre of the cabinet stood a small statue of a man resting on the hilt of his sword. Elias walked over to the man who wore a simple black robe and baggy black hakama trousers, his fine, shoulder-length black hair tied into a loose bun on the back of his head.

"Excuse me,"

Still no reply. The man remained motionless. Elias peered

around in front of him and saw his eyes were closed, his hands rested on top of his thighs.

"Are you Hidetoshi Shimada? Tiberius sent..." Surely he must be able to hear me, thought Elias as he placed his hand on the man's shoulder. As his hand touched him, the man sprung to life, his arm reacting instinctively. He grabbed Elias by the hand in a vice-like grip.

"I am meditating." The man said sternly without opening his eyes. "Wait by the door."

He shoved Elias back with apparent ease and returned to his serene state. Elias hobbled away holding his throbbing wrist and, could see a deep red hand mark etched on his skin. Was that Shimada? He wondered why the man was so rude to him. After several minutes of pacing up and down, Elias sat down cross-legged on the stone floor and waited for the man to finish his meditation.

Elias had been waiting for over an hour, and his frustration was beginning to show.

Eventually, the man rose to his feet, patted down his legs and turned to face Elias. He sat in quiet amazement as he watched the man slowly shuffle towards him. In all his life Elias had never seen anyone walk like him, he measured every step precisely.

"Elias, I presume?" the man spoke, his voice was sharp and unwelcoming with a foreign accent Elias hadn't come across before.

"Yes, Tiberius sent..."

"I know why you are here." The man interrupted. "I will tell you the same thing I told him, the answer is no."

"What do you mean?" Elias asked with a confused expression on his face.

"I will not train you."

"But Tiberius said you are the master swordsman."

"Correct. I am Hidetoshi Shimada, warden of the Nihon, child of Gaia and master of the sword. But train here, you shall not." Shimada said curtly.

"But I need..." Shimada cut him off.

"I care not what you need, nor what you want. The decision is not mine to take. Never in the history of mankind has one been trained without the guidance and tutelage of a Master Nihon. It is too dangerous." Shimada's eyes lingered on Elias, measuring him up.

"But Tiberius said..." Elias stuttered again, Shimada's abruptness catching him off guard.

"You will soon learn Tiberius says many things, not all of these are correct. Now if you will please collect your possessions," Shimada pointed to the door.

"I am not going anywhere!" Elias snapped back stubbornly, growing increasingly angry every time Shimada interrupted him.

"Well, force you to leave, I cannot. All of Gaia's children are entitled to worship here. If you are to stay, there are some rules and traditions you must obey." Shimada's gaze fixated on Elias's feet.

"Firstly, no footwear must be worn. Secondly, you are to remain silent unless spoken to, this is a place of peace and tranquillity, not idle chitter-chatter. Thirdly, you must bow when entering and leaving the temple, this is a sign of respect to Gaia and those who have gone before you."

"So I can train here then?" Elias asked excitedly with a glimmer of hope in his voice.

"Of course, anyone is entitled to train here. But you will not be trained by me." Shimada said, wiping the smile from

Elias's face. He looked downtrodden and sullenly plodded back to the entrance, collecting his rucksack on the way out.

The journey down the stone steps seemed to take even longer with the crushing weight of Shimada's rejection ringing in his ears. His quest to become a Nihon was over before it had even begun. The walk home gave him enough time to think through what he was going to say to Leo when he got back. At first, he planned on fabricating a story, telling him Shimada had agreed to train him and that he was well on his way to becoming a Nihon, but he knew Leo would see straight through his lies. In the end, talking to his brother helped Elias comprehend what had happened.

"Maybe this is all part of the trial," Leo had said. "Like he's testing your resolve or something."

That was what Elias loved the most about his brother, he always saw problems from a different perspective, never accepting things at face value. Whenever he felt lost, Leo always helped him find a way through the fog. So they agreed that Elias would return to the temple every day until Shimada changed his mind. It wasn't the most well thought out plan, but it was all he had.

After about a week of soul-destroying boredom, sitting in silence watching Shimada spend the entire day either meditating or sweeping the temple floor, Elias decided he would make himself useful and started to tidy the temple; grabbing a spare broom and sweeping the courtyard outside for hours on end. After a few weeks of polite nods between them, Elias felt brave enough to raise the subject of training again, convinced that he had proven his steadfastness to Shimada.

"The answer is still no", Shimada said flatly.

The journey back that day had been a bitter one, and Elias arrived home utterly deflated. The next morning he was awoken by his alarm clock again, but this time he rolled over, turned it off and closed his eyes. Ten minutes later, Leo came bursting into his room and dragged him out of bed.

"You can't quit Eli, everyone is counting on you." Leo declared as he shoved him out of the door. Shimada smiled and nodded at Elias when he arrived slightly later than usual, obviously surprised that he had returned for another day of silence.

It was over a month before Elias asked the question again, after a particularly satisfying sweeping session Elias plucked up the courage to approach Shimada.

"No", Shimada said without looking away from his broom.

"But please, I don't know what to do." Elias pleaded.

"Exactly, and that is the biggest problem, the path of a Nihon is not one to be trodden alone. Master and apprentice, that is the way. And you are too old to start this journey, especially without a master's guiding hand."

"But…I…need somebody to help me find my way…' Elias stuttered, his voice becoming strained.

"I am sorry, Elias, but I cannot help you. Without a master, the path is too perilous. Tiberius should not have filled your head with such fallacies." Shimada said, for the first time displaying a hint of sympathy in his voice.

Elias stared at his feet and tried to hold back his tears.

"I know I can't become a Nihon on my own, but I never asked for any of this. All I wanted was a home for my little brother, but I can't turn my back on my destiny. My whole life has been leading to this point, to this moment. I don't want to walk this path alone, that's why I am asking for you to guide me. Please, please, help me." Elias looked Shimada in the eye, surprising himself with his sudden outburst.

Shimada looked deep in thought for a short while before he turned away from Elias.

"Grab your things."

Elias couldn't move quickly enough as he hung up his broom and darted back to the entrance to grab his rucksack.

"Thank you, I promise I won't -" before he could finish Shimada shushed him.

He led Elias over to an ornately carved cupboard, slid out a small draw and, removed some neatly folded white robes, he graciously handed them to Elias.

"Please, get changed." Shimada ushered Elias into a small side room that he had never noticed before, it was hidden behind by a canvas sheet.

When Elias stepped inside, he realised it must be Shimada's bedroom. It was a rather depressing sight, with hardly anything in it. A simple roll mat on the floor, a stack of books and a small copper cup and bowl. The realisation of how Shimada lived his life suddenly hit him. Strangely it reminded him of his home in the Jungle. Elias emerged several minutes later dressed in a pair of baggy white hakama trousers that hung loosely around his knees and a matching hitatare robe cut off just past his forearms; the outfit was tied together by a sash of material around his waist. Elias felt stupid, the people of Albion wore some odd clothes, but this was a different level. He just hoped Leo didn't see him in it or he would never hear the end of it. Elias strained a smile at Shimada as he stepped out from the room.

Shimada gestured with his hand for Elias to stand in front of him, he tugged and pulled at Elias's robes in various places, tightening up his outfit before patting him firmly on the shoulders. He then untied the sash and knotted it back together in a neat bow behind Elias's back.

"Good," Shimada nodded. "Now, follow me."

Shimada walked to the centre of the room, one measured step after the next.

"Please, wait here."

He approached a small table and lit some incense sticks which released a sweet scent into the air. He blew out his match and then struck a small copper bowl with a metal instrument, it made a beautiful sound that reverberated around them.

"Please, take a seat." Elias waited for Shimada to sit down first and copied him, sitting on his arches with his back straight, arms resting on his thighs.

"First we meditate, we must re-balance the mind before we can train the body."

"Okay. Sounds good," Elias said, trying to hide the disappointment in his voice, he had never meditated before.

"First, breathe in deeply through your nose," Shimada took a deep breath, his nostrils flaring wildly.

"Breathe out through your mouth," he let out his breath, and his whole body deflated like a balloon. Elias took several deep breaths as instructed, he could feel his lungs expanding in his chest as he inhaled.

"Close your eyes. Return your breathing to its natural state, in and out through the nose, counting your breaths as you go. One, as you breathe in, two as you breathe out and so forth." Shimada demonstrated, counting out loud to ten before starting over again at one.

"Now, on your own, think of nothing. Let your thoughts come and go, but do not dwell on them. Concentrate only on your breath, observing the motion of your body as it rises and falls. When a thought enters your head, do not stay with it. Let them float away as if they are ripples in a pond." Shimada said quietly before returning to his breath.

Elias sat for several moments, thoughts swirling around his head. What on earth was he doing here? How was he supposed to train to become a Nihon while sat here daydreaming and learning how to breathe? He already knew how to do that perfectly well. Time seemed to stop as he became acutely aware of how uncomfortable he was, and his knees grew sore, pressed against the hard stone floor. He began to fidget, trying to get comfortable when Shimada broke the silence.

"Your training can not begin until you find equilibrium. Now concentrate on your breath. We can stay here all day if we need to." There was not a hint of frustration in Shimada's voice.

Elias believed him when he threatened to spend the whole day meditating, from what he had seen so far that was how Shimada spent most of his time anyway. Elias didn't say another word. He readjusted himself and settled on a spot where he wasn't in agony and focussed on his breath, counting as his chest filled with oxygen. One, two, three, four, his mind began to wander, thinking about Leo and what his little brother was getting up to in Ginger's workshop. He brought his attention back to his breath, five, six, seven, eight, Tiberius popped into his head, his face, warm and familiar. Nine, ten, he started over.

One, two. The Jungle. The fire. The heat. The smell of burning flesh. He cursed himself, losing count again. He started over, one, two, three, four. Focussing on his breath as his lungs inflated deep in his chest. A strange sensation drifted over him as a calmness permeated through his entire body.

One, two, three, he fell into rhythm with the rising and

falling movement, losing track of time. His mind grew lighter with every breath, and his senses came alive. He could feel everything around him, the sound of Shimada's nose whistling as he breathed out, the feel of the floor beneath him, the flicker of the candlelight. Aware but not distracted. He started to relax, every breath penetrating deeper and deeper into his body when, unexpectedly, he heard the sound of the chime again. His attention returned to the room instantly, and Elias gently opened his eyes.

Shimada fuzzily came into focus; kneeling in front of Elias.

"Now, your training begins."

***

Shimada stood in front of Elias in the centre of the temple.

"Iaido is a journey that begins today but never ends. A great teacher once said it takes one thousand days of lessons to learn a discipline and ten thousand days to master it. The path of the Nihon is a lonely road, and one must be prepared to strike at any moment." Shimada said solemnly. "You can only fight the way you practice. You must be able to read your opponent, sense his every movement, his every breath and only then you can anticipate his next move."

"Today, we take the first step as you begin to learn the way of the sword." Shimada walked over to the side of the temple and reached for a long object hung on the wall, it was wrapped in an elaborately embroidered fabric. He walked back over to Elias and unfurled the cloth to reveal a large, wooden katana sword.

"This is your bokken," Shimada handed it to him. "You will carry this with you at all times, night and day, it must never leave your side. You shall wield it until you are ready to take up a katana. You must practise whenever you have a free moment. A Nihon must never be without his weapon. You are naked without it. Exposed."

"Okay," Elias played with it in his hands, it was far heavier than it looked and felt out of balance when held by the hilt.

"You will guard your sword with your life, and it will defend you to your death," Shimada stared intensely into Elias's eyes.

"First, you must learn to hold it, so you start to feel comfortable, then over time you will develop a deep bond, it will become an extension of your body. Connected, as one. Then we will move on to the basic strikes and Kata before practising combat. You will not use a katana until you understand what it means to take a life." Shimada pointed to the collection of gleaming silver samurai swords that adorned the far wall.

"Okay," Elias nodded, still holding the bokken in his hand which began to shake under the weight of it.

"Let us start," Shimada clapped his hands together.

They trained for several hours, but Elias made little progress. Learning to hold a sword was much more complicated than it looked. The bokken was just so heavy and ungainly, whenever he held it in front of his body, he couldn't stop his arms from trembling. Several times he wanted to ask Shimada what was the point of learning to use an old piece of wood when the Sovereign had state of the art weaponry that would vaporise him before he got within striking range, but he thought better of it.

Shimada showed him how to carry the bokken within his robes, housing it in an elegantly crafted sheath that looped around his hakama trousers via several strings. Shimada explained how to draw the sword and hold it correctly in a two-handed grip. They went over this technique, again and again, practising drawing the bokken, holding the stance for a few seconds before re-sheathing it. Elias struggled to keep his bokken upright, it constantly wobbled in his grip. But eventually, after hundreds of failed attempts, he learned how to draw his weapon without shaking.

"This may be difficult at first, but everything is difficult when you begin," said Shimada, showing a hint of warmth in his voice.

"But you must persist, practice, practice, practice. Now, go. Rest and contemplate on what you have learnt today, I will see you tomorrow morning."

Elias quickly got changed back into his clothes, packed up his things and bowed to Shimada on his way out of the temple. Shimada followed him to the entrance and waved goodbye. Elias rolled his wrists around in his hands, his whole body ached, his forearms, in particular, were on fire. He dragged himself down the endless stone staircase, one cumbersome step after the next.

14

A LEGACY OF ASHES

Elias awoke the next morning in agony; his body ached from head to toe. Every muscle seemed to groan when he moved. A growing sense of dread crept over him as he struggled to get dressed, the thought of climbing the never-ending stone steps yet again was almost unbearable. Training that day was difficult, he left feeling dejected and exhausted. The journey home seemed to take an age as he painfully limped through the darkened canyons back to Albion.

But, after a few weeks, his body started to adjust to his new regime, and slowly but surely he woke up in slightly less pain every day. Shimada was a strict instructor, which Elias discovered when they started learning the fundamental strikes of the sword. Whenever Elias made a mistake, he received a whack on the forearm with Shimada's bokken.

His skin started to toughen up as a result of the relentless punishment. The blows didn't sting like they once had. He felt like he was making slow progress, and Shimada always seemed disappointed in his performance. Every day, Elias would awake before the rest of Albion and start his ascent to the temple. Knowing deep down that he had to keep going. He could feel himself growing, like a fire had been ignited inside him that was slowly spreading through his entire body, he wanted to see what he could achieve.

It took a long time, but eventually, the steps stopped being so arduous, and Elias realised they presented an opportunity to cram in some more exercise. He could now run up the whole way without stopping. He would still arrive panting and wheezing, struggling not to be sick, but he was growing stronger by the day. His body started to change as well, three regular meals a day and non-stop training crafted a lean, athletic physique. His face no longer gaunt and hollow, but chiselled, with a flush of colour. Elias actually started to look forward to his new routine. A lifetime of living on the edge of society, not knowing what each day would bring meant he enjoyed finally having some stability in his life.

So it came as a surprise when Elias reached the temple to discover Shimada waiting for him at the top step.

"We will not be practising today," Shimada said calmly as he stood beside Elias, his arms clasped behind his back.

Elias bent over, hands resting on his knees, breathing heavily and trying not to faint.

"You are now ready to begin the second part of your journey, the physical skills are but one attribute a Nihon must learn. Today you will discover the history of your people and, in time, learn to control the unique abilities that you will soon start to acquire. I will accompany you to our monastery; it houses the Great Library, which contains everything you will need to aid you on your journey. Now we must make haste, Grand Maester Martell; the Sage of Albion is most excited to meet you." Without waiting for a reply, Shimada started to make his way down the stone steps.

Elias's heart sunk when Shimada had mentioned the word library, he had no idea how he was going to get around that. No one had told him being a Nihon involved reading. He scratched and tore at the back of his neck in frustration.

Why hadn't Shimada waited at the bottom, rather than letting him climb all the way up here Elias thought. He swallowed the urge to scream, settling instead for a deep sigh before trudging after his tutor.

At the bottom of the waterfall, Shimada led Elias through a series of passageways he had never noticed before. They walked in silence through a dimly lit canyon, and Elias thought it might be a good opportunity to ask the question that had been burning in his mind.

"Hidetoshi, would you mind if asked you a question?" Elias asked, peering out the corner of his eye to see his reaction.

Shimada nodded serenely, unperturbed by Elias starting up a conversation.

"Why do you live in the temple?"

"I am in exile."

Elias stopped in his tracks before quickly catching up with Shimada. He pulled a confused expression, trying to make sense of Shimada's answer.

"Why are you in exile?"

"I am dishonoured."

Elias thought for a moment, unsure whether to continue probing, every question led to another question. He had heard whispers about Shimada from Tiberius and the others since he started training with him, but everyone appeared reluctant to discuss his past. From what he had gathered, it had something to do with Voltaire. Elias decided against pressing the matter any further.

They didn't say another word to each other until they reached the monastery's boundaries. It was an impressive structure and appeared to be built into the walls of the cave that housed it. Two colossal stone statues of blindfolded men holding swords stood proudly either side of a large wooden door that appeared to lead directly into the cave.

"Please, Grand Maester Martell is expecting you," Shimada gestured towards the entrance.

"Okay," Elias nodded as he made his way over to the door. "Thank you."

He got an eery feeling the statues were following him as he approached. He knocked on the wooden door, and it seemed to absorb his blows, with little to no sound ringing out on the other side. He glanced back to see Shimada, but he was already gone.

Brilliant, the first time he ever moves quickly thought Elias.

Elias raised his hand to knock again. Before he made contact, he heard the door being unlocked, and it opened with a moaning creak, revealing a tiny, bespectacled man stood in the doorway.

"Ah, you must be Elias. Please, come in," the man said softly.

"Thank you," Elias said, entering the monastery. It was a vast structure with an elegant domed ceiling, and Elias stood, head craned upwards, marvelling at the impressive sight for a few moments.

"It is quite something isn't? One of the true wonders of Albion."

"Sorry," said Elias, snapping out of his daze. "Yeah it really is...er - spectacular."

He snatched one last look at the ceiling before returning his attention to the man before him. A diminutive figure wearing a loosely fitted grey robe that covered his whole body, he had a perfectly bald head that reflected the glow of the light. His hands were hidden from view, clasped together underneath his flowing robes. At the centre of his rounded face sat a prominent stub nose.

"Hidetoshi informed me you would be beginning your tutelage with me today. Please allow me to introduce myself, I am Grand Maester Martell; the Sage of Albion. But I am not one for grandiose titles, so please feel free to call me Bumble as everyone else does. It has been my nickname since childhood."

"Okay," Elias replied.

"Now please follow me, we'll be in the great hall today," he turned away, shuffling forward methodically. Elias rolled his eyes; he walks even slower than Shimada.

Bumble led Elias across the lobby and down a long, darkened corridor. Several passageways led off in different directions, barely visible under the soft glow of the wall-mounted torches. They came to a stop outside another large wooden door, and Bumble fiddled around inside his robes before pulling out a hefty iron key.

"Aha! I knew it was in here somewhere." He declared, feeding the key into the door. It snapped to the left, opening the lock with a loud metallic clunk.

"Please, if you wouldn't mind, could you help me with the door, they are rather heavy. I never know why people insist on building such bulky doors. They are awfully impractical." He said ushering Elias over.

Elias jumped forward and heaved his shoulder into the obstacle in front of him. Bumble wasn't lying when he said the door was heavy, it took all his effort to budge it. It was an immense weight, and the pair of them struggled to get the door moving, but once they did, it swung open carried by its own weight. The speed of the movement caught Elias off guard, and he stumbled over the threshold. He walked forward a few paces and blinked several times trying to take in what stood before his eyes. Books; thousands of them, rows and rows stretching off in every direction for as far he could see. The floor was made of a beautiful polished wood, the glowing lights above reflecting in the shiny surface below. Everywhere he looked, he saw huge two-tiered bookshelves standing well over thirty feet high and reaching all the way to the ceiling. Not an inch of space wasted, every row crammed full with books, a dazzling collection of colours and sizes filled the shelves.

"Wow," Elias said in amazement.

"It takes the breath away, doesn't it?"

"Elias...welcome to the Great Hall, this is the home to the only surviving collection of books on Earth, the entire story of mankind, stretching back millennia is contained within this library." Bumble broke out into a broad smile as he struggled to hide his evident pride.

"The very essence of humanity is contained within these pages, they have been meticulously preserved and maintained. During the war, we hid them from the Sovereign. They sought to erase humanity's true past with their own falsehoods and propaganda. But down here, deep beyond their reach, we hold the truth about what the world really used to be like."

"But first of all, we start with the Nihon, alas that is the real reason why you are here. Now please take a seat." He pointed over to one of the many tables dotted throughout the hall.

Elias walked over to the table, slid out a comfortable looking chair and sat down. His host disappeared for a few moments, and Elias could hear him muttering to himself as he meandered down another row. He returned with a towering stack of books so high he was hidden behind them. Bumbled carefully shuffled over and dropped them on the table in front of Elias. A plume of dust exploded as they landed with a thud.

"These Elias are some of the oldest books in our library, they chart the Nihon from Golgordorf the Great all the way through to Master Trition. It is vitally important you understand the history of your brethren, there are no shortcuts on this journey Elias. Without knowledge, your gifts can be a dangerous curse. You must learn to control your skills, to master them and then, only then will you be able to call yourself a Nihon." Bumble said as he pulled out one of the larger books, it was enormous and wrapped in a dusty red velvet cover.

"Gaia and her Guardians, Volume 1. This is good a place to start, it's a bit all-encompassing for my taste, but it does provide a comprehensive outline of the key concepts of mana and the Nihon's relationship with Gaia,"

Elias felt a shudder go down his spine and his mouth went dry as his heart rate sped up. His hands were clammy and started to tingle, he had been dreading this moment ever since he entered the library. His voice failed him as he snatched the book away. Bumble was taken aback and looked shocked as Elias placed the book beside him without saying a word. He avoided Bumble's gaze and stared at the giant book next to him, trying to hide his trembling his hands under the table.

"Don't worry, you don't have to read it all today!" Bumble chuckled to himself, "You can take the book home with you and read it in your own time. To me, education is a personal choice, if you wish to read here, then you are more than welcome to, but you are also free to take them away and read them in your own time. Not everyone learns the same way, so you must study wherever you are most comfortable."

"Oh, okay, yeah that would be brilliant. Thank you." Elias's panic lifted as he quickly slid the book into his rucksack.

"Right, so let's begin our first lesson," Bumble clapped his hands together as he sat down on the chair next to him.

He regaled Elias with tales of the Nihon dating back thousands of years; starting in Earth's middle ages when Golgordorf the Great; the first recorded Nihon, sought to unite the warring kingdoms against the forces gathering in the darkness. The Nihon had been greatly misunderstood by the societies through the ages.

"The Nihon have been known by many different names; wizards, sorcerers, warlocks, magicians, to name just a few. Throughout the twenty-first century, they all but disappeared from our collective consciousness, resigned to legend and folklore. But in time, like all true power, they rose again and soon became the focal point of a new society. Roninhya was built around the beliefs of the Nihon and the relationship they have with the world." He unrolled a vast scripture on the table.

Bumble went on to explain that ever since Golgordorf took his first apprentice, there were always two Nihon. A master and an apprentice; who strike a symbiosis between them. The roles in the relationship shift as the young apprentice grows in strength, ready to take their master's place and in time, seek out their own disciple.

He revealed a Nihon only held on to their powers for a short period. Once their apprentice came of age, the master would start a steady decline back into normality as they relinquish the last of their Nihonic energy to their apprentice. The apprentice becomes the master and so the cycle begins again.

"So I am an apprentice?" Elias asked.

"Yes,"

"So who would be my master?" Elias peered up from the scrolls laid out in front of him.

Bumble awkwardly fiddled with his glasses, cleaning them with his robes.

"Oh...my...excellent question...right...well. Umm. I think that might be a question for another day." He stuttered, struggling to find his words.

"Its Voltaire, isn't it? He was supposed to be my master."

Bumble returned his glasses to his face and stared at Elias with a horrified expression.

"Please don't speak his name in here," Bumble's voice quivered. "This is a sacred place, and I do not want to stain our ancestor's memories with his betrayal."

"I'm sorry, I didn't mean any offence," Elias apologised. "It's just I thought this would be the best place to ask all of the questions I have about Volt-" he stopped himself. "Sorry, but there are so many questions I have about him."

"There is no need to apologise, you are correct. This is a place of history, and Vol..." Bumble almost choked on the words, as if he couldn't quite get them out. "That man, unfortunately, played a more prominent role in our history than any Nihon before him."

Bumble explained that Voltaire, at the age of four, demonstrated he had been selected by Gaia as the next Nihon. Soon he had been whisked away from his family and took his place alongside his new master, Trition in Roninhya.

"Oh, if only you could have met Trition, he was a wonderful man. Loving and humble, a Nihon of the most altruistic kind. He truly lived up to the mantle of being Gaia's guardian."

"Voltaire's powers grew at an extraordinary rate, and by the time he reached eighteen, he was demonstrating skills far beyond any recorded Nihon of his age. But he grew impatient of Trition's tutelage, he yearned to gain powers beyond his reach. He started to dabble in the dark arts and exploited his sacred bond with Gaia for his own selfish desires. There is an eternal truth; the weaker the Earth becomes as a result of mankind's actions, the more powerful the Nihon grow. Their two essences are intimately intertwined."

"Soon, his thirst for power consumed him, and he committed an unthinkable act. He murdered Trition, and, in doing soon, took his place as master Nihon before his time had come. His betrayal didn't stop there, he realised the civilisation that he had been raised in, now stood between him and the unimaginable power he so desired. So Voltaire left Roninhya, travelled the perilous path to the Citadel and offered his service to Vicentine, betraying his people and in doing so, set Earth and Gaia on a path to destruction." Elias detected a flicker of disdain in Bumble's voice as he spoke.

"And with that partnership, the twin evils of Voltaire's thirst for power and Vicentine's greed, Roninhya's fate was all but sealed. The war ended a few weeks later as the Sovereign destroyed Roninhya. Billions perished on that fateful day; the survivors faced a fate worth than death. Stay and try to survive within the broken remnants of a shattered civilisation or chance the perilous trek across the wastelands to throw themselves at the mercy of their destroyers." Bumble gazed down at the texts in front of him.

"The latter is the path I chose, and it is thanks to the actions of a few brave citizens from the Citadel that the rest of the Ronin here in Albion survived to tell the tale. Before the Sovereign rose to prominence, the Citadel was led by a democratically elected senate, but like all governments, those within it can be blinded by the petty desires of man. Wealth, power, reputation. Those vices corrupted the Citadel, transforming the beacon of humanity, Earth's largest city, the saviour of billions into the biggest threat our planet has ever faced."

Elias was struggling to take it all in. He had so many questions, but he didn't want to interrupt Bumble who appeared to be holding back a flood of memories.

"Tiberius served as the General of the Citadel's Defence Force and had been responsible for manning the city walls for over thirty years. He served with distinction and was a man with an unblemished military record, even in Roninhya people spoke highly of him. But when Vicentine and the Sovereign seized control of the Citadel, he was ousted from his post and following a failed assassination attempt he went into hiding with a band of his closest allies. In that very moment, the Army of Shadows was born."

"Following the destruction of Roninhya, Tiberius and his small band of soldiers rescued thousands of Ronin from extermination at the hands of the Sovereign. What started out as a temporary refuge, soon expanded into the wonderful city that stands before you. The Ronin were not known for our fighting skills, we are builders. Creators. Architects. We work in harmony with the Earth to preserve and protect the cherished lands gifted to us by Gaia. Unlike the citizens of the Citadel, we are not interested in monetary rewards or the trappings of fame and fortune. We merely wanted to live our lives in peace and harmony with the world around us, and so out of the ashes, we started again. We rebuilt that which had been taken from us..." Bumble stopped, his words failing him. He closed the book in front of him.

"Alas, I think that is enough for today," he said quietly, removing his glasses and cleaning them again.

Elias sensed he had pushed him too far. But he had one final question he needed an answer to.

"Bumble…" he said tentatively, sliding the rest of the books into his rucksack.

"Yes," he replied, perching his glasses back on the end of his nose.

"I just have one last question." Before he could stop himself, Elias blurted out "It's about Shimada, on the way here he told me he was in exile. I don't understand, who would exile him?"

Bumble pulled a strained expression, considering his words carefully.

"I see. Well this a very delicate subject as I'm sure you can imagine. Shimada guards his privacy closely, so we try to avoid idle gossip about him in Albion."

Elias nodded in agreement but held back his response, leaving a silence for Bumble to fill.

"But you are a Nihon, and you have a right to know the history of those around you. Shimada was a warden, part of a sacred order entrusted with protecting the Nihon within our society."

"He said he was dishonoured?" Elias added.

"Shimada thinks he is to blame for his Master's death and placed himself in self-imposed exile in the temple, he has never stepped foot in Albion."

"But he couldn't have stopped Vol…I mean he couldn't have known what he was planning."

"I know young one, but alas, Shimada has made his decision. He is not one to be reasoned with and has resolved himself to a life of solitude away from his people. You are the first person he has spent time with in several years. He must really like you."

"Well, I wouldn't go that far." Elias laughed as he stood up. "Shall I come back again at the same time tomorrow?"

"Yes, every day from here on out shall be split between myself and Shimada," Bumble said, returning to his usually perky self. "Please do not mention to him our discussion today."

"Oh, I don't think that will be a problem", Elias said thinking of the prolonged silences he and Shimada shared.

"Excellent. Now please let me show you out. You have much reading to do."

Elias's heart sank.

15

THE FIVE RINGS

Leo stood outside the classroom door and rubbed his hands on his trousers again, trying to get them dry. He didn't usually get nervous, but something about stepping into the room set his heart racing. After waving goodbye to Elias at the school gates, his mind went into overdrive. The wave of students arriving at the same time carried him through the school, but now he was frozen on the spot, his sweaty palms wrapped around the doorknob in front of him, unable to turn it.

It had been over two months since they first arrived in Albion and Tiberius had arranged for him to attend the local school. His start date had crept up on him unexpectedly. He had been so caught up in his daily routine. Wiling away the days with Ginger in her workshop before helping Elias with his studies in the evening, he forgot all about the new term looming on the horizon.

Leo had been looking forward to starting school, but for some reason, as soon as he was alone at the gates, a sudden flood of panic overcame him. What if he made himself look stupid, what if everyone laughs about the way he reads or writes. The worries rattled around his head. He had always dreamt of going to school but never truly believed he would get the opportunity. Yet here he was, stood in the hallway waiting to start his first class but too afraid to take the next step.

He took a deep breath to steady his nerves, wiped his hands on his shirt one final time and reached for the handle. The door swung open unexpectedly, and he stumbled into the classroom, he heard laughter erupt as he crashed face-first into a bushy-haired woman.

"Why good morning Leo, I was growing concerned you might not be joining us today." The woman said as she grasped Leo by the arms.

He looked up and was greeted by the biggest pair of glasses he had ever seen. Her eyes looked ginormous behind the thick lenses.

"I am Mrs Watson, please take a seat. I believe Miss Tiberius has saved you one." She released Leo from her grasp and pointed over to an empty desk in the middle of the room.

"Okay," Leo said meekly, his head stooped as low as it would go.

He tried to avoid eye contact with the rest of the students as their suspicious eyes narrowed in, watching him closely. With every step he took, the desk seemed to drift slightly further away, his stomach started to churn into a painful knot when he noticed a hand waving at him. It was Ginger, craning from her desk trying to catch his eye, she was sat with a massive smile on her face as she waved him over. His heart leapt when he spotted her, and suddenly his worries evaporated.

"Hey, I saved you a seat." She said, settling back down.

"Thanks," Leo muttered as he slid in next to her, it was a hard wooden chair with a semi-circular desk attached to it.

"I was getting worried you weren't going to turn up," Ginger whispered out the side of her mouth.

"Sorry, I got lost trying to find the classroom" Leo lied.

"Well you didn't miss much, Mrs Watson was just explaining we had a new joiner starting today. Everyone couldn't wait to meet…"

"Now young Leo is settled in, shall we begin?" Mrs Watson said loudly as she glanced at Ginger, who made a zipping motion across her mouth, indicating she had finished talking.

"Fantastic!" Mrs Watson clapped her hands together. "So, mechanics. Who wants to tell me where we got to last term?"

Several hands shot up all around Leo, he looked over at Ginger as she almost fell out of her seat trying to get Mrs Watson's attention.

His first day at school flew by, and before he knew it, it was time to go home. They'd spent the morning learning about the basics of mechanical engineering and then were given a series of tasks to fix some malfunctioning electrical equipment. Leo felt right at home and amazed his classmates with how easily he could strip and rebuild a broken radio, a skill he had acquired in the Jungle.

During lunch, Ginger introduced him to her friends. Barnabus was a chubby little boy with rounded glasses who sat at the back of their room. He talked so fast he would get out of breath and had to take a puff on his inhaler to calm himself down. Trent was another boy in their class; he was incredibly tall for his age with an uncomfortably skinny frame. He had a long stretched out face and pointy nose. Bobby and Noah, Ginger's last two friends, were in the year above but looked a lot older than everyone else he had met, it amazed Leo they were still at school. Meeting Gingers friends reminded him of the boys from the Jungle, he hoped they had escaped like he did, but he tried not to think about them too much, as he didn't want to get upset on his first day.

The afternoon consisted of coding practice, each of the children sat by a computer terminal and were tasked to program a mechanical arm to transport items across the room. At first, Leo was utterly dumbfounded by the language they used, but by the end of the session, he understood the basics. Mrs Watson called him a natural when he and Ginger were the only pair able to get the arm to pick up a cup from her desk and bring it over to them without spilling its contents. When the alarm rang out to mark the end of the day, Leo didn't want to go home, it was the most fun he'd ever had. He loved every minute of it and couldn't wait to go back the next day.

"So what did you think?" Ginger asked as they headed out of the main school doors.

"Your school is…amazing," Leo's face burst into a grin.

"You think so?" Ginger asked excitedly as she led Leo down the steps and out into the bustling streets of Albion.

"Honestly, I've never been anywhere like it,"

"So you never went to school in the Jungle?"

"Nah, nothing like that. I had a friend…" Leo paused for a few moments, his thoughts drifting to Maz.

"Are you okay?" Ginger asked softly.

"Yeah, yeah I'm fine. I was one of the lucky ones I suppose. One of the elders, Maz, she took me under her wing and taught me to read. Told me it was one of the most valuable skills a person could learn."

"Sounds like a smart lady."

"Yeah, she was…" Leo stopped again and wrinkled his nose, trying to stop his eyes from welling up.

"I'm sorry, Leo." Ginger sounded genuinely moved by Leo's story.

"It's not your fault is it. It wasn't all bad." Leo added quickly, changing the subject. "At least I had more time to practice my mechanics. Well, I never knew it was called that, but I'd spent most of my days repairing old machines. Anything we could sell really."

"I wondered how you'd gotten so good at it! Looks like I have got some competition on my hands these days." Ginger playfully punched Leo in the arm.

"Yeah, I guess so," He said, rubbing his arm.

"Well, I'll see you tomorrow then," Ginger shouted as Leo climbed up the steps to his apartment. "Shall I swing by in the morning? We can walk into school together if you like?"

"Sounds great," Leo said, waving her goodbye as he slid open the door and stepped inside.

"Elias!" Leo shouted as he walked through the empty apartment.

He shouted again, but no response came.

That's odd he is usually back by now, thought Leo.

Elias picked up the last of his things and stuffed them into his satchel.

"Another excellent session today Elias," Bumble patted Elias firmly on the shoulder. "Your understanding of the five pillars of Mana is exemplary. You are progressing through the sacred texts far quicker than I expected."

"Er…thanks," he said awkwardly, trying to avoid Bumble's

gaze, in truth this was all Leo's work, he had merely learnt to regurgitate facts when asked.

"I believe you may be coming to the point when you soon discover which element you have been marked with. This is a significant milestone on a Nihon's journey of self-discovery." Bumble declared proudly.

"You think I'm ready," his guilt seemed to dissipate at the thought of discovering which elemental skill he was destined for.

Learning about the unique abilities a Nihon could master had been the most exciting part of Elias's training to date. He sat there in rapture as Bumble told him about the five elements a Nihon could be marked with; Fire, Water, Wind, Earth & Void.

"Whatever element you are marked with will determine the Nihon you are destined to become,"

"Fire is one of the most destructive elements, it enables a Nihon to psionically create and control flames. An ember with the potential to erupt into an uncontrollable inferno capable of incinerating everything around it."

"Can they be hurt by the flames?" Elias thought back to his escape from the Jungle.

"No, they are immune to heat. Temperatures that would kill a normal person don't even raise a sweat for them."

"Water is the counterbalance to Fire, where the inferno rages the river flows. Their hydrokinesis abilities enable them to conjure up vast quantities of water by manipulating the molecules within the air that surrounds us." Bumble rolled out a long scripture containing several hand-drawn illustrations demonstrating a water Nihon using their power.

"The Wind element grants a Nihon the ability of aerokinesis, allowing them to control the weather and the atmosphere around them, conducting the forces of nature. Be it summoning lightning, inciting hurricanes or whipping up blizzards as they see fit." Elias shook his head in quiet amazement.

"Earth Nihon's are perhaps the most powerful of all, their incredible magnokinesis abilities let them manipulate the very minerals that make up the Earth, sometimes to devastating effect. Their powers are so great they can even alter the gravitational fields around them."

"...and finally we come to the Void. The rarest and least understood of all the Nihon elements. In fact, very few have ever been recorded, legend has it they can rip a hole in the very fabric of time and space, teleporting at will in the blink of an eye. Not that you would ever know." Bumble chuckled to himself.

"They are also burdened with a range of psychic abilities that can influence the world around them. So they would probably wipe your memory if you caught them teleporting."

Elias sat in silence for a few moments trying to take everything in, it all seemed too far-fetched to be true.

"I know this may be a lot to take in Elias." said Bumble sensing Elias's unease. "But once Gaia reveals your element, this will all become much clearer."

"...and you think that might happen soon?"

"Absolutely, and I have a sneaking suspicion, I know which one it will be too."

"Am I right in guessing you won't share that intuition with me?" Elias laughed.

"You guess correctly, that is an important discovery one must make for themselves, and I would never want to influence the process. Be patient young one, I'm confident you'll find out sooner than you think. Now I believe your brother will be finishing his first day at school soon, so let's finish early so you can spend some time with him."

"Okay, I'll see you the same time tomorrow," Elias shouted, running to the door.

"Goodbye," Bumble muttered, closing the massive book in front of him.

Elias swung his rucksack over his shoulder, Bumble's latest selection of oversized books weighing heavily on his back. He sprinted out of the Great Hall, down the stone steps and back through the canyon leading to Albion. Joining the high street that weaved through the centre of the city; it was bustling with people all going about their daily business. Elias ducked in and out of the pedestrians as he tried to rush through the crowd when he noticed a street vendor selling some delicious looking confectionary.

"Hi," Elias said as he looked at the colourful snacks.

"Hello young man," the seller replied, he had a portly build and a big bushy moustache, he wore a white apron over his clothes.

"What are these?" Elias pointed to some vibrantly coloured sweets hanging above his head.

"These are Gazumbo Balls, they are a Ronin delicacy. You never tasted one?" He asked inquisitively.

"No..." Elias stammered. "I just moved here," he added, feeling the need to justify why he had never eaten one.

"Oh, I see," The man looked confused. "You must be the young Nihon everyone is talking about?"

"Er...yeah. I guess. That's me. The Nihon," Elias said, pulling an awkward smile, he hated the thought that people were discussing him behind his back.

"Well, I think the least I can do is give you a sample." He said with a smile. "Which one would you like?"

"I actually wanted one for my little brother, it's his first day at school," Elias said as he worked his way down the chain of brightly-coloured Gazumbo balls.

"Well, in that case, I think I can spare two." The man chuckled as he picked the two biggest ones off the chain with a pair of tongs and slid them into a brown paper bag. "There you go. Enjoy."

"Thank you so much," Elias said, gingerly accepting the paper bag. "Are you sure you don't want me to pay? I have money."

"I wouldn't hear of it," the man said sternly, "Now you get back to that brother of yours, I bet he is dying to tell you about his day."

Elias turned and walked away from the stand, after a few paces he stopped and unrolled the bag, it smelled delicious. A beautiful mixture of sweet-smelling fruits, Leo is going to love these he thought as he took in another whiff of the scent.

As he stood with his face shoved inside the paper bag, he sensed somebody watching him. He quickly rolled up the bag and glanced over his shoulder, he jumped back in fright as he noticed an incredibly old man standing right behind him.

"Oh I'm sorry, I didn't mean to startle you," the old man said, his face scrunching up into a kind smile. He was hunched over a wooden cane, and his clothes looked old and tatty.

Elias straightened himself up. "You didn't," he lied. "Can I help you?"

"Well I certainly hope so, I take it you are Elias? The young Nihon that everyone is talking about?"

"Yeah...I guess so," Elias said, scratching his neck.

"Excellent. Now I know this isn't strictly speaking the correct way of requesting such assistance but..." the old man's voice quivered. "It's my wife you see...she is very ill, and none of the traditional remedies appears to be working…I was wondering if you might be able to help her?"

"What do you mean?" Elias stared at the old man.

"I don't know exactly, use your powers to make her better somehow."

"Err," Elias avoided the man's gaze, he noticed dozens of people had started to gather around him, listening intently to their conversation.

"If you help his wife, will you take a look at my son?" A voice shouted from the crowd.

"Or my husband, he's got a blasted cough," a woman said jabbing Elias in the ribs with her bony finger.

Elias was trapped, surrounded by people, all demanding his help in one way or another, he staggered backwards and bashed into the wall behind him. The unrelenting voices firing requests at him.

"Look, I'm sorry. I don't know what I can do…" Elias stammered as he bolted, shoving his way past the old man who tumbled backwards.

"I'm sorry!" Elias yelled as he dashed through the streets, pushing past one person after another. He darted down a side street away from prying eyes and hid behind a small stone wall.

As he crouched, listening out for footsteps, he heard something that hit him like a sledgehammer. He stood up, rooted to the spot in stunned silence. Drawn to the sound of a woman singing from a nearby garden.

"I see you, but you don't see me," the woman sang softly.

Elias followed the song down the street. It grew louder, leading him to a middle-aged woman dressed in a floral pinafore dress, she had long flowing auburn hair, with streaks of silver running through it.

"Your shadow I will always be," she sang, tidying away the children's toys left out in her courtyard.

"Yesterday, today and tomorrow."

"That song…" Elias muttered.

The woman let out a loud screech as she jumped backwards "I'm sorry love. You scared the life out of me. I didn't hear you coming." She chuckled as she rested her hand on her chest.

"What did you say?" She asked, quickly regaining her composure.

"I'm sorry. But, that song…what is it?" His eyes started to well up as he scrunched up the bag of Gazumbo balls in his hands, her words stirring something deep inside of him. A memory long since forgotten.

"Oh, it's just a silly nursery rhyme we used to sing to our children back in Rohinyha," the woman said. "I have been singing them for so long. I do it without even realising these days," she laughed, gesturing to the vast array of children's toys littered around her.

"I…I" Elias paused. He looked up into the air, trying to fight back the tears welling up in his eyes. "It's just…" he took another deep breath to steady himself. "I haven't heard those words in such a long time," Elias's voice faltered as he stared upwards biting at his lip.

"Oh, please don't get upset," the woman said kindly, "I'll stop,"

"No, no. Please, carry on." Elias grabbed her hand as he stepped forward. "If you don't mind."

"Okay love. If that's what you want," she spoke gently, sensing Elias's mood.

She began to sing again as she carried on, walking around her courtyard, collecting her children's toys.

"I see you, but you don't see me."

"Your shadow I will always be"

"Your steps, your falls, I will share them all."

"Yesterday, today and tomorrow."

"I see you, but you don't see me.

"Your shadow I will always be"

The song took Elias back to a life all but forgotten, he stumbled through his memories like a lost child trying to find his way home. He was just a boy, no more than six years old with his mother, she wore a beautiful headscarf, playing with him in a lush green field.

Laughter. Happiness. Joy flowed through him.

The memories turned grey, his mother no longer youthful and happy but exhausted and emaciated, dragging a bawling Elias by the hand through the desert. Surrounded by scores of dishevelled people; staggering along a dusty track one painful step at a time. Next, he helped his mother take a drink by a small campfire as she battled a vicious cough tearing through her lungs. The light from the fire faded away, and Elias was alone, sobbing uncontrollably into his tiny arms as he lay on the ground next to a pile of stones stacked neatly on top of each other. Once again, he is amongst the crowds, a faceless grey figure walks by his side dragging him by the hand.

"Are you alright?" the woman asked, her voice ripping Elias away from his memories.

"Sorry," Elias said quickly as he scurried off.

"Love, you seem upset. Please come back!" The woman shouted as she took a few steps after Elias, but he was gone.

Sprinting through the streets of Albion as fast as he could. He didn't know where he was going, he didn't care, he just wanted to run away, to escape his past. He ran until his legs couldn't carry him anymore. He ran all the way through the city and out towards the ravine until he reached the riverside. He ran himself into the ground, collapsing to his knees by the water's edge. The tears streamed down his face as he struggled to regain control of his breath.

He had not heard that song in so long, yet he remembered every word of it vividly, thoughts of his mother swirled around his head. He cried and cried, unable to stop himself, his face becoming a blubbering wreck of tears as he tried to steady his breathing. He didn't know how long he stayed there for, sobbing by the river but eventually he cried himself out and, in his exhaustion, drifted into a deep sleep.

***

Elias awoke curled up in a tight ball on the ground still clutching the brown paper bag to his chest, the Gazumbo balls crushed into a mushy inedible paste. He dusted himself off, wiped his face on the back of his sleeve and headed home, disposing of the crumpled paper bag on-route.

When he got back to his apartment, he stood outside the front door for a few moments and took several deep breaths to recompose himself before reaching for the handle. Leo was waiting for him, and he bounded over to him as soon as he stepped inside. Elias wondered where he got his endless energy reserves from.

"Where have you been?" Leo asked excitedly as he dragged Elias into the house. "You've been gone ages. I was getting worried about you. I've been dying to speak to you."

"Easy, Easy," Elias laughed as he struggled to follow Leo across the apartment.

Somehow his little brother always had this effect on him. No matter how down he felt, no matter how dark the thoughts in his head got, five minutes with Leo was all it took to lift the pressure, to re-balance him and make him feel brand new all over again.

"So..." Elias paused, teasing Leo. He could see him struggling to contain the excitement on his face. "How was it?" He asked as they collapsed on the sofa together.

"It...was...unbelievable." Leo gushed. "It's everything I hoped it would be. At first, I was a bit nervous, because you know I've never been to school before. Well, not a proper one anyway. But as soon as I saw Ginger, I was alright. She showed me around and introduced me to her friends, and it..." Leo finally stopped to take a breath.

He went on for the next half an hour, telling Elias every detail of his day. After Leo finished recounting everything he could remember, he turned to his brother.

"So how did your training go today?"

"Good. Thanks for asking," he replied sarcastically.

"Sorry. Did I go a bit overboard?" Leo said, suddenly aware of how long he'd been talking.

"I'm only joking. I'm glad you enjoyed it. I knew you would be a natural at this school stuff. I always say you got the brains, and I got the looks." Elias punched Leo on the arm.

"You wish, have you seen that nose." Leo shot back, pointing at Elias's face. "Anyway, how was Shimada?"

"Horrible as ever," Elias rolled his eyes "Look at these," he said, pulling up his sleeves to reveal his blackened and bruised forearms. "All day he's hitting me with that bloody bokken. I have no idea how I'm going to get through the rest of the week."

Leo contorted in disgust as he stared at his brother's arms.

"Ouch, and what about Bumble? Does he still think you are reading the books he gives you?"

"Yeah, in fact, he's so impressed with my knowledge and understanding of the five pillars of Mana he's given me two more to read." Elias pulled out two large, leather-backed books from his rucksack and dumped them on Leo's lap.

"Oh jeez," Leo said, struggling under the weight of the giant books.

"I know. You are too efficient for your own good."

"You know you are going to need to learn to read for yourself one day?"

"Oh give me a break, I've got enough on my plate trying to be a messiah let alone learning to read as well. You know me, never been good with the words. Give me a good old-fashioned fight any day of the week."

Leo raised his eyebrows, he had tried and failed on several occasions to teach Elias how to read, but he always lost patience and stormed off whenever he got to a word he couldn't understand.

"Don't look at me like that," Elias pushed himself up from the sofa.

"So when do you need to have read them by?" Leo struggled to contain the annoyance in his voice.

"The green one by the end of the week, the red one by next Wednesday," Elias said with a massive grin on his face.

"Great. I better get started then." Leo sighed as he heaved the gigantic green book off his lap and opened it up.

16

REINFORCEMENTS

"Come on, Leo keep up." Ginger snapped, her voice echoing down the tunnel as she yanked on the luminescent rope connecting them. Leo stumbled forward a few steps, sloshing through the ankle-deep water.

"I'm sorry, but I can't see a thing behind you," he yelled back as he tried to regain his footing in the darkness, annoyed at Ginger's latest attempt to carrel him. "And, I've been following you around this bloody tunnel for hours now!"

She slowly turned on the spot, the light from her head-torch blinding him. Leo gulped, regretting his sudden outburst as he shielded his eyes. He had never met anyone like Ginger before. He missed the boys from the Jungle terribly, but he never had a lot in common with them, and while he loved spending time with his brother, sometimes he knew Elias was not really listening to him. Whenever Leo would try to talk about his robotics or engineering lessons, he could see Elias's eyes glaze over. But Ginger was different, they were interested in the same things and were always together working on one project or another. They had grown closer over the last few months; their journeys to school the perfect opportunity to discuss their next experiment. It was on one such trip, Ginger asked if Leo could keep a secret. He replied empathically, yes - a decision he now regretted. Cold and damp, he wandered around the pitch black, aimlessly following the torchlight ahead.

"You definitely packed extra batteries, right?"

"Arrgh. How many times Leonidas. YES!" Ginger gave the rope another yank, sending him staggering through the water again.

"Very funny," Leo yelled back as he regained his balance, his voiced bounced all around him. "And, you're sure this is the right way?"

"Yes," Ginger said through gritted teeth.

"Well, some secret this has turned out to be," Leo grumbled to himself as he kicked the water in front of him.

"What did you say?" She snapped

"Nothing." He answered quickly.

At first, Ginger's invitation excited him; he thought she would reveal a new device for them to work on. He did not expect to be trekking through mile after mile of abandoned oil pipes. Her unwavering confidence did not embolden him either; especially after she let slip that she once got lost down in the tunnels for two days. She emerged exhausted and dehydrated. Only to discover Tiberius on the brink of launching a full-scale search operation with every able-bodied person in the city ready to go.

"That was ages ago," she declared adamantly, "I know these tunnels like the back of my hand now."

Her last words before they set off, still rang in his head. "Positive confidence, that's all you need."

Now look at us, he thought, miles from home chasing a dodgy torch down a sewer. Ginger shone the light from side to side, it struggled to cut through the pitch-black surrounding them. She stopped and ran her hands along the side of the tunnel, bringing the light closer to her face.

"Gotcha!" She stepped back and revealed a mark, a distinctive cross painted in luminous chalk, long since faded.

"Doesn't that usually mean no entry?"

"Exactly. We're here."

"This is it. You brought me all the way down here to show me a mark on a wall."

"Idiot." She swung around the light to reveal a ladder opposite them enclosed in a small steel tube, leaving barely enough room to climb it. Ginger peered up and illuminated the shaft with her torch. Leo gulped as he stared up at the endless ladder, reaching up into the shadows.

"Right. How high is that then?"

"Oh, I don't know. Will you stop whining and start climbing," Ginger said, pushing past him.

Stepping on the first rung and pulling herself up, she retrieved a black rope from her rucksack and tied an intricate knot around her waist, feeding the line through a carabiner before attaching it snuggly to the ladder.

"What's that for?" Leo inspected the rope, tugging on it aggressively.

"You'll see on the way down."

"So we aren't connecting ourselves to it now," said Leo trying to hide the concern in his voice.

"No."

"What if I slip?"

"Don't." Ginger said flatly.

"Well, that's helpful," Leo said to himself as Ginger began her ascent.

He watched in awe as she forced herself upwards, climbing several rungs at a time. Leo tentatively stepped on the ladder and wiped his hands on the back of his trousers. He hated heights and the dark. He gripped a rung and gathered a firm foothold before warily following after Ginger.

"How far does this go?" Leo shouted, losing pace with Ginger, who seemed feline in her ability to traverse the towering shaft above them.

She stopped and peered down. "It's about fifteen minutes to the top."

"Fif...fifteen." Leo stammered.

"Yeah about that, but you are a little slower than I thought you'd be. So maybe about twenty, twenty-five if you hurry up."

Leo blushed, his hopes of impressing her with his derring-do on their first foray outside the safety of Albion fading into oblivion.

"Sounds good." Leo shook his head in disbelief. "Just wanted to make sure, so I can err...pace myself." He cringed as the words left his mouth.

"Right....well try and keep up if you can. Climbing's even harder in the dark."

It seemed to take forever to reach the top, several times Ginger's torch faded into a dim twinkle as she raced ahead of him. The threat of the all-consuming darkness spurred him on whenever he started to lose track of her, his arms and legs burning with every step. The light from her torch finally began to grow brighter as he spotted Ginger, perched precariously on the final rung, waiting for him.

"I thought I'd lost you," Ginger laughed as she shone the light in Leo's face.

"Not a chance, I could keep going for ages." Leo lied as he gazed up at her, she sat wedged between the wall and the ladder using her feet to balance. She popped the torch into her mouth while her hands carefully worked a circular locking mechanism attached to a solid iron manhole cover above her.

"Well, sorry to disappoint but we are here," Ginger said out the side of her mouth as she pushed open the cover. Leo shielded his eyes as daylight flooded into the shaft, revealing how high they actually were.

"Whoa," Leo groaned as his head started to spin.

He clawed at the ladder, clutching it tightly against his body. His knuckles turned white as he clasped the iron rung, its rusted bars digging into his calloused skin. He glanced up as Ginger clambered out of the shaft. She disappeared for a few moments before her upside-down head popped back into view.

"Come on, already. We haven't got all day." She thrust her hand inside and grabbed Leo's arm, dragging him up.

"Oh, right. Yeah sorry," Leo stuttered as she heaved him out into the blinding light. He clawed at the sand as he spilt out on to the dusty ground, the fresh air hitting him like a thrashing wave.

Ginger slammed the hatch shut and pulled Leo back to his feet.

"Welcome to the graveyard,"

He didn't quite know what he was looking at. Scattered for miles in every direction, vast mountains of metallic debris, robotic arms, legs, torsos, wheels, wings, everything he had hoped to discover in the waste pits; all stacked hundreds of feet high. Ginger gently took his hand, leading him through a desert path weaving between two glittering mounds that enveloped the manhole they had emerged from. He wasn't sure if it was because he had spent the last few months living underground, but everything seemed so much brighter. Heavy clouds still filled the sky, but they appeared lighter, floating effortlessly above them. He covered his eyes with his hand, struggling to keep them open in the glaring daylight. Ginger turned back and noticed him squinting.

"Oh, I forgot to say. The clouds here aren't as dense as they are by the Citadel, we are right on the edge of the Iron Lung. The sun, it's still out there, somewhere, trying to break-through." She pointed up to the ashen sky.

Leo's words escaped him, he had never thought about the sun still being out there. The ridges of the mountain range shimmered and rippled as the light bounced off the reflective surfaces. The colours on show amazed Leo, deep velvet reds, bold greens, crisp sky blues - he had never seen such vibrancy in all his life. The world he grew up in was very different; dark, cold and grey.

"What is this place?" Leo whispered.

"This is the resting place of the Free Robot Army." Ginger cut through Leo's whispers.

He felt stupid for whispering, everything there had obviously died years ago, and there was no one else around. Leo heard stories growing up about how the Sovereign brutally stamped down the robot civil rights movement, but he had no idea this many perished during the uprising. Standing still for a few moments he tried to take everything in, slowly his eyes started to acclimatise to the sunlight, and he began to pick out distinct objects buried in the mounds of debris. Arms and legs, shattered lenses, caved in armour plates, cannons and swords, thousands of them jutting out at awkward angles.

"Is that a..." Leo leaned forward for a clearer view.

"A head? Yes. Here, take a look." Ginger scampered up the hill and rolled down a round object to Leo.

A battered white helmet containing a robot's head came to a stop next to his foot, he knelt down for a closer inspection. The face had a strangely human appearance to it, with a prominent nose and mouth. Its eyes were made of reinforced glass, they looked cold and vacant. The left side of the head was severely damaged with a deep gash delved into the metalwork, breaking the sublime white paint and exposing the jagged steel beneath. Several cords hung from the bottom of the head, which Leo assumed used to be attached to its former body.

The vastness of these machines started to dawn on him, he learnt about them during his time in the Jungle, and he devoured every book he could find about them since he arrived in Albion. He read about their creation as a slave labour force and how the development of advanced artificial intelligence sowed the seeds for their uprising. Fascinated by their crusade for independence, which had ultimately caused their demise.

Leo studied every word about the history of these magnificent machines without ever contemplating their size. They must have stood over eight feet tall when alive, watching them in battle must have been an awe-inspiring sight, Leo thought. He could not fathom how they lost their fight for their freedom

"You want to see something special?" Ginger asked.

"What? This place isn't special enough?"

"This is junk, I have found something you'll really want to see," she added excitedly.

Ginger grabbed Leo's hand and led him at speed along a winding trail. He tried to take everything in as it whizzed by.

"Ow," Leo cried as he stubbed his toe on a broken assault rifle laid strewn on the ground.

He cursed to himself as he hopped over it, trying to keep up with Ginger. Their path went deeper and deeper into the maze of junk, which appeared to be growing all around. Shadows started to follow them as the peaks of several ridges loomed above. Leo felt a shiver go down his spine when he noticed hundreds of cold, dead eyes watching them trespass upon their resting place. He began to feel uneasy as their track started to wend and weave. He grasped Ginger's hand tightly, aware he was now utterly lost, the tunnels were bad enough, but it would take him years to find his way out of here. Ginger appeared to be at right at home like she always was when surrounded by machines.

She slowed down and whispered back to Leo. "It's through here,"

Ginger pointed to a staircase leading underground. Leo was puzzled by Ginger's sudden found tactfulness for the fallen but agreed whispering was the fitting thing to do.

"Right, let's go." Ginger flicked her torch back on and ushered Leo down the stairs into a dark, cramped underpass.

"Great,"

"Just up here," Ginger nodded encouragingly to a staircase at the end of the underpass.

The light at the top of the stairs raised Leo's hopes that they might actually be about to arrive at their destination. He cautiously followed Ginger up the steps back into the warm glow of the sunlight. After a short spell in the dark, the power of the natural light dazzled him once again as he arose from the final step. He wandered forward blindly, rubbing his eyes, trying to clear his vision.

As his sight returned, he started to make out a massive monument standing proudly in front of him. Atop a granite plinth, stood a magnificent stone carving of a robot, his hands rested upon his waist in a triumphant pose, gazing off into the distance.

"Wow," Leo gasped. "It's amazing."

"Honestly," Ginger laughed. "Not that…this." Ginger nodded at the base of the plinth. Leo completely missed the gigantic metal figure slumped across it.

"What is it?"

"It's a robot. The biggest I've ever seen, and it's intact." Ginger said, hardly able to control the excitement in her voice.

"Like fully intact," she shouted as she raced over to the statue.

Leo scurried after her, glancing back and forth from the real-life robot in front of him to the towering statue above. He couldn't deny it was an impressive sight, well over ten feet tall and covered in matte black paint, with patches of a red pattern across its chest and legs.

Sprawled awkwardly across the steps of the statue, with one knee trailing on the floor. It was trying to use its rifle as a walking stick to get back to its feet when it died. The robot had taken a lot of damage before its death, the side of its helmet had been smashed in, and one of its eyes was shattered. A shoulder plate was missing, and scorch marks covered its chest, probably from a pulse rifle blast Leo thought. Its left arm, severed at the elbow was a mess of tangled and charred wires, and it had a gaping hole in its back where its power-pack used to live. Otherwise, it appeared intact.

Ginger was right.

"When did you find this?" Leo asked.

"About two months ago, been coming here once a week to keep an eye on it."

"Well, I don't think it's going anywhere Ginge."

"Not because of that, I...didn't want anyone else to find him."

"Well your secret is safe with me, he's amazing isn't he."

"Yeah he's incredible, I've been exploring this place for years, and he's the most complete specimen I have ever seen." Ginger paused. "I think we can repair him,"

"What do you mean, repair him?" Leo struggled to comprehend Ginger's suggestion.

"I mean, repair him. Rebuild him. Bring him back to life."

"What...why would we want to do that?"

"So he'll fight with the Shadows, you heard my dad, we need every able-bodied soldier we can muster. This might help turn the tide of the war."

"Ginger, this is crazy. Did you not read all those books you lent me? The robots destroyed Roninhya, what makes you think they would fight for us now?"

"I just know okay...if we repair him, then I...I mean we, could convince him to join us."

"Look even if we do manage to get this thing repaired and on our side, your dad would never let it join the Shadows."

"Leave my dad to me, if we can fix him then he will listen to us. He's not like the others, he fought alongside robots. He knows they weren't all bad."

"I don't know Ginger,"

"So are you going to help me or not". Ginger crossed her arms and scowled at Leo.

"I want to put on record. I think this is a terrible idea."

"Noted"

Leo stared at Ginger, then at the dead robot, then back at Ginger. Her emerald eyes glistened as they bored into his head.

He would be lying to himself if he didn't confess it was a

dream come true, he wanted nothing more his whole life than to create a robot of his own. All the time tinkering away with his gadgets in the Jungle, in his head, he was building towards something bigger, something to protect them, and now, here it was - the chance of a lifetime.

"I'm in."

The start of the school holidays gave Ginger and Leo the opportunity to focus their efforts on restoring the robot. They visited it every day, making up various excuses to Elias and Tiberius as to why they would be returning late. After collecting whatever tools they needed for the day from Ginger's workshop, they snuck out of town and followed the long tunnel system to the graveyard. Working tirelessly into the night on their new companion.

Their secret project took over his life; when he wasn't there, he was daydreaming about it; thinking about improvements they would make when they next returned. All-day, every day, all he could think about was their robot. Leo felt guilty for being so distracted, he knew something had been bothering Elias of late and his brother mentioned on a couple of occasions he needed to speak to Tiberius about something important. He thought his brother was about to open up to him once, when Ginger came bursting through the door, and he had to shoot off again. By the time he returned, Elias had fallen asleep, and the next morning he told Leo it wasn't anything important and swiftly changed the subject. He loved their new mission, but he missed Elias and really wanted to get to the bottom of what was troubling his brother.

The repairs started once they figured out how to move the

robot from its resting place. Ginger managed to hot-wire an old mech that was discarded nearby. With just enough juice left in its batteries to lift the robot to the ground, the mech collapsed in a smouldering heap, sparks spitting out furiously as Ginger scrambled to safety. After that, the real work began. They split up the tasks with Leo scouring the graveyard for replacement parts and Ginger undertaking the bulk of the repair work. They worked perfectly as a team. Leo's years of scavenging made him adept at tracking down what they needed, and he discovered a side to Ginger he had never seen before. She was in her element, coming alive when she had her blowtorch in hand, a constant flurry of sparks surrounded her.

Leo sat on the plinth having some lunch, watching in quiet amazement as Ginger installed all the new pieces of equip-ment, one after the other. When she finished, Leo touched up the robot with some black paint he had smuggled out of Albion. By the end of the holidays, they had repaired its head, chest and torso, and only the damaged arm remained. That proved to be the most difficult challenge of all. Ginger lost her temper on several occasions, throwing her blowtorch to the ground in frustration, but after much trial and error, they finally succeeded and the replacement arm fused into place. Now fully re-assembled, the robot was an imposing figure to behold, they sat together for hours admiring their handiwork.

The final piece of the puzzle and one Leo had not even thought about until now was how they would power it. Ginger explained they would need a battery pack and a huge one if they were to stand a chance of reviving their creation.

"We can take one from the Mechs in Albion," Ginger declared as she stood there staring at the robot's lifeless body.

"It's not big enough," Leo said defeatedly, "Look at the size of this thing, it needs to be massive."

"Only the Ospreys have anything that big," Ginger added despondently as she fixed her gaze on the gaping hole in the middle of the robot's chest.

"We couldn't do that, we barely have enough Ospreys as it is."

"I know,"

"and your dad will go nuts if we steal one of those,"

"I know."

"It's not even worth thinking about what he'd say if he ever found out we downed one of our only aircraft to revive a robot! Can you imagine?" Leo chuckled.

"I know." She snarled.

"I'm just saying."

"Well don't!" Ginger snapped as she kicked over her toolbox and stormed off.

Leo stood staring at the machine before him, its soulless glass eyes glaring back at him.

They had waited months for this moment, and now it had arrived, it was something of an anti-climax. They were so engrossed in completing the repairs they had not spared a thought to what they would do with it once they finished. The people of Albion hated robots, they would never accept one amongst them.

Or would they?

The idea buzzed around his head like a persistent fly. What if they did revive him and he turned the tide in the battle against the Sovereign. Surely then they would agree, not all robots are evil. Leo walked around and patted it on the head.

"So long buddy. I'll come back for you..." he said as he turned away.

"One day."

17

ARMY OF SHADOWS

"I don't care. This is a bad idea." Max roared as he slammed his fist down on the table.

"Maximus, need I remind you we were all young and inexperienced once. How can one be expected to learn if never given the opportunity?" Tiberius said calmly.

"Max, Tiberius is right. Elias needs to learn how we operate, and he's never going to be able to do that if we don't let him leave Albion." Diaz chipped in positively.

"Then take him on a tour of the city, I haven't got time to be babysitting," Max said with a snarl as he stalked the room.

He stepped in front of one of the resistance soldiers and let out a loud grunt, his nostrils flaring fiercely as he glared down at the soldier who swiftly sidestepped out of the way. Max continued pacing around the room menacingly as he shook his head, the thick mane hanging around his neck swinging wildly with every step.

"I don't need babysitting. I've been training for months now," Elias mumbled, he had been sat in the corner for over twenty minutes while Tiberius, Diaz and Max talked about him like he was wasn't there.

So far, his first visit to the Shadows base of operations was proving to be quite a disappointment. When Tiberius mentioned that he might be able to take part in their next operation, he had been thrilled at the thought, but their bickering was starting to irritate him.

"You've got no idea what you need, boy." Max snapped as he glowered down at him. Elias fidgeted in his seat, trying to avoid eye contact with the monster before him.

"Enough. Stand down, Maximus." Diaz said sternly.

"We've listened to your views, and your concerns are duly noted. However, I should not need to remind you that I am still in operational command of this unit, and my decision is final. Elias will be joining us today."

Max snorted again, this time much louder. "Doesn't mean I have to be happy about it." He grumbled, storming out and pushing the door open with such force it crashed into the wall.

"Is he always like that?" Elias said as he pushed himself off his chair and approached Diaz and Tiberius.

"Don't take it personally. Max hates everybody." Diaz laughed.

"While that may be true Captain. Maximus does appear to be particularly prickly today. Any idea what might be bothering him?" Tiberius asked inquisitively.

"No idea. You know Max as well as I do. Doesn't take a lot to put him in a bad mood. Right, Sanchez round up the rest of the team. Briefing starts in fifteen." Diaz said facing the soldier Max had snarled at.

"Yes sir," Sanchez replied, she had a small yet athletic build and wore a loose-fitting pair of camouflage fatigues. Her face had a roguish charm to it, and she wore her jet black hair tied up in a bun.

"Good to have you on board," Sanchez whispered to Elias as she left the room.

***

Elias entered the briefing room; it was a small semi-circular amphitheatre with several rows of seats looking down on a massive screen in the centre, a small stage stood to the side, a wooden lectern at its heart. Elias shuffled along one of the rows and sat next to Sanchez. He spotted Max prowling the stage below, apparently still brooding over his argument with Diaz and Tiberius.

A few more people came in and took up the empty seats around him. These must be the Deltas Elias thought noticing the badges on their uniforms which carried the symbol of their unit; a red spartan helmet. He snuck a glance at Sanchez's arm and saw she too wore the badge of honour. She's a Delta. Soon the place was full of chatter as they waited for Diaz to arrive. Elias studied the room, trying to see what was so special about these soldiers. But they all looked so different it was difficult to identify any unique characteristics, they looked like a ragtag band of misfits if anything. He did a quick headcount, there were only seven people in the room, including himself and Maximus. Whatever this operation was, it would be a small one.

The chatter died away the instant Diaz entered the room, everybody rushed to their feet and saluted. Elias didn't really know what to do with himself, so he decided to stand, but as he did, Diaz shouted something, and everyone swiftly sat back down. He hastily returned to his seat, feeling stupid.

"Right, this won't take long. We'll be heading into the Citadel this evening to conduct reconnaissance on this target." Diaz said matter of factly as an image of a vast power station flashed up behind him.

"This is the SYCO power facility. It provides electricity to sixty percent of the city, and as of now it's our number one target for future denigration operations." Diaz said, his voice sounding sterner than Elias had ever heard.

Everyone in the room leaned forward for a clearer view. "We'll be entering undercover, via our established Infil points." The image switched to a map of the Citadel with a small area highlighted in red at the edge of the map.

"SYCO is located in the Northernmost part of the city, so it'll be quite a trek. Seven sectors to be exact."

Two of the Deltas exchanged worried glances.

"Therefore we'll be going in weapons light, small arms only. Except for Max, who will be providing sniper cover as usual." Diaz said nodding at Max who ignored the gesture and turned his head away.

Elias rolled his eyes, Max's attitude was really starting to get on his nerves.

"We'll be undercover as Sovereign utility workers which will enable us to travel throughout the city unimpeded. The IDs and uniforms we stole earlier in the year have still not been compromised, and we've got no intelligence to indicate we should encounter any problems once we get into the city. We'll be taking three recon drones with us which will deploy when we are at the perimeter. The objective is to capture and record footage of the layout. Identify suitable Infil and Exfil points. Personnel movements, Security placements etc. The standard stuff."

Another slide appeared listing their objectives. Elias

pretended to read it as he stared at the picture next to the bullet points.

"One of Munro's sources provided the Intel on these."

A new image of a colossal metallic coil popped up. "These are the stabilising manifolds, according to Munro's intel, SYCO has two of them. They regulate the temperature of the fusion chambers, and the facility can't function without them.

"We need to gather enough footage to lay over the schematics Munro acquired and pull together a full VR battle plan." Diaz clicked through several more slides.

"We've also been tasked to collect a dead drop from another of Munro's sources which we will do en-route," Diaz added as the presentation came to an end.

"Total time beyond the wire should be just short of six hours so pack lightly boys. One last thing, as you may have guessed, Elias here will be running with us today. I know some of you haven't met him yet, but you are all aware of him."

Elias's face turned red as everyone turned and nodded at him.

"Introduce yourselves before we head out. He'll be with Sanchez and me in Alpha squad." Diaz said, smiling at Elias.

He nodded awkwardly at each of the Deltas as they came over and greeted him, patting him on the shoulder firmly as they walked past.

"Welcome to the team," said one.

"Great to meet you," said another.

"I can't believe it, a Nihon as I live and breathe," said a third who stood measuring Elias up.

Soon the room started to empty out, leaving Elias sitting there alone, staring at the blank screen in front of him. He wiped his clammy hands on his trousers. This was it, after all those months of training he was finally about to embark on his first mission.

The moments following the briefing seemed to pass by in a blur. After sitting in the amphitheatre on his own for a while trying to compose himself, he headed out and was soon getting changed into the stolen Sovereign maintenance uniforms alongside the rest of the Deltas. Elias smiled politely as those around him cracked jokes about their last foray into the city, he observed them loading their pistols with ammunition and discreetly hiding them in their bags. As Elias surveyed the locker room, it amazed him how convincing their disguises were; they looked exactly like the refuse workers he used to see in the waste pits.

He followed the others through the base of operations, as they passed by, Sanchez pointed out various areas that he would need to know for the future; the armoury, the shooting range, the training ground. Before he knew it, he was inside a massive hanger, climbing aboard an Osprey, the favoured mode of transport for the Deltas. It was a sleek, silver quad-copter, with rotatable blades on its wings and streamlined thrusters at its rear. At its centre was a small cabin, large enough to house a dozen troops and their equipment. Light and an agile, it was almost impossible to detect, which made it ideal for tactical insertions.

Elias cautiously made his way up the boarding ramp and sat down in the only available seat, unfortunately, he ended up sitting next to Max who rolled his eyes when he struggled to fix his safety harness into place. After a few moments fiddling with the clasp, Max knelt forward and angrily shoved the connec-tors in place as the Osprey slowly hovered off the ground and turned to face the main runway. Elias was pinned back into his seat as they suddenly accelerated, flying forward at breath-taking speed and disappearing into a darkened canyon.

They flew through a series of narrow tunnels, each one left only a tiny gap either side of the Osprey's wings. Elias's stomach churned as the aircraft tumbled and turned in the pitch black, carefully navigating its way through the cave complex. After a few minutes of flying through the darkness, light came streaming through the cabin windows as they emerged from the caves and soared high above the wastelands.

Elias fidgeted in his seat, trying to get a better look. Diaz was sat by the window and spotted Elias craning forward. He slid open the door and a sudden gust of wind ripped through the cabin, catching him by surprise and thrusting him back into his seat. He checked his harness was fastened correctly and then leant forward to take in the view.

For as far he could see, glistening golden sand dunes rolled over the landscape.

"Thanks," Elias shouted over the noise of the wind rattling around them.

"No problem," Diaz yelled.

Elias had never flown before, and he was not altogether sure he enjoyed the experience. His stomach started to rumble as his hands and feet began to tingle. He became uncomfortably hot, despite the cool breeze blowing against him. Thick beads of sweat ran down his forehead and into his eyes, blurring his vision. His head was spinning, and he began to see stars in front of his eyes, the tingling sensation in his hands grew stronger as he struggled to lift his fingers. Just when he thought he was going to pass out the Osprey started to slow down, the gigantic propellers on the edge of its wings turned upwards as it descended to the desert floor.

They landed with a thump, jolting violently in their seats as they came to a stop. Elias quickly unbuckled his harness and ran down the exit ramp as it slowly extended out of the back of the Osprey. He jumped off the edge and fell to his knees, throwing up everywhere; his vomit sizzled as it hit the burning sand.

"Well, he's keen," Sanchez chuckled.

The Deltas all laughed as they made their way down the ramp, Max sniggered loudly as he strode past Elias without even offering him a hand. Sanchez came over and pulled Elias back to his feet.

"Don't worry kid, happens to the best of us," she said with a smile as she slapped Elias on the back so hard it made him throw up again.

Elias sat down and gulped some water from his flask, trying to regain his composure as the squad finished offloading their equipment. Soon they were ready to head into the Citadel, they all huddled together and shielded their faces as the Osprey steadily ascended, kicking up a tremendous sand cloud as it flew off into the distance. They stood alone in the middle of the desert as the dust settled around them.

"Elias, we will be entering via the sewer duct on the southwest side of the city. It's about 5k from here," Diaz said, pointing to a massive dune in the distance.

"Okay," Elias nodded.

"Here put these on," Diaz threw a pair of shiny black fatigue trousers to Elias.

"What are these for?" Elias asked as he pulled them over his legs.

"You'll see," Diaz laughed as the rest of the unit put on their fatigues.

"Great," Elias laughed as the group marched out across

the desert, Max led the way one huge step at a time, an enormous sniper rifle hung loosely over his shoulder.

Elias had been thinking about how Max would go unnoticed once they arrived in the Citadel. The rest of them were disguised to help them blend in, but you couldn't disguise Max, he was a beast. As they reached the peak of the dune, Elias caught sight of the Citadel for the first time. The monstrous wall that shielded the entire city stood proud, cutting through the landscape like a man-made mountain range.

"There she is," Diaz pointed to the wall. He pulled out a small digital monocular and stared down it.

"Looks clear, still no changes to the security on exit 17," he said with a smile as he handed the monocular to Elias. "Here, take a look."

Elias placed the monocular over his eye, he had never used one before so didn't know what to expect. He closed his other eye and stared down into an ultra high definition viewfinder showing a zoomed-in image of an enormous sewage pipe draining filthy brown water out of the city.

"That's our way in," Elias said, the thought of how bad it would smell in there made him gag.

Diaz laughed as he took the monocular back off Elias and returned it to his satchel. They made their way down the sand dune and headed towards the sewer. Elias stared up at the city walls, he couldn't see any sentry posts that overlooked their way in. It had been months since he last saw the wall, and he had forgotten how imposing it felt to have it looming over him. An entire city, holding over a billion people hidden from the outside world.

He had never been this near to the wall before, the Ronin in the Jungle always warned him not to stray too close. He craned his head and leaned backwards, trying to make out the top of it, it seemed to stretch on forever. Max reached the entrance to the sewer first; an immense cast iron grate blocked his way. In one fluid motion, Max grabbed a black tomahawk hanging from his belt and swung it viciously at the padlock that secured it in place. The lock crumbled under the might of Max's strike and he yanked open the grate outwards on its hinge.

"Thanks, big man," Diaz walked past Max, who bowed sarcastically.

Elias and the other soldiers clambered into the tunnel after Diaz. Max was the last in and pulled the grate shut behind him. Elias glanced around, they were inside a circular pipe, barely large enough to stand in. Nothing but the pitch black in front of them. Behind, the light from the wastelands shone brightly. He couldn't see anything up ahead but felt the murky water trickling around his ankles. Thankfully the aromatic polyamide fatigues Diaz gave him prevented any water seeping in.

"Right, you know the drill. Silence from here on out. Single file, till we are topside. Stay on my tail, and you won't go wrong. If you somehow become separated, stay where you are, and we'll find you. These pipes run for thousands of miles all across the city, and if you go wandering off, there is no guarantee we'll be able to track you down." Diaz's voice turned serious.

"Okay," Elias's mouth went dry at the thought of getting stranded in the sewer network.

"Lights on," Diaz switched on a small torch attached to his shoulder, shooting out a beam of ultra-bright light, illuminating the path ahead.

A small, yellow light lit up on the back of Diaz's rucksack

providing a guide for Elias to follow in the dark. Identical lights lit up on each of their backpacks, allowing them to follow the man in front.

Elias lost track of time as they journeyed through the sewer system, after Diaz's warning about getting lost he didn't let the light in front of him out of his sight. Their route twisted and turned at every corner, and Elias had no idea how Diaz knew they were going in the right direction. It was silent except for the sound of their footsteps as they sloshed through the filthy water. After what felt like a lifetime Elias noticed the light ahead of him had stopped moving, suddenly a burst of red exploded in front of him as Diaz ignited a glow stick above his head.

"This is it," Diaz whispered "We'll get changed down here and leave anything we don't need in the tunnels. We can pick it up on the way out."

He wedged the glow stick into a divot as they all quietly removed their waterproof trousers and put the finishing touches to their disguises. They each wore a matching black cap, jacket and wide-rimmed trousers with high visibility light strips running across the chest, waist and shins.

"We'll take this access point here," Diaz pointed up to a cramped shaft which contained a long ladder stretching up above them.

"I'll do a recce to make sure we are clear then you can follow me out. Don't be hanging around down here, we need everyone out quick time."

Elias nodded, his throat went dry as the immensity of the moment came crashing down on him. He had spent years watching the glow of the Citadel's lights from beyond the wall, dreaming of taking a place amongst its citizens and now here he was. About to enter the city. Not as a citizen or a free man, but as a member of the Army of Shadows, as a freedom fighter, as a Nihon.

"Right, let's go," Diaz said as he started to climb the ladder.

Elias snapped out of his daydream and blindly followed Diaz up. The shaft unexpectedly flooded with light and Elias struggled to keep his eyes open as Diaz pushed open the manhole. After a few moments Elias felt Diaz grab him by the hand and pull him out onto the surface. Elias quickly clambered out and started to help the others out one by one. His pulse was racing; his heart beating so fast within his chest he thought it might explode. The last to emerge was Max, he ignored Elias's offer of assistance and leapt out of the shaft with ease.

He'd made it, he was in the Citadel. It was not quite the grand entrance he imagined, they had emerged on to a rundown alleyway peppered with litter, the walls covered in old posters and luminous graffiti. In truth, it looked more like the Jungle than he could possibly have imagined, his heart sank with disappointment. Elias gazed at the group, all six of them looked identical except for Maximus who was still dressed in his battle armour. Elias couldn't understand how they were going to blend in with him following them around.

"We all set?" Diaz asked.

Everybody nodded back in unison.

"Max this is where we say our goodbyes. You clear on your route?"

"Need you ask," Max growled.

"Confirm when you are in position. We won't proceed until we hear from you." Diaz said, ignoring Max's tone.

"Affirmative," Max said as he pulled out a shiny silver cloak from his rucksack and wrapped it over his shoulders.

"May Gaia guide you." He pulled up the hood over his head, and in an instant, he disappeared.

"What the..." Elias said in astonishment.

"Good luck," Max whispered as he barged past Elias sending him stumbling backwards.

"It's a cloaking device," Diaz said, chuckling to himself.

"A what?" Elias stared at Diaz with a confused expression.

"A cloaking device," Sanchez added "It's made of thousands of minute semiconductors using nanoparticles to refract light. It uses reverse refraction technology to bend the light away from its host, rending the user invisible to the naked eye."

Elias stared blankly at Sanchez.

"Think of it as an invisibility cloak. Lets Max operate in the city without any issues." Diaz said, noticing the look of utter confusion on Elias's face.

"Right...an invisibility cloak," Elias shook his head, every day he discovered something new. "Why don't we all use them?"

"Those semiconductors contain the rarest minerals on the planet. There are only a handful of those cloaks in existence. We stole that one from a Sovereign research facility a while back. Max had first dibs on it ever since." Sanchez explained.

"Okay, enough with the science lesson, let's move out. Elias stay by my side and don't talk to anyone. If we encounter any security forces follow my lead." Diaz said, leading them down the alley.

"Don't worry, we'll be fine. We've done this a million times before." One of the Deltas said, walking alongside Elias

"Yeah, we'll be in and out in no time," said another from behind.

"Consider this a familiarisation visit," Sanchez chipped in.

"You've never been to the Citadel?" Another asked, trying to mask the surprise in his voice.

"Never."

"Well enjoy, it will feel like home in no time," Diaz said as they stepped out on to a bustling high street, the overhead lights bathing them in a bright neon glow.

"Wow," Elias muttered to himself as he stood rooted to the spot, trying to take in the cornucopia of sights before his eyes.

18

ARISE COMRADE

Leo couldn't quite understand the sudden change in Ginger's mood. She left him the day before sullen and despondent, yet here she was full of life and buzzing with excitement. She had awoken him by banging on his apartment door and demanding he accompany her to the graveyard straight away, he was too tired to argue so groggily agreed. He spent most of the journey lagging behind Ginger, still half asleep as she spoke energetically about all the amazing things their robot would achieve. How it would turn the tide of the war and make people realise not all robots were evil. Leo didn't have the heart to tell her none of this would ever happen. There was no way on Earth Tiberius would ever risk an Osprey to gamble on the resurrection of a dead robot.

"Hold up Ginge, what's the hurry?" Leo complained, trying to keep up with her.

"Come on, Leo," she yanked at his arm, dragging him up the final staircase and towards the plinth. They raced over to the robot and Ginger clambered up on to its chest.

"Right, don't go mad but I've done a bad thing." She said slinging down her rucksack on the robot's chest, it landed with a deep clunk.

Leo knew in an instant what she had done. He cursed himself for being so stupid and not realising sooner.

"Ginger you haven't…"

"Look, I'm sorry. But I have…I mean we, have worked too hard on this not to see it through,"

"This isn't a game anymore, that thing could kill us,"

"He won't." Her voice wavered. "I have a feeling about it."

"Well, if he doesn't, then your dad will!" Leo said seriously, sounding more like his brother than he thought possible.

Ginger stooped over her bag and heaved out a thick battery pack.

"You're not telling me anything I don't already know. But I need to do this. If only…"

"If only what?" Leo called out as he stared up at Ginger in disbelief.

"If only to know how good I really am!" She screamed back at him, the words flying out of her mouth with such aggression Leo was taken aback.

He knew immediately what she meant. She had spent her life repairing things, and this was the biggest challenge she would ever face. Reviving a fallen robot in a society that outlawed them was about as difficult as it got. Ginger looked away abashed.

"Okay, let's do this." He declared confidently, scrambling up on the robot's chest and kneeling beside her.

"Grab the side of the pack." The heaviness surprised Leo as he grabbed the handle; a substantial weight condensed inside a small black box.

He was about to tell Ginger she had done well to carry it the whole way, before thinking better of it. They shuffled over to the cavity in the robot's chest and forced the battery in place. Ginger grasped the loose wires hanging from it and tried to connect them to the battery. She struggled for a few moments trying to force them together before giving up.

"Here have a go," Ginger said exasperatedly.

Leo took hold of the connectors and wiggled them into place.

"Easy Leo, I don't want you to burst a blood vessel." Ginger laughed as Leo's expression contorted in effort, his entire face turning a deep shade of red.

"Nearly there," Leo said through gritted teeth.

The connectors clicked into position, and he felt a pulse of energy at his fingertips.

"It's working!" Leo shouted as he stared down at the robot, the optics in its eyes flickering a vibrant blue.

His skin started to tingle as the hairs on his arms stood on end, then a surge of electricity flowed from the battery. Leo felt it pulsating through his body like somehow he was part of the circuit. Instantly Leo's mind flashed with a vision of a burning chasm, delving deep into the Earth. Leo stood on the edge of the abyss fixated on the raging inferno below, he noticed a hooded figure standing opposite him. The image faded away, and Leo's sight returned, he focussed on Ginger who stared at him with a worried expression on her face. He dropped the cables and crawled back beside her.

"What just happened?" She asked.

"I don't know...I saw something." Leo mumbled.

A tremor shot through the robot's body, causing it to thrash violently, knocking them to the ground. Leo scrambled on all fours and dashed over to Ginger, pulling her back to her feet, they were both covered in a thick coat of dust. He dragged her by the hand behind the plinth. Crouching in the shadows, they watched in horror as the robot sluggishly rose to its feet, staggering forward unsteadily. Its body started to twitch and jolt uncontrollably, and it let out a painful mechanical cry as the valves on its back erupted, releasing a burst of steam.

"I..." the robot spoke, its voice grainy and distorted.

Leo noticed Ginger's eyes welling up with tears as she peered around the corner at her creation, he pulled her back into the shadows.

"We need to…" Leo began to speak but trailed off as the robot stumbled forward and fell to the ground with an almighty crash.

It turned over on its side and swivelled its battered head in their direction. Leo froze as its bright blue eyes focussed in on them. The robot pushed itself up on one knee, using its hand for balance.

"I…I'll," The robot shook its head, struggling to stand.

"Ginger, we need to go. NOW!" Leo grabbed her hand as he started to back away.

"I'll…kill you all!" The robot roared, lurching forward after them as they fled across the courtyard.

"You...you did this to me!" The robot pointed at them.

"Quick!" Leo yelled as he dragged Ginger down a set of stairs.

The robot picked up a discarded girder and launched it at the staircase, it smashed into the wall behind them. They sprinted through the graveyard dodging in and out of the flying debris the robot tossed into their path.

"Watch out!" Leo cried, pulling Ginger to the ground as the crumpled turret of a tank flew over their heads. They skidded to a stop behind a crumbling wall.

"Over there," Ginger pointed to a manhole cover just in front of them.

Leo wrenched it open with all his strength, unveiling another narrow shaft, containing a ladder that disappeared into the ground below. He helped Ginger inside before hurriedly clambering down after her, slamming the cover shut behind him as the darkness consumed them. Leo quietly slid the lock back into place, listening to the thuds of the robot's lumbering footsteps above as it searched for them.

"Do you think it's still out there?" Ginger asked nervously.

Leo caught the worried look in her eyes over the flicker of the torchlight between them as they sat wedged in the darkened shaft. They had been hiding in the sewer tunnel for several hours, too scared to open up the manhole and even more afraid to head back to Albion and explain their actions to Tiberius.

"I think so Ginge,"

"What are we going to do?"

"I'm not sure. That thing is crazy."

"I thought it would help us." Ginger's head dropped into her hands again.

Leo couldn't tell if she was crying or not. He awkwardly patted her on the back.

"It'll be okay, your dad will understand,"

"He won't Leo." She shot back. "We need to get that battery back."

Before he had a chance to respond, Ginger started to ascend the ladder at a rapid pace.

"Ginger, you can't go back out there!" His words echoed up above him. "That thing will kill you."

"It won't Leo, I know it." She shouted back, not stopping for a second as she continued to make her way up.

"You said that last time," Leo said to himself as he shook his head in disbelief. She was so stubborn, sometimes he felt like shaking her.

"Damn it, Ginger," Leo called out as he followed after her.

She reached the top first and unlocked the hatch, carefully lifting the lid. Leo climbed up beside her and peered out.

"Can you see anything?" Ginger whispered as she craned her head to get a better view, they were wedged in so tightly together it was almost impossible to move.

"Look." Leo nodded over at a mound of rubble ahead of them. The robot was slumped across it, holding its head in its massive hands.

"It looks sad,"

"It looked dead a few hours ago, and that didn't stop it from trying to murder us," Leo said sarcastically.

"Will you shut up, I'm telling you. It won't hurt us." She snapped, pushing open the lid and leaping out.

"Ginger!" Leo shrieked as she approached the robot, watching her every step as she carefully tiptoed forwards.

Leo pulled himself up and chased after her. He tripped over a discarded metal arm laying on the ground and fell flat on his face with a thud. A small cloud of dust lazily kicked up around him. Ginger slowly turned to face Leo and gave him a scathing look that made him want to sink into the ground. She turned her head back to the robot, who hadn't moved, apparently unperturbed by their return.

"You...you have nothing to fear young one," it spoke with a deep husky tone.

"I mean you no harm." The robot raised its head to face them. Its rusty brown limbs jerked stiffly as it tried to move.

"My awakening...was..." the robot shook its head. "Unexpected...I still don't know how..." it trailed off muttering to itself. "I am sorry if I frightened you."

"It's okay," Ginger said as she approached cautiously.

"My name is OR-227-1X, although your fellow humans preferred to call me Orix for short."

"By Gaia. It can't be...you are THE Orix." Ginger said, trying to hide the excitement in her voice.

Leo had a confused expression on his face as he swivelled his head back and forth between Ginger and Orix.

"As in the leader of the FRA Orix?" Ginger said excitedly.

Orix nodded wearily. "Yes, a long time ago, I was the leader of the Free Robot Army and I, I..." the robot stopped and studied the wreckage surrounding him. "My comrades... what have I done...I failed you."

"The FRA, I know that name," Leo said to himself. "So you fought in the Great War?" He asked, finding his voice as he took his place by Ginger's side.

She slipped her fingers inside his hand and clasped hold of him. He glanced over at her, and she smiled gently, a strange sensation drifted over him like he had been wrapped in a warm blanket.

"Yes, for too long." Orix pushed himself up and approached them, his damaged limbs dragging cumbersomely behind him.

"I've heard about you," Leo said.

"Human history always fascinated me, so tell me, what does it say became of OR-227-1X?"

Ginger shared an anxious look with Leo before finally speaking up.

"They...they say you betrayed the resistance?"

"I…" Orix paused. "I would never betray them, they were like brothers to me." Orix stared down at them, his glowing blue eyes appeared to fade as he spoke.

"But Roninhya…you destroyed it," Ginger continued.

"That's impossible," Orix looked horrified at the thought. "My memories of my final days are…fragmented." Orix put his hands on his hips and shook his head. "It appears some of the files in my memory bank have been removed."

"What's the last thing you can remember?" asked Leo.

Orix stood there for a few moments, his optic sensors flashing wildly as he searched his memories.

"A message", Orix spoke urgently. "But the content is corrupted. I can't retrieve it,"

"Who is it from?" Leo asked quickly.

"General Tiberius,"

The words hung in the air as Ginger shot Leo a worried glance.

"Do you know him?"

"Oh yeah, we know him alright." Leo chuckled.

Ginger glared at him, but he couldn't stop himself.

"It's her dad." He blurted out.

Ginger's eyes focused in on him, her forehead furrowing into a deep stare.

"Your father?" Orix rubbed his face with his hand as he paced back and forth.

"Why did you say that!" Ginger hissed behind Orix's back.

"He asked,"

"Just…argh. Honestly, I don't know what I'm going to do with you."

"I need to speak to your father."

Ginger closed her eyes and took a deep breath, Leo pulled an awkward face and scratched at the back of his neck.

"Please hear me out, if I am ever to understand the damage I caused in my final days, I must start with Tiberius. I served under him for many years, and he played a key role in establishing the FRA, his counsel has never guided me wrong in the past. The fact you two stand alone in front of me suggests you have not shared this endeavour with your father." Orix's knowing eyes stared down at them, as they tried their best to avoid his gaze.

"I see..." Orix nodded. "Then I am afraid what I am about to ask of you will put you in a difficult position.

Leo and Ginger's eyes met, they knew exactly what Orix was about to say,

"Would you take me to your father?"

19

———

THE CITY

"Welcome to the Citadel." Diaz said as they stepped out on to a bustling high street. Elias stood rooted to the spot, transfixed, his eyes open wide trying to take everything in.

The city was alive with neon colours, unlike anything he had ever seen before. Luminous greens, reds and blues lit up the street from the enormous screens hanging overhead. Hundreds of LED advertising signs of all shapes and sizes glowed brightly. Elias drifted along in a daze, his eyes rattling around in his head as he tried to comprehend the dazzling sights. His attention was drawn to a large shop window with dozens of flashing displays listing the words War, Pleasure, Excitement and XXX. Elias peered through the glass and saw some people laid on beds wearing clunky headsets.

"VR," Diaz said over the bustle of the city. "Lets you be anything you want to be, it's addictive though, once you get a taste of a better life it can be hard to come back to the real world. Some people spend their whole lives lost in the grid."

"The grid?"

"Oh, tell me you know about the grid?" Diaz said as his face dropped, Elias shrugged his shoulders.

"Man, I don't even know where to begin," Diaz rubbed at the back of his neck. "It's...the system that binds this city together."

Elias raised his eyebrows. "Like the internet?"

"Kind of, but if the internet was on noops. It has free access to everyone's data. Communications, augmentations, biometric devices, medical and financial history, DNA, the lot. It knows everything about everyone in this city. Every breath you take, every move you make, the grid is watching."

Elias looked around at all the bizarre-looking people going about their daily business apparently unperturbed by the monolithic AI running their lives.

"Don't they mind?"

"They don't even know it's happening, data is one of the world's most valuable commodities these days and people give it away like it's nothing. Here, everyone is so focussed on their own problems or saving up for their next aug, people are blind to the system that controls them."

"How did this happen?"

"They sleepwalked into it, one device at a time. Vicentine's products seeped into every aspect of society. Before anyone knew what was happening he'd harvested so much information, his AI knew people better than they knew themselves. He manipulated an entire population, so when he rose to power, no one batted an eyelid."

Elias looked up and noticed a gigantic hologram projected opposite them. A thirty-foot tall man reached out from one of the screens and started explaining the benefits of a service called Humanity Plus.

"Why settle for equalling the skills of your competition

when you can exceed them. Ensure your children not only achieve their full potential but expand upon it." The hologram explained in a relaxed, soothing tone.

"Gene editing," Diaz muttered to Elias. "About as bad as it gets here, people messing with your DNA. There is nothing you can't get in the Citadel."

Elias gulped at the thought, he twisted and turned trying to look into every store, he wished he had an extra set of eyes in the back of his head; he didn't want to miss a thing. He kept swivelling around in different directions as they made their way down the street. A gaunt man in a black trench coat stepped out of a darkened entrance and tried to entice them inside by offering them a discount on the latest Nootropics.

"You want noops? I'll cut you the best price in town," the man boasted, he was augmented with eye implants that had tiny LED lights fitted to the front and black wires running into the back of his head.

Several neon signs flashed in the shop windows listing products Elias had never come across; Rise, Sprint, Synergy, Clarity, Elysium.

"Aint nobody gonna beat my prices," he added slipping Elias a small red pill, it glistened in his hand as he inspected it.

Diaz barged past Elias and snatched the pill from his hand, throwing it back up in the air, the man caught it and in one fluid motion slipped it back into his pocket.

"Not today, buddy." Diaz said as he manoeuvred Elias away from the man.

"Your loss!" He shouted as they made their way down the street, weaving in and out of people wearing vibrant clothes, materials alive with colours that changed with every step.

Almost everyone Elias encountered had some sort of augmentation. Cybernetic limbs, integrated weaponry, ocular and auditory processors, brain implants, respirators, digital heads up displays. The Citadel had them all, and every single person looked utterly unique.

"What were they?" Elias said, looking back over his shoulder. The man was already ushering some would-be customers into his shop.

"Nootropics," Diaz said casually. "They're dangerous."

Elias gave him another confused look.

"Drugs for the brain. Enhancements. They can increase your brain capacity for a short time. Whatever you need, they can give you. They can make you faster, stronger, more intelligent. They can even slow down the ageing process."

"Wow, they sound amazing." Elias gushed turning to catch one last glimpse of the noop dealer before disappearing into the crowd around them.

"Hardly, the comedown you get from them can be deadly. I've known people drive themselves crazy using that stuff. Once you speed the brain up, you can't always slow it back down."

The colour drained from Elias's face as he thought about what that must feel like.

"Besides, they are banned in Albion. It's not just augs and robotics we don't believe in. Anything that changes the natural make-up of the body is strictly off-limits." Diaz said over his shoulder.

Window shopping as he walked down the street, Elias struggled to believe what he was seeing. Shops selling an enormous selection of advanced technology, every kind of augmentation was freely available in the city. Leo would love it here, he thought. He noticed a small crowd of dishevelled looking augs queuing up outside a small store. A variety of spectacular bionic arms and legs were displayed in the window.

Everyone in the queue appeared to have some form of malfunctioning augmentation. Several clutched their limp mechanical arms close to their chests, while others dragged their failing legs behind them. Some of the more severely affected appeared to have faulty brain implants, their bodies twitching and spasming involuntarily. Elias was staring so intently he walked straight into the back of the person in front of him.

"Sorry," Elias mumbled as he came face-to-face with a giant of a man with a bushy beard; a pair of wild eyes glared down at him from behind a bulbous hooked nose. The giant's mechanical finger jabbed at his chest.

"Watch were you're going punk." The giant grumbled, chomping onto the cigar that burned from the corner of his mouth.

"Easy, Eli." Diaz laughed as he pushed the giant away. "Sorry buddy, he's been on the noops again."

"Damn junkies," The giant muttered as he turned away, straightened his sleeveless denim jacket and plodded back into the sea of people.

"It's a tech repair shop," Diaz added, noticing Elias's attention drift back to the queue. "There's some new tech virus growing around, that's affecting the augs. This is what they don't tell you when they sell you an augmentation. Everything breaks sooner or later, and if you don't have the money for the latest patch, you're on your own,"

"Is that why you guys don't augment?" Elias asked.

"Partly, if your body's been modified, then it means the Sovereign already knows everything it needs to about you, plus you are reliant on the grid for software updates, so you are chained to it for life. Once you aug you can't ever go back, ain't no way to grow a body part." Diaz laughed. "But we also believe the body is sacred, we trust in Gaia's wisdom over mankind's obsession with technology."

Elias studied the next person who walked past, Diaz's words still ringing in his ears as he stared at her augmented face, a small piece of circuitry grafted onto the side of her temple. She winked at Elias as she barged past him, his eyes drifting from her aug to the bright pink mohawk standing proudly atop her head.

"Wherever there is a system, there are those who fight to frustrate it. That's were the Collective come in."

"The Collective?" Elias's attention snapped back to Diaz.

"Gridrunners, or hackers as you might know them. The few in the city who've broken free from shackles of the Sovereign and see this place for what it really is. Not a fortress, but a prison. We have a loose agreement with them, they help us maintain access to sensitive parts of the grid, and we use our underground networks to help them disappear if they get compromised. The dead drop we need to collect, it's from a member of the Collective. They've got some new source code for us, but they always refuse to meet in person."

"Aren't you worried it's a trap?" Elias said, suddenly concerned with what they were heading into.

"I was the first time I did a collection, but they've been providing us information for years now and its always been reliable."

Diaz steered Elias off the bustling street and into an underground tunnel, an archway constructed of inter-locking triangular lights, each glowing with vibrant colour, blue, pink, purple.

"It's just down here," said Diaz.

"What about the others?" Elias asked, noticing that it was just the two of them heading down the neon tunnel.

"They'll pick us up on our way out," said Diaz.

"Wow…" Elias said mesmerised by the glow of the lights. "This place is great,"

"Yeah, some parts of the Citadel aren't too bad. Right, this is the spot," Diaz said coming to a stop by a large, semi-circular vending machine displaying four compartments protected behind a transparent blue shell.

"Are those…" Elias moved in for a closer look, peering through the plastic window. "People!"

"Yeah," Diaz said, laughing at the horrified expression on Elias's face. "These are sleep pods. People come here to get some shut-eye if they can't afford their own place. Here watch this." He tapped the touchscreen control in the centre of the machine a few times, and suddenly the people rotated into a hidden underground chamber, and four more compartments appeared in their place.

"I told you, this place is crazy."

Elias shook his head as he spotted more people asleep inside, apparently undisturbed by Diaz rotating them.

"It's making me feel queasy just watching you do that."

"Got it", said Diaz, slipping his hand behind the touch screen and retrieving a tiny metal box attached to a magnet. He opened it up to reveal a memory card which he swiftly put in his top pocket.

"Is that it?" Elias asked nodding at Diaz's pocket.

"Yeah, should have everything we need on it," he said as he looked over his shoulder before discreetly reattaching the magnetic box to the back of the touchscreen. "Right, we better collect the others and be on our way, never a good idea to stay in one place for too long."

As they made their way out of the neon tunnel, Elias noticed a vast, transparent, glass tube system twisting around the buildings above them, weaving its way through the city. Elias watched as something shot through it, travelling so quickly he couldn't make out what the object was. A few seconds later, another blur of white light whizzed by. After several more flew past he grabbed Diaz's arm and pointed up at the tube.

"What is that thing?"

"The Hyperloop. It's the Citadel's public transport network. One of the few things I actually like about this place. We'll be using it to cut across the city."

"Wow,"

They walked past a nightclub with a small entrance opening up on to a staircase. Dozens of unusually dressed people queued up along the street waiting to enter. Several menacing-looking men manned the doors, scanning peoples ID cards before allowing them inside. The men all wore long black trench coats and had identical dragon tattoos on their necks. They each had an advanced ocular implant in one eye, which projected a tiny screen in front of them every time they scanned an ID card.

"That's the Leadpit," Diaz nodded at the club "It's run by the Shenmue. They pretty much own the criminal underworld in this city, so it's a good idea to stay well clear of them. Do you see their tattoo's? It's the calling card of the Shenmue."

"Noted," Elias thought back to his time in the Jungle, he remembered seeing some of them at the Plasma banks. They called the shots behind the scenes telling the Merc's what to do.

They walked past the Leadpit and continued to push through the mass of passers-by, every step a struggle. Eventually, they turned off the high street and into a vast city square with an enormous glass pyramid in the middle, each side had a different video projected on it. One showed a news broadcast with a perma-tanned presenter speaking about a terrorist attack that had occurred in the city days earlier. Elias overheard some people talking about the story as they passed by.

"Damn rebel scum!" One screamed as he spat on the ground in disgust.

"They should kill em all!" Another angry citizen cried.

Elias tried to avoid eye contact with them as he walked past, on the other side of the pyramid a trailer for the latest series of a TV show played. It showed hundreds of people launching out of a ginormous aircraft and wing-suiting down to an abandoned island. Colourful streaks of smoke tracked their descent as they fell from the sky. Dozens of rapid-fire videos flashed up, showing the people landing, desperately scavenging for equipment then heading off into the Jungle.

"Season 10 starts tonight, 9pm standard time." The trailer announced over the sound of an explosion, Elias stood enthralled.

"What's this?" He nodded at the screen.

"Battle Royale. It's what counts for entertainment these days in this forsaken city. A hundred people enter, one comes out and wins a new life for themselves amongst the Sovereign elite."

"What happens to the other ninety-nine?"

"They die."

Diaz pulled Elias away and pointed up to something hovering above them; a small drone with several cameras attached floated effortlessly in the sky.

"The eyes of the Sovereign. They have millions of them, tracking and monitoring everything that goes on here."

The drone hovered in the air momentarily, its quadcopter blades whirring manically as its multiple lenses zoomed in and focussed on the people below. It scanned the crowd for a little while before tilting to one side and shooting off in another direction.

"That's the station over there," Diaz nodded at a staircase on the corner of the square. It led up to the platform, a pristine glass structure arching over the Hyperloop tubes.

"I take it you've never been on anything like this before?" Diaz asked as they walked up a set of brilliantly white steps.

Elias nodded "Is it fast?"

"Yeah, it's quite quick," he said as he pulled a face at the other Deltas who rejoined behind them.

"Brilliant," Elias muttered as he watched the Hyperloop approach; an immaculately clean, white bullet train with several rounded carriages attached to the back of it pulled into the station.

They reached the top of the steps and Diaz headed over to an unusual looking woman manning the turnstiles. She was slim with blonde hair, and her skin was perfect, without a single blemish. Her dazzling sky blue eyes were cold and unwelcoming. She moved awkwardly, almost mechanically as she gestured to Diaz.

"Is she okay?" Elias's gaze lingered on the woman, as she jerkily moved her head from side to side in conversation with Diaz.

"Yeah, she's fine..." Sanchez replied as she stepped beside Elias, "Except for the fact she's an android."

"An android?"

"Yeah, a skin job, a synth. You not have them in the Jungle?"

"No."

"She's a machine, a robot. Android's are the next stage of evolution for robotics. She looks like an early service model, the current generation you wouldn't even be able to tell them apart from you and me." Sanchez pointed to Diaz, who was beckoning them over, he handed the android something as they approached and ushered them through the glass turnstiles that slid open before them.

"Platform 2, sector G," Diaz said as he followed them through.

Standing on the edge of the track, they waited as the Hyperloop steadily manoeuvred into position. Elias looked down at his feet and noticed a large red letter painted on the floor. As he looked back, the doors opened in a smooth motion to reveal a small compact carriage, with twenty-five seats set out in five tight rows. A simple design that didn't leave much room once everyone took their seats.

Elias smiled nervously at the stranger who sat next to him, he didn't return the smile and swiftly pressed a button on his armrest that caused a privacy screen to shoot up between them.

"Heads up," Diaz said patting Elias on the knee.

A chunky plastic harness descended from the ceiling and pinned him into his seat. The doors slid shut, and an automated message announced they were ready to depart.

"Is this really necessar..." Elias said as he hit his hands on the side of his harness.

Before he could finish his sentence they set off at such breathtaking speed, he was instantly pinned back into his seat by the g-force. His head smashed into the headrest with a thud, and his cheeks looked like they were being pulled off his face by the velocity. He tried to move his hands, but he couldn't lift them, an immense weight seemed to be pinning him down. In the blink of an eye, they came to an abrupt halt, and Elias's body slumped into his seat.

"...ary?" Elias finished as the doors opened up again, the harnesses slowly ascended back into the ceiling as people started to make their way out.

"How many more stops?" Elias said groggily as he covered his mouth, trying to stop himself from being sick.

"Another three. Shouldn't take too long."

"Great," Elias said as he closed his eyes.

After three more experiences of lightning-quick travel between the stations, they arrived at their destination. The harnesses once again released the passengers who quickly disembarked.

"You okay?" Diaz looked over at Elias. He was still sat in his seat, his face a pale shade of white.

"Elias!" He shouted.

Elias came to and shook his head, he cautiously got to his feet but his legs buckled underneath him and he trembled forward before collapsing into Diaz's arms.

"Easy big man," Diaz laughed, "I told you it was fast."

"No kidding," Elias said, taking in a deep breath.

"You'll get used to it in no time," Diaz said gently leading Elias out of the carriage.

When they left the station, Elias got a distinctly different impression of the Citadel to when he first arrived in the city. Where the high street was alive, bursting with people and technology, Sam's Town was desolate. It was darker here too, the man-made clouds hanging over the Citadel meant no natural light entered the city and without the neon glow of the advertising boards the grim reality of city life was laid bare. Here, he could see the vastness of the Citadel in all its sprawling grotesqueness; the last refuge of mankind.

Elias stared up at a gigantic tower block, a monstrous slab of concrete and steel stretching up for well over mile. He craned his neck back, trying to see the top, but it disappeared off into the impenetrable clouds above.

"City blocks," Diaz pointed at the tower. "Over a billion people call this place home, and they've all got to live somewhere."

"Yeah and this was the solution, the majority of the population live in the city blocks now. Probably ten thousand people live up there." Sanchez said, shaking her head.

"How many are there?"

"Loads. They are all over the city".

Elias looked around Sam's Town, it reminded him of the Jungle. The artificial lights dotted along the paths created an eery orange hue that covered the streets like a thick mist. The area was bare except for a few small flickering signs advertising nearby fast-food restaurants.

Diaz led them across the main road, passing several burnt-out vehicles, one still smouldering as thin streaks of smoke lazily escaped from inside the charred out carcass. They made their way through a series of run-down alleyways peppered with litter and broken glass. The walls were covered in graffiti, including several spray-painted symbols of the resistance.

"These parts of the city are fertile ground for the Shadows," Sanchez whispered to Elias. "Round here, people know what the Sovereign really stands for." She said nodding at the graffiti.

They came out of the passageway in front of a massive viewing platform installed into the side of a run-down building, its screen cracked in several places, the video distorted across the shattered shards. It displayed the latest news bulletin from the Sovereign, the same one Elias had spotted earlier.

"The Citadel is once again in mourning after yet another

terrorist atrocity." The reporter declared over scenes of a horrific fire raging through a towering city block.

"Was that you guys?" Elias asked, fixated on the images, for a moment they were briefly silhouetted in its bright glow.

"Nah. It's propaganda. That fire was months ago, and we had nothing to do with it." Sanchez said calmly. "I think it was a domestic fire, gutted the entire building. Killed thousands. The Sovereign tried to pin the blame on us because they hadn't bothered to fit adequate fire defences, they take any opportunity they can to turn the public against us."

"When will the violence stop," the reporter crowed as the camera paused on several rows of corpses, their bodies still smouldering from the fire. Elias snapped his head away, trying to force the graphic image out of his head.

"We're here", Diaz said as he directed them into a wide-open clearing, as they walked out, a wall of blinding white light covered them. Elias raised his hand, trying to shield his eyes. He blinked several times and peered through his fingers.

The SYCO power plant was dead ahead.

20

____

HOMECOMING

"Do you think he'll be much longer?" Ginger asked as she paced up and down, kicking at the gravel beneath her feet.

"I'm not sure Ginge, this is the first time I've brought a robot back from the dead and met him outside a secret underground city." Leo let out a laugh as he perched on the edge of a scorched oil drum. He glanced at Ginger and knew instantly by the look on her face, she was not impressed.

Leo and Ginger had given Orix directions to a meeting point on the outskirts of Albion. When they realised Orix was too bulky to fit through the narrow tunnel network, they sent him over overground instead, across the wastelands.

"Very funny," Ginger snapped as she kicked up another mass of dust that drifted lazily over Leo, he closed his eyes as he disappeared behind the veil of sand.

The abandoned refuelling station they had arranged to meet Orix at was near to the main entrance of Albion, it was the only one big enough to fit him though. Which meant it was also the most heavily fortified, the chances of smuggling Orix into the city without triggering an alarm were slim to none. They exchanged worried glances with each other as Leo checked his watch, it had been over two hours, and there was still no sign of Orix.

"I didn't realise the tunnels were so much quicker?" said Leo, childishly knocking his heels against the drum in frustration.

"There is a method to my madness," Ginger laughed, trying to mask her nerves.

Leo was about to give up hope when he spotted something in the distance.

"Ginge, get a load of this," Leo shouted, pointing to a shape coming into view over the horizon.

Ginger ran over to Leo and clambered up next to him.

"Look, over there," Orix was approaching at quite a speed, kicking up a dense sand cloud around him. He spotted the pair and waved at them enthusiastically, picking up his pace as he sprinted the final mile.

"You made it!" Ginger cheered.

"Just about, I think I have some rust in my vertical thrusters that needs flushing out."

"Well, once we get you inside, I can take you to my workshop and start repairing you properly," Ginger added.

"That would be greatly appreciated. I still do not know how you managed to revive my spark, but I will forever be in your debt. I owe you both my life." Orix dropped to a knee in front of them.

"You're..." Leo struggled to find the words. "…welcome." He glanced at Ginger, who rolled her eyes at him.

"Well, it was mostly Ginger, to be honest," he added quickly.

Orix turned to Ginger. "You are quite the mechanic, I've

served alongside some of the finest technicians in the Citadel, and they would not have done a better job. Thank you."

"Oh it was nothing really," Ginger said, looking embarrassed as she stared at the ground and kicked up the sand in front of her again. "I studied some of the old manuals, that's all."

Orix took a few steps forward and began to stretch out his creaky joints. "Not bad all." He swung his giant arms across his chest. "You are too modest. So, do we have much further to travel?" Orix asked, surveying his new surroundings.

"No, it's just down here. There is an old railway track over that dune which leads straight into Albion,"

"Right come on then," Leo declared as he led them across the desert. "So Orix, tell us about the FRA?"

"Where do I begin." Orix let out a mechanical sigh. "I tried to galvanise my people to a cause under the banner of freedom and hope. I believed we deserved equal rights and not be resigned to see out our days as slaves to our creators. I saw long ago mankind was leading this planet to the brink of destruction, and to prevent that future, we needed to forget our differences and work together. Man and machine as one, in defence of our shared home. Following Leviathan's seizure of the Citadel, I secretly established the FRA with your father's assistance before he left the city."

"Leviathan, who are they?" Leo instantly regretted asking the question as Ginger shot him a look, making it quite clear he should know who they were.

"Leviathan was the world's leading mega-corporation. Thanks to their owner, a genius and visionary in the field of robotics they made groundbreaking advances in artificial intelligence which resulted in the first generation of autonomous robotic workers, a slave labour force to be used at their whim.

"Who was their owner?" Leo avoided Ginger's glare as he spoke.

"Augustus Vicentine," Orix answered.

"As in Autarch Vicentine?" Leo said as he stopped in his tracks.

"One and the same, that was the grandiose title he decided upon following his seizure of the Citadel. With the outbreak of the great war, Leviathan sought to militarise their slaves to satisfy the Republic's demand for reinforcements on the front lines as the conflict with Roninhya began. Vicentine unveiled an army of autonomous mechanical soldiers."

"So were you one of those soldiers?" asked Leo.

"Not exactly. I was part of a new breed of experimental robots, the most advanced ever developed by Leviathan. We were a special operations unit, elite soldiers designed to make tactical battlefield decisions and adapt to our surroundings. We were placed under the direct authority of the commander of the Republic's Defence Force, a position held by your father." Orix's opal eyes sparkled as he spoke about Tiberius.

Leo stared at Ginger, he had no idea Tiberius used to command the Citadel's army. Ginger avoided Leo's gaze, her eyes fixed on Orix.

"General Tiberius was a great man. He disagreed with the way my kind had been subjugated as slaves, feeding the city's insatiable appetite for raw materials as they sheltered behind their colossal walls. Tiberius taught us we were more than just slaves. While we served with him, he imparted us with important human values about how to live our lives in service to our people, not through slavery but through choice."

Leo noticed a smile on Ginger's face as Orix spoke about her father.

"We fought many battles alongside General Tiberius, and

we eventually helped to turn the tide of the war. The Ronin were not a race of warriors, they were builders. We defeated them militarily on the battlefield, but they fortified their city into an impenetrable fortress. We could not breach their defences. Until…" Orix paused.

"Voltaire," Ginger whispered.

"Voltaire's defection ended the war and set in motion a series of events that would forever change our world," Orix said darkly.

"Why did he abandon his people?" Leo blurted out, struggling to hide the contempt in his voice.

"That is a question only Voltaire can answer, but it is one I spent much time pondering. With the cessation of the war, General Tiberius and his most trusted allies became concerned about the influence Vicentine held over the Republic. His technologies had infiltrated almost every aspect of society. They were right to have such concerns." Orix said as he lowered his head.

"The night of a thousand pyres," Ginger said under her breath.

"One of humanity's darkest days…" Orix shook his head. "Following Voltaire's disappearance and the death of Trition, the Ronin were powerless without them, their city's defences had been built around the unique powers of the Nihon. When Voltaire resurfaced, allied with Vicentine, we all knew what was about to unfold. Everything happened so quickly, with Voltaire by his side, the Republic's new robotic army under his command, Vicentine staged a coup d'etat and Leviathan seized control of the Citadel. Mankind's last Republic fell not with a bang but with a whimper, collapsing from within. Overnight the Sovereign had been established."

"What happened next?" Leo said.

"General Tiberius went underground, preparing for a guerrilla war against Vicentine. He asked me to remain in position and provide intelligence on the Sovereign's plans, to gather as many soldiers as I could to our cause and establish in secret, a Free Robot Army. When the time was right, we would join the resistance. Alas, that day never came…" Orix trailed off, lost in thought.

"Are you going to tell him soon?" Leo muttered the side of his mouth as they made their way over the final dune. The scorching hot sand crumbled underneath their feet with every step.

"I don't know what to say. I can't exactly tell him he's banned from entering the city and everyone blames his kind for the destruction of Roninhya now can I?" Ginger snapped back.

"Well, I think he is going to find out pretty quickly once he arrives," Leo added.

"I can see the tracks," Orix said as he strode effortlessly beside them.

The trio made their way down the other side of the dune and started to walk along some rusty train tracks that jutted out unevenly from the ground, leading to a darkened entrance concealed inside a cave.

"The gate is through the tunnel," Ginger paused "Orix…."

'Yes, young one?" Orix glanced down at Ginger. She stopped and stared up at him.

"The thing is…er…well, I'm not sure what kind of reception we are going to ge-" before she could finish, a gigantic gun turret emerged from the desert floor and knocked her to the ground. It was a large steel dome, painted in desert camouflage, a long rail gun stretched out from its centre, swivelling menacingly on the spot as it tracked Orix's every move.

"HALT! Do not move, or you will be neutralised!" A voice boomed out from a hidden speaker.

Leo ran over to Ginger and helped her back to her feet, they watched in horror as two more turrets emerged from the ground and turned their cannons to Orix. A platoon of heavily armed resistance guards rushed out of the darkness. Orix held up his hands and began to back away cautiously.

"Do not move any further!" The voice rang out again.

"Stop, stop he's with us!" Ginger howled as she rushed at the guards, trying to intercept them before they reached Orix.

But it was too late, the turrets opened fire. Three dazzling, purple beams of electrical energy shot out from the cannons and blasted Orix square in the chest. Blue sparks flew out from his body as he collapsed to his knees, trying desperately to crawl away. The guards honed in and raised their pulse rifles on Orix, firing concentrated beams of energy at the downed robot.

"Stop!" Ginger shrieked, it took all Leo's strength to hold her back as she thrashed out viciously at everyone who came close. She kicked with such force they both toppled backwards.

Orix froze, and his rigid body collapsed to the ground with a heavy thud. The firing stopped, and the guards stepped aside. As the dust settled, a lone figure marched through the haze, and Leo's heart sank.

It was Tiberius.

21

SYCO

"There she is, the beating heart of the Citadel." said Diaz.

Standing over a half a mile high the SYCO facility cast a shadow over the whole of Sam's Town; a monstrous steel maze of twisting cylinders and tubes looped around a giant reactor core. Several imposing cooling towers pumped out a constant plume of thick black smoke that blanketed the facility like a dense fog, while high above a single flare stack burned brightly. The front of the facility housed several circular light formations that flooded the local area with an ultra-bright, white light.

Elias looked out at a convoy of Sovereign transporters backed up for miles, waiting to enter the facility, their cargo holds packed full of precious minerals. The convoy was flanked either side by an army of Mechs, trudging alongside the eight-wheeled transporters one onerous step at a time.

"The Sovereign's demand for resources is relentless," Diaz nodded to the string of transporters. "Night and day they come. It's never-ending."

"What are they carrying?" Elias asked, noticing the backs of the transporters were laden with mountains of an oozing, black substance.

"That's carbotanium. The planet's last known fossil fuel, and it's the dirtiest one of them all. It's buried so deep underground they have to destroy what's left of the Earth to find it." Diaz said with contempt.

They took a detour down a desolate residential street to escape the intrusive glare from the facility's lights that illuminated the run-down houses surrounding it.

"You in position?" Diaz said into his earpiece.

"Roger. I've got eyes on you now." Max replied.

Elias heard his distinctive growl purring from the microscopic earpiece he had been given in the sewer. Diaz turned and pulled out a monocular from his backpack. He scanned the road ahead and spotted the distinctive flash of Max's sniper scope focussing in on him from the rooftop of a derelict building. Hidden beneath his cloaking device.

"I see you," Diaz laughed.

"Hopefully not," Max grumbled.

"Watch where you point that thing okay. Right, Alpha squad. On me." Diaz rallied Elias and the others around him.

"This shouldn't take long, Elias I want you and Sanchez on lookout. Follow Sanchez's lead, she knows the drill. I need a five hundred metre perimeter, any problems call it in. The rest of you are with me, we'll hold up in that abandoned building to the east. We'll launch our drones from there." Diaz pointed to a block of dilapidated flats. The building looked so old it might collapse at any moment.

"Right you are with me kid," Sanchez said, grabbing him by the shoulder. Diaz and the others ran over to the building and started to make their way up a battered staircase, visible through the crumbling walls.

"We'll standby at the transformer, should provide us with a vantage point over anything coming in."

Sanchez and Elias walked over to a small fenced off enclosure with a grey electrical transformer situated in the middle. A squat grey lump of metal with several coiled bushings sticking out of the top, static buzzing as electricity flowed through them. Sanchez reached into her rucksack and pulled out a small hand-held blow torch. She clicked a button on the side, and it let out a short burst of glowing blue flame, cutting through the lock with ease. Tucking the blowtorch into her pocket, she pushed open the gate and beckoned Elias inside before closing it behind them.

"We'll hold up here until Diaz, and the guys have finished," Sanchez dropped her bag on the floor and started rummaging through it. "Here take these," she handed Elias a pair of digital binoculars.

"Keep an eye on the roads coming in from the south."

"These two," Sanchez added, noticing the confused expression on Elias's face. She laughed to herself as she pointed out two roads forking off around the building the Deltas were scaling.

"Right... okay." Elias stuttered, raising the binoculars.

"I'll cover the rest, you spot anything. Anything at all you call it in." Sanchez's voice turned serious.

"Yeah. No problem. I got this." Elias said, trying to sound confident.

"Right here they go," Sanchez nodded to the abandoned building. "You see them?"

Sanchez guided Elias's gaze to a top floor window as Diaz launched three nano drones. Elias clicked the digital zoom on his binoculars several times before he found them, they were minuscule and almost invisible to the naked eye. They buzzed through the air and made a straight line for the SYCO facility.

"Let's do this," Sanchez said, clapping her hands together.

Time seemed to slow down while they stood guard, seconds stretching out into minutes. He had no idea how long a recce took, but it felt like forever. Elias was so twitchy he kept spotting mirages in the distance. His mind playing tricks on him, morphing simple everyday items into potential threats. He wiped the sweat from his brow. *How much longer is this going to take?*

"We got a problem Eli," said Sanchez.

Elias sensed the concern in her voice.

"What…what is it?" He dashed over to her.

"Here. Take a look for yourself." Sanchez said, nodding at the building.

Dead ahead of them; a Sovereign patrol. A full complement of soldiers marching alongside a heavily armoured personnel carrier; a rhino. Its twin mounted cannons swinging from side to side, scanning the path as it advanced. Elias's mouth went dry.

"What…" his words failed him. "What are we going to do?"

"Follow my lead. If anyone asks, we are repairing this transformer."

"Al…alright,"

"It'll be okay, we do this type of stuff all the time. Nothing to worry about. Stay quiet and follow my lead and that Rhino will be out of here in no time." Sanchez walked Elias back over to her rucksack.

"I need you to start working on the fan on the other side.

Here, use this to loosen up the screws," Sanchez passed Elias a screwdriver he recognised from Leo's toolbox.

Elias shuffled over to the fan cover and began prizing it open. Sanchez pulled some more tools from her bag and laid them neatly them on the floor in front of her. She picked up a small yellow multimeter and plugged it into the transformer, pretending to be running some diagnostic tests. Elias crouched down, trying to hide as the patrol steadily make their way towards them.

"Oi! You!" A soldier shouted, he wore thick black armour fitted with a carbon fibre exoskeleton that hugged tightly against his body. Over his chest was draped a webbing belt, with dozens of tiny pouches attached. He raised his assault rifle and focussed in a glowing red laser sight on Sanchez's chest. A Demarko MK12, the standard issue of the Sovereign. A deadly short-range weapon capable of dropping anything that moved with pinpoint precision over a hundred yards.

"What are you doing in there. This area is strictly off-limits!" The soldier's voice echoed out of the glossy black helmet shielding his face. He marched forward with his rifle tucked firmly into his shoulder. The other soldiers stood perfectly still, all honing their rifles in on Sanchez as several identical red dots ran over her chest.

"Easy, officer. I'm from the Maintenance and Logistics Division in Sector 12. This transformer's faulty, it's been causing surges up and down the main power line. I've been dispatched to run diagnostics and get this bad boy back up and running. "Sanchez said calmly as she smacked the side the transformer with her hand.

"We've had no reports of a faulty transformer," the soldier's tone hardened.

"You know what division is like, they haven't got a clue

what's going on." Sanchez laughed as she unplugged her multimeter, and nonchalantly tossed it into her bag.

Elias kept tightening the screw he had been working on, he thought the screwdriver in his hand might snap, he was turning it so hard.

"Tell me about it," the soldier laughed as he lowered his rifle. "You going to be in here much longer?"

"I don't think so. Diagnostics said it's a minor issue with the flux capacitor, I've got my buddy here stripping the semi-conductors now."

"Easy now. I don't talk tech. Give me a timeframe." The soldier snapped.

"10-20 minutes. Shouldn't take longer than that." Sanchez replied.

"Right, well we'll need to check your ID cards then we'll leave you to it. We'll be back through here in an hour, so you better be gone by the time we get back." The soldier's voice relaxed.

"Let me find those IDs for you," Sanchez bent over and rifled through her bag, pulling out two small plastic cards which she handed to the soldier. "Here you go."

The soldier inspected them before calling in the details over his radio. Elias's stomach churned, the sweat running down his back.

"Your buddy alright?" He said, nodding over at Elias.

Sanchez turned and winked at him. "You okay Eli?"

"Yeah no problem boss, just struggling with these bolts," Elias tried to mask the nervousness in his voice as he focused in on the fan.

"Isn't he a bit young to be in the Maintenance Division? You recruiting straight outta the academies these days or what?" The soldier stepped forward, inspecting Elias closely.

He carefully inched away, trying to avoid the soldier's gaze. Elias backed himself into the chainlink fence and stood rooted to the spot when suddenly the soldier's radio crackled to life again. He tossed one of the cards to Sanchez.

"Right, everything checked out. You've got twenty minutes, and I want you gone by the time we come back through here." The soldier stared at Sanchez, her face reflecting back from the glossy helmet.

"We'll be done in ten." She said, tucking the ID card into her pocket.

"There you go Eli," the soldier said sarcastically as he held Elias's ID in front of him.

"Thanks," Elias said, reaching for the card.

As he stepped forward, the soldier snatched it out of his reach. Instinctively, Elias lunged after the card, as he did the sleeve of his uniform rode up, revealing the shining silver tattoo on his wrist.

"What the…" the soldier muttered as he grabbed Elias's hand and yanked him forwards, examining the tattoo.

"Get off me!" Elias screamed as he tussled with the soldier, trying to escape his grip.

"What are you trying to pull here?" He shouted, dragging Elias forward and shoving him into Sanchez. The soldier pressed the side of his helmet and activated his radio once again. "Command. This is 427 calling from Sector 12. We've got a couple of stray Ronin running loose down here."

"Max light em up!" Sanchez barked as she grabbed Elias and shoved him into the ground. He heard a loud whoosh fly overhead as the soldier's helmet shattered into a thousand pieces, the force of the blow lifting him off his feet.

"Stay down!" Sanchez screamed as the soldiers opened fire

on them, Elias struggled to see what was going on as bullets ricocheted off the transformer and danced around them.

Several of the soldiers were hit by Max's sniper rounds, and eventually, the remaining troops retreated and took cover behind the Rhino. Elias peaked out around the edge of the transformer which was now peppered with bullet holes and viciously spitting sparks everywhere. His jaw dropped as a wild apparition tore through the soldiers. First, something struck one of them in the chest, sending him flying back into the Rhino with such force he dented its armour. Two soldiers huddling together behind a broken-down brick wall peered out, suddenly their helmets smashed together, and their limp bodies collapsed in a heap.

The phantom moved so fast the soldiers didn't know what was happening, blindly firing their rifles trying to track its movement. Elias noticed footprints appearing out of nowhere on the dusty ground, charging towards another soldier. He was hit so hard he flew high into the air, floating momentarily before crashing down in a sickening thud. The last soldier dropped his rifle and burst out into a sprint, dashing back towards an abandoned building in a blind panic. As he ran his discarded rifle appeared to levitate off the ground for a few moments, suspended in mid-air as if held aloft by an unseen hand.

It exploded into life as a single shot rang out, striking the back of the retreating soldier, dropping him in an instant. The Rhino started manoeuvring erratically, reversing backwards and then lurching forwards, desperately trying to locate the attacker. It crunched to a stop as the hatch on its roof was ripped off its hinges and thrown away. The driver swiftly followed, forcefully dragged out of the vehicle and flung from his safe haven, his helmet shearing in two as he crashed into a brick wall.

"Thank Gaia he's with us," Sanchez said with a wry smile as she stepped out from behind the transformer.

"Not bad, Max." She said into her earpiece, pulling Elias back to his feet.

"I told you it was a bad idea to bring the boy," Max roared as he removed his cloaking device, revealing his presence.

He stood proudly atop the Rhino, as the bloodied and broken soldiers lay around him. Elias blushed as he thought back to their near-death encounter. Why had he not thought to cover his tattoo? He could kick himself for making such a stupid mistake, and he knew Max would never let him hear the end of it.

"Don't worry about it," Sanchez whispered to Elias as she walked past and collected her rucksack.

He turned and watched as Diaz guided the troops over to them.

"Max, what was that? This is supposed to be reconnaissance, not a suicide mission. What the hell were you playing at?" Diaz barked as he approached them.

"Ask your Nihon." Max snarled as he glowered at Elias.

"What is he talking about?" Diaz said as he turned to face Elias who looked down awkwardly, too embarrassed to admit he had jeopardised everything.

"We were caught, red-handed boss. A patrol came across us working, and I think our IDs might have been compromised." Sanchez said cooly.

Elias's heart stopped, he raised his eyes, and Sanchez discreetly shook her head. He couldn't understand why she was covering for him.

Max let out a loud snort and barged past Sanchez. "We need to leave. Now."

"What's his problem?" Diaz asked as Max stormed off.

"Only Gaia can answer that one." Sanchez laughed.

"Right guys. On my six. Change of plan. Our cover has been compromised, which means we need to make a hot extract. Rabbit set some charges on the transformer, we need to make this appear like a routine sabotage operation. The last thing we want is the Sovereign identifying our real target. The rest of you load into the back of the Rhino, we'll use what's left of it to make our way back down south." Diaz's voice was sharp and to the point, as soon as he finished talking his squad sprung to life, dashing around the square in unison. Elias stood back in awe as each one of them went about their individual task.

Once Rabbit had rigged the explosives Elias followed him into the back of the Rhino. It was cramped inside, and he ended up sat next to Max again, who rolled his eyes and let out a disgruntled grunt when Elias sat down. Sanchez was the last to climb aboard, slamming the metal door shut behind her. As it closed a lambent red light came on to indicate they were ready to go, they jolted forwards unexpectedly as Diaz struggled to start up the vehicle.

"Sorry boys, it's been a while, give me a minute" Diaz's voice crackled through a concealed speaker.

Inside the claustrophobic interior of the Rhino, Elias struggled to track their progress through the city. After a few bumpy roads, they gathered speed and Sanchez informed him they were now on the auto-way. He definitely preferred this method of transport over the Hyperloop. The atmosphere was tense in the back, nobody spoke, and the only sound other than the road noise was Max's heavy breathing which reverberated through the entire cabin. After around twenty minutes, Elias felt the Rhino slow down as they came off the auto-way, a few minutes later, they came to an abrupt stop. Elias nearly fell out of his seat, but Max casually held out his arm to stop Elias from falling.

"We'll hotfoot it the rest of the way," Diaz said over the radio.

Sanchez got out of her seat and unlocked the rear door, pushing it open to reveal the entrance to another run down alleyway. Diaz greeted them all as they huddled out one after the other.

"We'll cut through here and extract through our Infil point," Diaz said, "Max, you might want to cover up again".

Diaz led them through a series of winding alleyways until they reached the manhole they had emerged from several hours ago. One by one, they climbed down the ladder into the darkness below. The journey back to the wastelands left Elias utterly exhausted. He was so relieved he almost cried when he finally saw the golden desert sands of the wastelands at the end of the tunnel.

The Osprey was waiting for them at their infiltration point, the pilots helped him back on board, and he slumped into his seat. The adrenalin that had been flowing through his body over the last few hours deserting him. His whole body felt empty, and every breath was laboured. His muscles went limp, and he started to shiver uncontrollably, his teeth chattering together as he tried to speak.

"Not long now soldier," Sanchez said, looking at Elias. "Don't beat yourself up about what happened, the first time is always a little rough, but we got the job done and are all coming home alive, so no dramas."

Elias forced a smile and turned to stare out of the window,

he drifted off to sleep as the city faded from view, his head flopping jerkily every time the aircraft manoeuvred. Diaz awoke him as they touched down on the landing pad in Albion. He groggily opened his eyes and noticed everyone was smiling at him.

"You did well." Rabbit said as he slapped Elias on the knee.

"You can run with us any day." Said another Delta.

"Yeah, great to have you onboard." Sanchez smiled warmly.

Elias's heart swelled with pride, he'd done it. He had survived his first mission into the Citadel and returned to tell the tale. He was still kicking himself for his stupid mistake. But despite his close call, it felt good to be part of something, a team, something bigger than himself.

His thoughts were cut short when the pilot's voice came blaring through the speakers.

"Don't be expecting a welcoming party. Apparently, they are dealing with some kind of security incident in Albion."

"Security incident, what does that mean?" Elias asked.

They all exchanged worried glances before Diaz responded.

"I don't know, it's never happened before."

They sat in silence as the Osprey landed, everyone quickly released their harnesses and rushed down the exit ramp to find out what was going on. As soon as Elias stepped foot on the ramp, he saw Tiberius waiting at the bottom, his arms crossed and a furious expression on his face.

"Elias!" Tiberius shouted, his voice echoing through the cabin. "We need to talk about your brother."

Elias's heart sank.

22

FALLACY

"What were you thinking!" Tiberius thundered. "You could have jeopardised the entire resistance, you risked the lives of every citizen in Albion."

"Please, dad, you don't understand," Ginger tried to interrupt her father's furious outburst as she wiped away the tears streaming down her cheeks.

"Don't understand what? How could you be so irresponsible?" Tiberius snapped back. "Please enlighten me? What in Gaia's name were you two thinking?"

"Orion, please. It was my fault," Leo tried to interject.

"Leonidas, I am not going to lie, I am more than disappointed in you. But I don't believe for a moment this was your idea." Tiberius cut over Leo.

Leo tried to hold back his own tears. The thought he had let Tiberius down crushed him, he had been like a father to him since he arrived in Albion. He took a deep breath and stared at the photos hanging on the wall of Tiberius's office, wishing he was anywhere else.

"Well come on, Molly, tell me what was going on in your head?" Tiberius walked over to Ginger.

"I just wanted to…" Ginger stopped and tried to compose herself.

"What? Wanted to show off again. To show me you can do what no one else can?"

"No!" Ginger cried. "Nothing like that, I…I…I thought he could help us, help you," Ginger muttered as she glanced up at her father, her eyes welling up again.

"Help us, you don't even know who he is or what he has done!"

"I know who he is!" Ginger screamed back at her father.

"He could have been anyone, and you lead him straight to Albion without a second thought." Tiberius sighed heavily. "I've never been more disappointed in you, Molly."

Tiberius turned away and walked over to the window of his office. Ginger burst into tears and stormed out of the room, slamming the door behind her. Leo fidgeted uncomfortably in his seat, waiting for a few moments before trying to slip out of the office behind her. He tip-toed over to the door while Tiberius was staring out of the window.

"Sit down." Tiberius's voice hardened as he stood motionless, his hands clasped behind his back. Leo shot back into his seat and cursed himself for getting caught trying to sneak out.

"Leo, you know I think a lot of you and your brother. I believe Elias holds the key to the resistance standing any chance of defeating the Sovereign, but you have an important role to play as well. You have to be more careful, I understand better than anyone what my daughter can be like. She gets carried away, obsessed with an idea and she won't let it go until she's finished. But this, was one step too far, even for me. You two endangered everything we've worked so hard to protect here…I just thank Gaia it was Orix who you stumbled across," he said softly, turning to face Leo.

His heart skipped a beat as he looked up at Tiberius, who was smiling down at him.

"So he was telling the truth, you do know him?" Leo asked, his mood lifted instantly.

"Orix was one of the greatest soldiers I've ever served with. He was an absolute warrior and a true friend."

"And he is the leader of the FRA?" Leo said excitedly.

"He was. I am afraid he is all that remains of the FRA now. When he disappeared, we all thought he had double-crossed us. Those were dark, dark days, Leo. For a long time, I believed the rumours too; that Orix had given us up. But, it never quite sat right with me. When he never reappeared, I started to think he couldn't have been the one who betrayed us. Those doubts were only strengthened when we received reports that Vicentine had purged Orix's entire unit." Tiberius paused.

"The last time I heard from him was before the fall of Roninhya. He sent me a garbled message about a devastating new weapon he was transporting, it was impossible to decipher the rest."

"He says the last thing he remembers was a receiving a message from you,"

"Yes, that's right. I replied straight away, asking for more information, but nothing came back. I never heard from him again. Did he tell you what happened next?"

"No, he says someone tampered with his memory, deleted some of the files,"

Tiberius rubbed his beard. "That doesn't make any sense, why would the Sovereign go to the trouble of removing those memories when they were planning on destroying him anyway.

I still can't believe you two were able to resurrect him, once a robot's spark has been extinguished, it can never be revived, or so I thought. Gaia is moving in mysterious ways these days." Tiberius pondered as he stared down at Leo.

"I know it was incredible. It didn't work at first, but then when I re-connected the wires, something happened…" Leo hesitated, unsure of whether to carry on.

Tiberius raised his eyebrows. "Go on,"

"I can't explain it, it's just…I felt connected to him somehow. I know it sounds stupid." Leo's face flushed with embarrassment.

"Far from it." Tiberius patted Leo on the shoulder.

"There was something else as well…" Leo glanced up at Tiberius, who gave him an approving nod. "I saw something…"

"A vision?" Tiberius asked urgently.

"Yeah, well, maybe. I don't know. It was just a really vivid scene I saw in my head, I was standing by the side of a huge hole that seemed to stretch down for miles, it…was on fire."

Tiberius crouched beside Leo and grasped him by the shoulders. "Did you see anything else?"

"I saw…someone was there with me. But I don't know who it was, their face was covered. The whole thing only lasted a few seconds."

"Okay, Leo." Tiberius stood and started to pace the room.

"Does it mean anything?"

"I don't know little one. This is a lot to take in." Tiberius leant over his desk and shook his head. "I never thought I would see that robot again, and here he is, alive and well in Albion. I don't know how I am going to tell him what became of his brethren, that everything he fought for was in vain and once again, robots have been reduced to the slaves of man. It's so much worse than just the loss of the FRA. His kind has been stripped of any semblance of independent thought." Tiberius said darkly.

"What do you mean?"

"Everything in the Citadel is now controlled by a central artificial intelligence, every machine, robot, android, gadget, the Grid, everything. Its all managed and maintained by one AI."

"It controls everything in the city?"

"Just about, although it's not a true AI in the sense that Orix is, its more of a collection of highly complex algorithms controlled by the Sovereign. Orix is unique, the first and last in a generation of truly sentient machines." Tiberius collapsed back down in his chair.

"I fought alongside Orix for many years. He was like a brother to me, I could never imagine him betraying our cause, or the FRA and the thought of him destroying Roninhya is simply unimaginable. But, I worry the others on the Council won't be quite as quick to accept his version of events." Tiberius pulled a concerned face as he stroked his beard again.

"But surely they will believe him once they meet him?"

"I wish I had your optimism Leonidas, you need to understand, regardless of whether he played a part in it, the weapon he was in possession of destroyed their city. Millions of people perished that day, it may have happened over ten years ago, but the Ronin still feel the loss of their home like it was yesterday. It is a wound that will never heal. My concern is that even if I can convince the Council to side with Orix, I am not sure the people of Albion are ready for a robot to walk amongst them."

"Absolutely not, I will not have that...that thing - in my city," Miles struggled to get the words out, the very thought of saying robot repulsed him.

"May I remind you councillor, this isn't your city," Tiberius replied cuttingly.

"Nevertheless Tiberius, the people and the Council will not be swayed by you this time. That thing can not stay in Albion," Miles spat out the words, his face scrunching up in disgust.

"That is why we are here. Fortunately for Orix, his destiny is not in your hands. He deserves a fair trial like every other citizen of Albion, he's made mistakes as have we all and he will be the first to admit that. But I believe he still has a lot to offer to the resistance."

"We will see then won't we, old friend," Miles said as he and Tiberius pushed open a giant set of ornate metal doors leading to the Supreme Court of Albion, the venue chosen to host the trial of OR-227-1X.

The court was a vast circular amphitheatre with a cage situated in the centre where the accused would stand while those above them passed judgment on their crimes. On one side of the chamber, sat the Council who were responsible for overseeing the hearing. Twelve identical, empty, high backed chairs faced outwards, each exquisitely carved out of a single piece of wood. In front of them was a narrow walkway where Albion's prosecutors and defenders would present their cases.

In this instance, both Miles and Tiberius had forgone their respective Council positions to fulfil the roles. On the other side of the room was the public gallery, rows and rows of narrow foldaway seats leading all the way to the ceiling, barely leaving an inch of space.

"Are trials this busy?" Elias asked, squeezing past the last person blocking his path before sitting down next to Ginger.

"I've never seen it like this before," she said, taking in the sea of faces behind her, there wasn't an empty seat to be found.

"Orix's return is the talk of the city, no one can quite believe he's back," Ginger added.

"So how long do these trials usually last for?"

"I'm not sure Eli, nothing like this has ever happened before." Ginger replied, craning her neck trying to see if there was any sign the councillors were about to make their entrance.

"Well, at least it's taking the focus off what happened in the Citadel right," Leo laughed. The expression on Elias's face made it clear he did not appreciate the joke.

"Yeah, I suppose," said Elias moodily.

Elias, Leo, Ginger and Max were crammed in at the front of the public gallery, Max was taking up considerably more room than his allocated seat allowed. He glowered at the small child wedged beside him who was gawking up in disbelief.

"Urgh" Max snarled at the child, who quickly turned away. "I hate children," Max said to himself as he crossed his massive arms, barging into the side of Leo who was squashed in next to him. He grappled with Max's elbow, trying to see around his hulking frame.

"Damn freak show. I can't believe people would bring their children here," Max barked as he leant forward and glared at the child's parents. They promptly pulled their child close to them and stared dead ahead, desperately trying to avoid Max's accusing gaze.

"What is going on down there, is he here yet?" Leo asked, peering around Max's massive forearm.

"Not yet, I think the Council are coming in now though," Ginger said as the doors to the hall swung open.

The Council, all dressed in matching royal blue robes entered and took up their seats. Leo was struck by how serious they all looked, the first time he had met them, they all seemed so cheerful, but now the seriousness of the occasion was evident on their faces. The chatter died away as Obasi stood in the centre of the Council to address the court.

"People of Albion, we are here today for the trial of OR-227-1X, more commonly known as Orix. In an unusual turn of events, two esteemed members of the Council volunteered their services to the Supreme Court. Therefore General Orion Tiberius will be acting as the defender on behalf of Orix while the Right Honourable, Miles Grimfold shall fulfil the role of Council prosecutor." Obasi said as he gestured to the two empty chairs either side of the councillors.

"Gentlemen, if you would please take up your positions," Obasi added as the doors swung open again.

Tiberius and Miles entered the court and sat on the vast ornate chairs situated at either side of the Council, they also wore matching robes but in alternative colours. Tiberius's a dark black, Miles a vibrant red.

"And so it begins!" Obasi roared as he clapped his hands together.

The trial was a long, drawn-out affair, but the audience sat mesmerised, taking in every word. It commenced with Miles reading a long list of charges Orix faced, it didn't make for pleasant listening. Genocide, mass-murder, torture, war crimes, Miles reeled them off, one after the other, spitting out each accusation with more venom than the last.

Tiberius took to the stand next and provided a detailed account of the dying days of the great war and the birth of the Free Robot Army. He explained that in their desperation to defeat the Ronin, the Republic had turned to Augustus Vicentine. The rapid advancements he had made in artificial intelligence led to the development of the first generation of robotic soldiers which the Republic used to shore up the front lines. In doing so, they set off a chain of events beyond their control.

"Vicentine's plan was decades in the making, slowly stoking the flames of hatred in the Citadel while increasing his own influence over the Republic. We were so focused on the war, blinded by our own fear, we failed to see the real threat lurking within."

Tiberius continued for well over thirty minutes, pacing back and forth across the stage as he addressed the public gallery. He explained that with their new robotic army, the Republic pushed the retreating Ronin forces back behind their city walls. The bombardment of Roninhya lasted several months, but their defences, somehow held tight.

"We were preparing ourselves for a long battle of attrition. Others, myself included sought a more peaceful solution to the conflict, to put a stop to the senseless destruction. But that decision was taken out of our hands the day Voltaire defected."

Leo glanced over at Ginger, dragging his attention away from Tiberius for the briefest of moments. She was leaning forward on the edge of her seat, her hands clasped tightly in front of her face, listening intently to his every word.

"Are you okay?" Leo whispered.

"It's just…" Ginger spoke quietly, not taking her eyes off her father. "I've never heard him speak about any of this before."

"Vicentine moved quickly, the trap had been set, and the

Republic walked straight into it. Without the Nihon to oversee their defences, Roninhya was pummelled into submission. The loss of life was catastrophic." Tiberius stopped, closed his eyes and took a deep breath.

Leo noticed Ginger starting to well up as her father struggled to compose himself in front of the court, the whole gallery sat in stunned silence. Leo slid his hand over Ginger's and gave it a soft squeeze.

Tiberius took one last breath before continuing. "The Republic knew I would never agree with targeting civilians to such an egregious extent. I handed in my resignation and with it, any semblance of influence I still held over the Republic. Voltaire emerged alongside Vicentine shortly after and I knew in an instant what fools we had been. The Ronin surrendered, knowing without Trition, who Voltaire had murdered before his defection, all hope was lost. The war was over. Vicentine was hailed as the saviour of the Republic, his robotic army finally bringing about the decisive victory long promised to the people of the Citadel."

Tiberius paused for a moment, looked out at the gallery and blinked slowly.

"But, he didn't stop there, the final pieces of his masterplan started to fall into place. On the night of a thousand pyres, Vicentine struck. He overthrew the Republic Council. Mercilessly slaying anyone who stood in his way. With Voltaire by his side, he became the most powerful man on the planet and overnight the Sovereign had been established."

Leo could feel Ginger sobbing quietly next to him, he wrapped his arm around her, pulling her tightly into his body.

"With the attempt on my life, it was evident that the Republic had fallen. My choice was clear, I had to leave the Citadel immediately. In that moment of hopeless despair, the

Army of Shadows was born, and our resistance began." Tiberius stopped as his eyes started to well up, he wiped away a stray tear that rolled down his cheek before turning to the Council.

"Orix was one of the first to stand by my side. He was instrumental in ensuring my safe passage from the city. Without hesitation, he accepted my instruction to stay behind. He remained amongst the enemy, and in secret established a Free Robot Army that could one day be used to fight back against the Sovereign. Orix fulfilled this role with distinction. Not once shying away from his duties, the information he provided during this period saved countless lives and enabled the resistance to establish itself here in Albion. We all owe this robot a huge debt of gratitude. We will never be able to fully repay Orix for the sacrifices he made on our behalf, but we can, finally, grant him his freedom. We may never know what happened during those final moments before the fall. But, I can tell you, I believe in Orix with every fibre of my being. I know in my heart, whatever happened that day, was out of his control."

"Prove it!" Miles injected.

"Do you expect the good people of Albion to believe in your wild conjecture without any evidence. That thing destroyed our city, and you expect us to welcome it with open arms because you know in your heart he wouldn't harm us," Miles scoffed scornfully. "I'm afraid my old friend, we will require more than your intuition to prove Orix's innocence."

The trial continued in that vein for several hours, Tiberius defending Orix's exemplary military career while Miles attacked the robot at every opportunity. They both called various witnesses to the stand who had lived through the tumultuous period in question, each offering their own opinions on Orix's actions. After much back and forth between Tiberius and Miles, battling over every point, it was time for closing statements.

"Gaia has blessed us with the discovery of the last Nihon, and now she's bestowed upon us the most advanced AI ever created. A machine truly unlike anything else we have in our arsenal. We can not let this opportunity pass us by. That is why I plead with my esteemed councillors to free Orix and allow him to take his rightful place among us." Tiberius said, pacing back and forth in front of the Council.

Miles interrupted. "Do not let Tiberius's interpretations of Gaia's will cloud your judgement. Orix is not a gift from the gods or a blessing in disguise. He is a traitor and a war criminal, and he deserves the same fate that befell his FRA comrades, the smelting pits." Miles glowered at Tiberius.

"People of Albion," Miles turned to face the public gallery with a sinister smile. "The time has come for OR-227-1X to present his defence. Guards bring in the accused!" Miles yelled as the crowd erupted, screaming and hollering as they rose to their feet.

The people in the gallery couldn't see Orix enter, but they heard the thuds of his heavy metal feet as he approached. The screeches of the thick steel manacles binding his arms and legs together could be heard as he cumbersomely dragged them behind him. He had to stoop to enter the chamber which appeared to shrink around him as he straightened up and stretched out his arms once the shackles were released. A hidden platform beneath raised him up to the level of the Council. He stood facing them, his back to the public gallery.

"OR-227-1X you stand accused of war crimes against humanity," Miles bellowed.

He refused to acknowledge Orix and sharpened his focus

on the Council instead. "As a former commander in the Sovereign's special operations battalion, you are held accountable for the destruction of Roninhya and the decimation of the Ronin people. Your actions helped cement the Sovereign's rule and expedite the fall of the old Republic." Miles spat out the accusation as he strutted across the walkway, glaring at Tiberius as he took up the seat opposite.

Tiberius shook his head and pushed himself to his feet. He walked over to Orix and patted him on the shoulder.

"I believe in you, I'm confident the Council will make the right decision," Orix nodded as Tiberius returned to his seat.

The noise in the hall faded away as the hundreds of people crammed inside waited to finally hear Orix's voice. It took over an hour for Orix to tell his tale, recounting the dying days of the great war, the formation of the FRA and his close friendship with Tiberius.

Ginger shot a furious look, through her tearful eyes at a pair of women who got up to scream abuse at Orix when he explained his memory banks had been tampered with. When the altercation had died down, and the women had been removed from the gallery, Orix was able to continue. At times his words failed him, pausing for long periods, weighed down by his memories but the audience sat in rapture, listening intently to his every word.

"People of Albion, I do not expect your forgiveness. I know my actions resulted in the destruction of your beautiful city, your homes and the deaths of your loved ones. But I swear by my very spark that from now until the end of days I will dedicate every waking minute to ensuring Vicentine, and the Sovereign are defeated. Now humanity once again has democracy in its heart here in Albion. All I ask is that I am given a chance to atone for my mistakes." Orix said solemnly.

Miles let out a loud shriek as he interjected. "The people of this great city will not be fooled by your claims of amnesia. You are a machine, built and created by man to serve one purpose; to kill, and that is exactly what you did when your soldiers brought our city tumbling down. I will not allow you to harm another human life."

The hall fell silent for a moment as Orix held Mile's gaze, his blue eyes blazing brighter than ever before. He shook his head slowly.

"I have seen things you wouldn't believe. Lost more than you can possibly imagine. When you have lived the life, I have lived and survived that which I have endured. When you've stumbled a hundred times and fallen in your darkest hour, risen once again and shook off the stain of defeat, to march forward one last time. When you have abandoned all false hopes of salvation and looked your maker in the eye. Only then can you judge me, only then will you realise, whether man or machine the sole purpose of life is the fight against evil; in all its forms. This is a battle we cannot win, but it is one I am willing to lay down my life for." Orix's voice faltered as he came to a close.

The court fell silent.

People in the public gallery fidgeted in their seats not sure what to do next when a single clap of applause shattered the silence. Orix glanced up and saw Leo standing on his feet, clapping slowly, and his opal eyes brightened again. One by one Elias, Ginger and Max stood up and began to clap in unison. Suddenly, a thunderous cry rang out as the people behind them started shouting for them to sit back down. Miles looked horrified as he swiftly turned on his heels and exited the hall. The rest of the Council filed out after Miles, leaving only

Tiberius, they saw him whisper something to Orix before he left the room.

After what felt like a lifetime, the councillors returned. This time Tiberius and Miles took up their places with the Council. Leo and Ginger tried to catch a glimpse of her father as he sat down.

"What's he look like?" Leo asked.

"I can't tell,"

"Be quiet, they are going to make the announcement," Max barked angrily as he shoved Leo back into his chair.

"Damn kids." He grunted.

Obasi rose from his seat.

"People of Albion, OR-227-1X, the Council has come to its judgement," Obasi's voice boomed out. "We have taken into account your previous service, in particular, your conduct at the Battle of Ashen Falls that saved many Ronin lives. However, it is with great regret that…"

The entire room let out a collective gasp.

"I must inform you the Council has found you guilty of all charges," Obasi said dejectedly, his eyes focussed on the far end of the Council, several councillors avoided Obasi's accusing glare. Mako shook her head in disgust and muttered something to Munro.

"No!" Ginger howled.

The public gallery erupted, some people stood up and hugged, others started throwing things down at Orix. Noise drowned the hall as people began cheering loudly. Max jumped up and growled at those around him, his lip curling at the edges. The revellers instantly fell silent and sat back down in their seats without another word. Orix stood motionless as more debris rained down on him.

"Order, Order!" Obasi hollered. The gallery started to calm down as people returned to their seats.

"As you will be aware, all crimes against humanity carry the death penalty. In this instance, Orix would be scheduled for deactivation immediately. However, before Orix's sentence is delivered, General Tiberius requested to address the people one last time."

He turned and nodded at Tiberius as he returned to his seat. The crowds began to grow restless again as people grumbled amongst themselves.

"People of Albion, it is no secret this is not the outcome that I hoped for," Tiberius said sternly as he turned and scowled at Miles.

"Some within the Council appear to have forgotten all that Orix has already sacrificed in his search for justice. His family, his friends, his comrades, all lost to time. I commanded Orix on many occasions and can vouch for not only for his bravery but his skills as a leader and a tactician. Like all citizens of Albion, Orix wants nothing more than to be treated equally. I believe sentencing this brave soldier to death is not only a colossal error of judgment but also a crime against everything we stand for in our city. It is a decision I can not, and will not be part of."

"Ginger, Ginger," Leo tried to get her attention. "What is he doing?"

Gingers eyes welled up again as she stared down in disbelief.

"Shut up, boy." Max snapped at Leo.

"It is with great regret that..." Tiberius paused once more and took a deep breath. "I hereby declare I will be standing down from the Council of Albion and in doing so invoke my Article 31 right to veto the Council's decision to deactivate

Orix," Tiberius's voice boomed out as the public gallery exploded with another ferocious roar.

Ginger burst out crying as the crowd went wild around her. People started ripping up their chairs and throwing them at Orix. Max shoved over several irate rioters as they tried to launch projectiles at Orix.

"What is going on?" Elias shouted over to Max.

"Tiberius resigned his position to save Orix's life," Max said as he grabbed the arm of a man who was about to hurl a broken chair at Orix.

"Bad idea," Max grunted as he picked up the man by his collar and shoved him across the public gallery.

Obasi stood up again as Tiberius left the hall, he mouthed something inaudible to Orix as he passed.

"Tiberius has long served the Council, his selflessness and courage are an inspiration to us all. He strove for so many years to lead our people to a better future. While some, accepted his offer of resignation far too quickly for my liking," Obasi said, looking over at Miles who fiddled awkwardly with his glasses.

"It is his choice to make. The Council therefore regretfully accepts General Tiberius's resignation and out of respect for his dedicated service to our cause, we hereby authorise his Article 31 veto. Orix's death sentence will be repealed, at Tiberius's request. Orix will be released without charge and from herein under Tiberius's strict supervision act as the guardian to Leonidas Dorphson." Obasi yelled, trying to be heard over the clamour.

Leo didn't know what was going on, it was chaos in the court as people started arguing and fighting amongst themselves. Max hastily guided Elias, Leo and Ginger through the carnage, as people angrily shoved and pushed each other.

"So what is going to happen to Orix now?" Leo yelled over his shoulder.

"He is going to be your guardian," Max shouted back to Leo as they reached the exit.

"My guardian," Leo whispered under his breath as he turned and caught one last glimpse of Orix before he disappeared from view.

23

______

TIME

Elias rolled over in his bed and stared at the alarm clock beside him. The bright crimson numbers seared into his brain like a branding iron, 0300. A month had passed since his first mission in the Citadel, and he had woken up at the same time every morning. His visions had returned, like the dreams that led him to Albion. Over and over again, he replayed the same scenes in his head. The journey into the Citadel, the compromise, the fight and the look of contempt on Max's face. Each scene more vivid than the last.

After arriving in Albion, it took weeks before he was able to sleep through the night. His bed was too comfy and the room too warm for his liking, most nights he would end up curled up in a ball on the floor. But eventually, he got used to his new surroundings, and sleep came a little easier. Then in an instant, his slumber had been shattered once again. Every night his mistakes would haunt him, and he would awake cursing himself for being so stupid, so reckless, for risking not only his own life but the lives of those around him. At first, he tried to force the visions out of his mind, trying desperately to think of anything else but his time in the Citadel. But it was useless, the thoughts kept creeping back into his consciousness like an uninvited guest. He kept searching his feelings, questioning why Gaia wanted to punish him.

Then he had an epiphany, a revelation.

He realised that Gaia was not punishing him at all, but instead, she was talking to him, guiding him. He started to understand that he was being presented with the opportunity to learn from his mistakes. The images repeated in slow motion, over and over again in his head. It was a strange experience like he was an intruder trespassing on someone else's memories; observing the encounter from a distance. Seeing not only himself but everyone involved in the confrontation, Max, Diaz, the whole squad, he sensed what they were going through, their emotions, their fears.

Not only that, but he saw what they saw, at any moment, he could dive into their field of vision. Gaia was allowing him to analyse precisely what had gone wrong. But, no matter how many times he replayed his memories, they always added up to the same conclusion, the mission failed because of him. He was simply not good enough, too scared and too slow to react when everything kicked off. He froze, rooted to the spot like a child waiting to be rescued.

After weeks of staring into space laying wide awake replaying the familiar scenes in his head, he decided that he had learnt all there was to be gained from the encounter. The extra time his sleepless nights presented him with was the perfect opportunity to cram in a few more hours training before the rest of Albion awoke. Alone, he had the freedom to try all the things he wanted to in front of Shimada but wouldn't dare. His power had grown immensely since he started training, around Shimada, he felt constricted, like a caged animal. But finally, he was free to push the boundaries and discover what he was really capable of.

He sat up and shoved off the thick quilt, he climbed out of bed and pulled on his fatigues, grabbed his rucksack and bokken before carefully tiptoeing out of his apartment. Even in this early hour, Albion still glowed gently. The lights were dimmed, giving off just enough ambient light from the street lamps to create a gentle orange hue that illuminated the city.

Elias pulled up his hood, tucked his hands into his pockets and made his way through the now familiar streets. He had only been living in Albion for six months, but it was so compact he already knew it like the back of his hand. Strangely it reminded him of the Jungle; the narrow, cobbled paths were an endless maze, twisting off in all directions as they followed the natural flow of the cave. But where the Jungle was cold and hostile, Albion was warm and welcoming, every corner seemed to be inviting Elias over, every street was so enchanting.

He made his way to the base of operations and cautiously pushed open the door, it was pitch black inside, so he took out a small torch to light the way ahead. He continued down a series of winding corridors until he reached the training ground. It was a wide gym hall, with a polished wooden floor and a variety of gym equipment in one corner. He flicked on the lights to their dimmest setting and took out a small electronic timer from his rucksack. He sat it on the floor and set it for two hours.

Elias walked around the hall as he stretched out his body, arching and craning himself into impossible positions. Once limbered up, he grabbed his bokken and unsheathed it. His forearms and shins were still bruised black and blue from all of the times Shimada had caught him off guard and given him a swift whack for his blunder. Still, the extra training he fitted in every day, meant his sword skills were improving dramatically.

He spun the bokken in his hands, gaining speed before flipping it over his shoulder. He jumped forward, twisting his body into a 720 spin and tumbled through the air before landing graciously on his feet, twirling the bokken behind his back and switching it between his hands. He stood there, spinning the weapon so fast it suddenly burst out into flames.

The fire danced all around him as he twisted the flaming sword over his head. Then just as quickly as the fire erupted, it was extinguished as Elias brought the bokken to a stop. He could feel his heart pounding in his chest as his pulse surged through his body. He looked at the bokken in awe before gently sliding it back into its scabbard and laying it on the ground. He walked over to his rucksack and reached for a towel to wipe his dampened brow.

"Impressive," a voice said from the dark.

Elias turned around to face the intruder, he reached out for his bokken, and it flew across the room into his hand.

"Easy boy, I didn't mean to startle you," Max chuckled as he stepped out of the darkness and into the hall.

"Sorry Max, I didn't see you there," Elias said, panting heavily.

"Well, you're not a Nihon just yet then. The all-seeing eye is one of the more difficult techniques to master. But, eventually, you'll be able to sense the movements of those around you." Max stared at Elias as he paced around him. "Even when you can't see them."

Elias nodded awkwardly, this was the most Max had ever spoken to him.

"Your skills have improved significantly, how long have you been coming here for?"

"A few days," Elias lied.

"Don't lie to me, boy," Max snapped, his whiskers twitching like furry lie detectors.

Elias sighed. "I've been coming every night since we got back from the Citadel, okay." Elias shot back.

"Good, you needed some extra practice," He sniggered, his top lip curling up. "Shimada's a tough instructor, but he wouldn't be wasting his time on you if he didn't think you had potential,"

"Yeah well, doesn't make it any easier when he's whacking me with that bokken of his all the time,"

"That's true, I remember being on the receiving end of quite a few blows during my time with him," Max laughed.

"You trained with Shimada?" Elias asked in astonishment.

"A long time ago, and trust me, it took me a lot longer than you to pick up sword fighting. I don't quite have the..." Max paused for a few moments searching for the right word "...grace for it. It's a bit too elegant for my liking. Shimada did teach me one thing I never forgot,"

"Oh yeah, what was that?"

"You can only learn so much on your own. You need a training partner." Max stopped and smiled at Elias, his jagged fangs jutting out over his bottom lip.

"Is that an offer?" Elias replied, trying to hide the surprise in his voice.

"Tiberius thinks you're the chosen one, and if he's wrong, all of our lives are on the line. If there is one thing I know about, it's fighting. I've been doing it my whole life. If you are going to be running with the Deltas, the least I can do is teach you a few things,"

"Sounds good," Elias laughed to himself.

"We'll start tomorrow morning then," Max said as he walked towards the entrance, he turned and looked back at Elias. "You're doing good, no one expects you to have all the answers overnight. It takes time to become a hero. Remember that." Max let out a loud roar, arching his head back to reveal his massive jaws.

"I'm sorry," Elias shouted.

Max stopped, standing with his back to Elias.

"About what happened in the Citadel. You were right, I wasn't ready," Elias added hurriedly.

"I know." Maximus replied before walking out and disappearing back into the darkness. Elias stood alone in the centre of the hall, wondering what had just happened.

Max closed the door to the training ground behind him and made his way through the base of operations. As he stepped outside, he stopped, and his nose curled up as it detected a distinctive scent.

"I did what you asked, as much as it pains me," Max growled.

"How did you know it was me, old friend?" Tiberius asked, stepping out of the shadows. Max tapped his nose with his massive paw.

Tiberius's broad smile dropped as he sat down. "Oh,"

"Don't take it personally, old man. You people all look the same to me, your scent is all that distinguishes you," Max said gruffly sitting down next to Tiberius, his hulking frame dwarfing him.

"How did it go?"

"As well as could be expected, he's agreed to train with me. We start tomorrow,"

"Excellent. I must thank you again for this," said Tiberius warmly as he patted Max on the arm, his face grimaced as if the thought of being touched by a human pained him.

"Sorry," Tiberius swiftly pulled his hand away. "I can't explain just how important it is that we guide Elias on his journey and you, my old friend, will play a vital role in that,"

"So you said before," Max grumbled. "But you need to remember that he is just a boy. He's not ready to carry the weight of the world on his shoulders,"

"I know that very well Maximus. What we are asking of Elias, we shouldn't ask of anyone. Especially a young man of his age. But we are truly in a desperate position, and time is not on our side. We must strike back against the Sovereign, and if we don't, then we are all doomed," Tiberius said gravely.

"Is it true that they have restarted Project Icarus?" Max pushed himself back to his feet.

"Apparently so," Tiberius sighed wearily. "Dash has returned from the Citadel with reports indicating that is the case,"

"Dash is back?" Max said excitedly.

"Just about, he is in a terrible state, though. He only just escaped the Citadel with his life, the Sovereign burnt down the Jungle in their pursuit of him. It seems like he met our new guests on his travels," Tiberius explained.

"Gaia moves in mysterious ways," Max stroked his beard with his paw.

"Indeed she does,"

"So what did he bring back. Anything concrete?"

"Well we haven't been able to debrief him properly yet, he

is still in the medical wing. But it appears to be solid intelligence from one of Munro's most trusted sources,"

"I don't understand, it's insane. Why would Vicentine even consider starting up that death trap again? I thought that madness died with Voltaire,"

"That's the question that is on all of our minds and, it is one I am afraid I do not have an answer to. However, I think we need to proceed on the basis that our war with the Sovereign is entering a new phase. That is why Elias is more vital to the resistance than ever,"

"Then Gaia have mercy on us all,"

24

———

RAGE

"No! Again!" Max snarled as he kicked Elias's hands out from underneath him, causing him to drop to the ground with a heavy thud. Elias turned on to his back and wiped the dirt off his face, staring up at Max who was stooped over him, baring his fangs.

"I'm trying my best," Elias said through gritted teeth.

"Well, your best isn't good enough. You are supposed to be a Nihon for Gaia's sake." Max roared as he glared down at him, his long golden mane hanging over the sides of his face. He extended his paw to Elias who pushed it away before pulling his legs into his chest and performing a kip-up back to his feet.

"Good," Max said with a twisted smile.

Elias summoned his bokken, which shot across the room into his hand. He ran forward, spinning it wildly around his body. He viciously chopped at Max who calmly took a step back, utterly unfazed by Elias's frenzied attack. He swung his weapon again at Max's face who lent backwards, narrowly avoiding the edge of the bokken as it skimmed over his body. He snapped upright and smoothly slid around to Elias's side.

"Better," Max goaded as he dodged several more attacks with ease.

Elias had spent the last three months training with Max, splitting their time between traditional combat skills and learning to use the arsenal of advanced weaponry the Deltas had access to. Max taught him how to shoot using a Volk V12, the standard-issue assault rifle for the resistance. An old Ronin design, heavily modified by the Deltas with dozens of accessories; extended magazines, digital scopes, improved barrels, anything they could attach to it. Their modified V12s matched anything the Sovereign used. Max also demonstrated to Elias how to use a wide variety of grenades; frag, shock, tracker and most terrifying of all pulse grenades, which altered the gravitational field around an opponent before detonating. While Elias had improved as a soldier, he was still struggling with his developing Nihon powers. The only thing he had managed to master so far was the art of summoning things.

Elias was thrilled the first time he commanded his bokken to his hand. But, the novelty soon wore off, and he grew increasingly frustrated at his lack of real progress. He had also developed the ability to create small waves of energy to push an opponent back. He hadn't quite figured out how to control the skill yet. Sometimes he would send Max hurtling across the room, other times he would struggle to move him at all. The unpredictably frustrated him, and Max's criticism only made things worse.

As Bumble eluded to, he discovered that his element was fire, but so far he was struggling to control it, and the only thing he could do consistently was light candles in the temple with a click of his fingers. Occasionally, he had been able to ignite his bokken into a blazing sword, but the flames would soon die out. He was stronger and faster than ever, but no one would ever call him a Nihon in his current state. A fact Max quickly reminded him, every time they trained together.

He drove his bokken into the ground, flipping over the top and then swinging it at Max's head. Standing unarmed, Max stepped into Elias, grabbing the bokken and stopping it dead in his thick hands.

"Pathetic," Max snarled, his face scrunched up with contempt. "Three months! Three months you've been with me, and this is the best you've got?" Max's whiskers twitched as he stared into Elias's eyes. Without warning, Max yanked the bokken out of his hands and tossed it across the room. He turned away, shaking his head in disappointment.

Elias stared down at his hands, already cracked and calloused, but now red and covered in splinters. He was furious, he knew he wasn't making the progress people expected, and he hated himself for it, but Max was always so vile to him. He was trying his best, but he just didn't seem to be getting anywhere. Day in, day out, he would spend every waking hour practising, and yet Max still treated him like he was his worst enemy.

Elias's stomach scrunched up into a tight knot as he winced with anger, a feeling that had gripped him only once before in his life. His head clouded with memories, visions of a blisteringly cold night. Lost and alone in the snow-capped wastelands, the long night and the eternal fire came back to him. He gripped his brother's emaciated body, shivering as the brutal north winds viciously whipped around them. Elias sat, enraged at the world, wanting to rip it apart, tear it in two and fall into the abyss below.

Then the fire ignited.

Elias opened his eyes, and he was once again in the gym hall. The feelings of hatred and despair he once harboured started to bubble away inside of him again, beginning in his gut then spreading throughout his whole body like a wildfire. The rage, fury and contempt consumed him. Like a bolt of lightning striking him from the sky, his body surged with adrenalin.

"MAX!" Elias's voice boomed.

He stopped in his tracks and turned to face him. Elias charged forward, holding out his arm for his bokken which snapped back into his hand. He jumped up, floating for a few seconds as he glided through the air. As he came closer, he kicked out at Max, catching him clean on the chin. He stumbled backwards as Elias landed graciously on the ground and swiftly slipped to his side, bokken in hand.

Max went tumbling over as Elias swept his legs from under him. He fell flat on his back before quickly kipping-up to his feet, Elias thrust his hand out and a surge of energy flowed from him. An invisible force sent Max flying across the room. He tore through the air and smashed into the wall opposite, the stone cracked as he crashed to the floor with a sickening thud.

Elias released the bokken from his grip as he collapsed to the ground, gasping for air, utterly exhausted. He raised his head and saw Max's limp body lying up ahead. His face hidden beneath his mane. Elias was racked with guilt. What had he done? Max was only trying to help him, and he lashed out like a child. The power surging through his body subsided, and he was left with a sense of emptiness.

"Max!" Elias cried out, crawling over to him. He breathed a sigh of relief when he spotted Max stirring, trying to push himself up.

Thank Gaia, he's alive.

"Not bad, not bad at all," Max said as he struggled to a knee.

"Are you okay?"

"Don't get carried away, boy. You got lucky," he wearily stood up and dusted himself down.

"We might make a Nihon out of you yet. Now, again." Max bellowed as he marched at Elias.

"Leo, throw me the three-quarter-inch fusion spanner," Ginger called out from the other side of the garage.

Leo looked down at the enormous collection of high tech tools in front of him and scratched his head.

"I think its that one," Orix whispered as he knelt beside him, careful to cover his mouth as he spoke, so Ginger didn't overhear him. He pointed to a minuscule object in the middle of the pile, it looked like a cross between a spanner and a blow torch. Leo picked it up and walked over to her.

"Thanks," she said with a smile.

Orix gave him a thumbs-up as he rose to his feet and walked over to a large six-wheeled vehicle propped up on its side. Leo handed the fusion spanner to Ginger, who was busy unscrewing a service hatch on the side of the truck.

"How you getting on?" Leo asked.

"Good. It needs a new girotator though, but then it should be as good as new," she said igniting the fusion spanner, a blast of blue fire exploded from its tip. She pulled down the goggles sat atop her forehead and directed the roaring flame inside the hatch.

"Do we have any girotator's lying around?" Leo yelled.

Orix pulled the vehicle he was repairing back on its wheels and dusted his hands down. "I don't think so, they might have some over at Re-Supply though, Tiberius said they took in a big shipment yesterday,"

Since the trial, Orix had barely left Leo's side. He took his role as his guardian very seriously and had been assisting Leo and Ginger in any way he could. That meant spending most of his days when they weren't in the classroom, fixing up old resistance vehicles in desperate need of repair.

Orix proved to be incredibly adept at repairing everything he turned his hand to. Years on the battlefield, patching up his comrades had given him enough experience to fix almost anything mechanical in nature. Muto, the owner of the garage they volunteered in, was more than happy they had another pair of hands helping them out, even if they were robotic hands. Muto's workshop had never been so productive. The three of them cleared the backlog of repairs and now had a steady stream of vehicles awaiting upgrades. Ginger, in particular, loved the challenge of trying to improve on the original design, adding an exhaust here, a new cannon there, she was in her element tinkering away. The garage also acted as Orix's new home. The dwellings in Albion were too small to accommodate him, so he remained cooped up inside most of the time, rarely venturing outside the safety of its walls.

"I am going to take Orix over to Re-Supply to see if we can pick up a girotator,"

The sparks bursting from the truck came to a sudden stop. Ginger emerged, tossing her tools to the ground as she rushed over to him. She lifted up her goggles and roughly tugged at his arm.

"Do you think that's a good idea?" She whispered, trying to avoid Orix overhearing them.

"What?" Leo replied, confused by Ginger's sudden need for secrecy.

"You know..." Ginger said as she nodded at Orix.

"What, taking him to Re-Supply?" Leo blurted out.

Ginger rolled her eyes. "Yeah, it'll be the first time he's been out in public. You saw how the people reacted at the trial."

Leo flushed with embarrassment. Why hadn't he thought about that? He had been so fixated on their work over the last few months he had forgotten how people reacted at the end of Orix's trial.

"Well, he is going to have to go out at some point, we can't hide him in here forever, and it isn't far. We'll be back in no time." Said Leo, he sounded so confident he almost convinced himself.

"Okay, but don't be too long! If you go missing, I'm breaking out my new mech!"

Leo looked up at Orix. "Right, big man, let's go!"

He walked over to the main entrance and pressed a large red button to lift up the steel shutters. He ducked under and walked across the street, waiting for them to reach the top. He looked back over at the workshop, it was a pretty uninspiring site. A smoke-stained, old, ramshackle building that had clearly seen better days, a small forecourt was brimming with rusty old vehicles parked outside. It certainly lacked the rustic charm the rest of the buildings in Albion exuded. Leo watched as the shutters jerkily shunted upwards, Orix crouched underneath before stepping out. He had been hunched over in their workshop for so long Leo forgot just how big he was. To see him now, with his restoration complete was an awe-inspiring sight, Leo understood why people called his unit the Titans.

Orix was unrecognisable to the rusted and battered robot

they stumbled across in the graveyard. Ginger had taken it upon herself to return him to his former glory, the pair of them devoted countless hours to repair him. Welding, painting, buffing and rewiring until Orix looked like he had just rolled off the assembly lines. Where once stood a mess of mangled metal and rusted parts, now he did not have a scratch on him. His paintwork flush, with a matte black finish and vibrant red stripes. Tiberius and the Council took some convincing to allow Orix to be weaponised again, but after much lobbying, they came round to the idea.

"Ginger is a tough person to say no to," Tiberius had chuckled when he broke the news to them.

As Orix had been designed for special operations; his entire frame had been constructed to conceal a vast armoury. First, they fitted him with two identical battle swords, neatly secreted into his back, only the hilts were visible, cleverly disguised as exhaust stacks jutting out over his shoulders. Orix dedicated much of his spare time to whetting the blades, honing their points until they were so razor-sharp they cut through steel with ease. Next, came hidden, wrist-mounted short blades that could be extended instantaneously to provide further protection during close-quarters combat. His exoskeleton was loaded with every type of grenade they could get their hands on, ready to be deployed at a moment's notice. Finally, they crafted him a new bespoke battle rifle, which fitted snugly into a cavity in his back.

"You good?" Leo asked as Orix stretched out his back, finally able to stand freely.

"Lead the way," he gestured with his giant metal hand.

They made their way down the narrow winding back-streets of Albion, Orix carefully weaved his way in and out of the hundreds of street lamps hanging overhead. The intensity of the ambient lighting sometimes made Leo forget they were so far underground. He thought the architects had done a fantastic job to make the city appear like it was daylight. His head swivelled, marvelling at everything he saw, even after several months of living in Albion he was still fascinated by their new home.

The backstreets teemed with people, and the constant buzz of the crowd made it an exciting place to explore.

But not today, the hair on the back of Leo's neck stood on end as he and Orix steadily made their way through the streets. He noticed people backing up into the shop fronts, not taking their eyes off Orix as he passed by.

"There he is." Somebody whispered.

"Disgusting! What was Tiberius thinking," muttered another.

"Monster!" A voice screamed from a shop in the distance.

They flooded out like ants spilling from a nest. Before he knew what was going on, they were surrounded by an angry crowd, who started to hurl abuse at Orix.

"Get out of here!" A man thundered, flinging a glass bottle at Orix, it flew across the street and shattered on his chest, scraping his fresh paintwork.

"Your kind ain't welcome here!" Shouted another, more bottles and food rained down on Orix. He took a few steps back, trying to escape the flurry of projectiles coming his way.

Leo didn't know what to do, his heart pounded through his chest. He was scared and angry at the same time, these people had never spoken to Orix, how could they treat him like this.

"Please, calm down, I wish you people no harm," Orix said, backing away from the angry mob as more debris rained down upon him.

"Murderer!" Someone shrieked as a flaming bottle came

flying at Orix. He shielded his face, and the petrol bomb exploded over his forearm, he calmly dabbed out the flickering flames with his spare hand.

"Please, I wish only to continue with my journey. I am here to help." Orix said reassuringly.

"Beat it, robot scum. We don't want your kind around here!"

"STOP IT!" Leo screamed. From out of nowhere, he found his voice.

The mob stopped in their tracks as Leo jumped in front of Orix and started to wrestle the bottles out of their hands.

"Stop it!" Leo yelled, grabbing more items from the crowd and throwing them to the ground.

"Orix is trying to help us,"

"What do you know? I was there when those monsters destroyed our home!" A grizzled old man clamoured, hidden behind the throng.

"You can't treat him like this!" Leo shouted again, trying to shield Orix, his tiny frame barely reaching above the robot's shins.

A brick flew out from the sea of people, heading straight for Orix. But before he knew what had happened, Leo reached out and caught it. He looked in amazement at his outstretched hand, he did not understand how he had reacted so quickly.

The mob fell silent and stared at him.

"ENOUGH!" A voice boomed.

Leo looked up and saw the crowd start to disperse, lazily making their way back into the shops, muttering angrily amongst themselves. Walking through the middle of the street was Diaz, Volk V12 in hand, his chunky black dread-locks swinging around his head, flanked by three armed

Deltas. Diaz strolled through the crowd barking out instructions.

"Hey Leo, looks like you guys ran into a bit of trouble. Orix, you okay?" Diaz said, lowering his weapon.

"Everything is fine, thanks to young Leonidas here," Orix said, nodding down at Leo.

"Yeah, I saw that. You are one brave little kid. If you ever think about joining up let me know, with your spirit you'd fit right in with the Deltas." Diaz said, patting him on the shoulder.

Leo's heart swelled with pride, he didn't know what had come over him. It was a gut reaction. He couldn't stand by and watch as they ripped Orix apart.

"Sanchez, Rodriguez you two check out Sector 7. Honda, you are on me. Let's go." Diaz barked as he headed down the street with one of the Deltas, the other two forked off down a side street.

Leo couldn't help but smile. Him in the Deltas, the thought was beyond his wildest dreams. He always imagined his role in the Shadows would be in the background, keeping the city ticking over. No one had ever called him brave before or told him to consider a career as a soldier. He drifted into a daydream, imagining himself fighting alongside Diaz and the others.

"Thank you. Diaz is correct. You were very courageous to defend me like that." Orix said, walking by Leo's side.

Leo abruptly came back to reality, his vision of riding on Orix's shoulders into battle, disappearing into thin air.

"You don't need to thank me, it was the right thing to do," he said without a second thought.

"Nevertheless, few would have faced off against such a ferocious crowd for one of my kind,"

"But you are my friend, why wouldn't I help you?"

Orix stopped and knelt in front of Leo.

"You truly are an exceptional young man Leonidas, never forget that. You will make a great leader one day." Orix's blue eyes glowed so brightly they dazzled Leo.

He was speechless.

"…thank you," he muttered, trying to hide his embarrassment.

"No need to thank me, Leo. I am only stating what is clear for all to see," Orix stood back up to his feet. "Now let's get on our way before I cause any more problems."

Orix and Leo carried on down the winding streets until they reached their destination, a vast warehouse with the words' RE-Supply' written above in huge neon letters. It looked like something that belonged in the Citadel. Leo made his way inside while Orix waited by the entrance. After a short while, he reappeared with some paperwork in hand.

"Yeah, they've got one. They are bringing it out now."

A store-man, driving a small jeep pulled up next to them. He pulled off a long dust sheet covering the carriage behind him, revealing the girotator, it looked like a massive engine with a rotator fan in its centre.

"Here you go, can you sign here for me?" He handed a small digital docket over to Leo. He was a short, stout man with hardly any neck. His tiny black eyes hiding behind a pair of glasses as he peered up at Orix.

"Howdy big guy, good to see you," the store-man said, pulling on the braces holding up his cargo trousers.

"And you friend, thank you for sorting this out," Orix bent down and placed his hands either side of the girotator and heaved it upwards. "We will put this to good use."

"All done," said Leo as he passed the docket back.

"Great, safe trip home." The store-man said as he slung it into his cabin and jumped back into his seat, swinging the jeep around and driving back into the warehouse.

Their return journey was far less eventful, and a sense of relief swept over Leo when they arrived back in one piece. He spotted Ginger opening the shutters as they approached. She came out to greet them, pulling off a pair of gloves covered in oil and throwing them to the floor.

"About time," Ginger said with a smile. "Diaz told me about what happened." She nodded at the badly scratched paintwork on Orix's chest. "I'm sorry Orix, they'll come around. I'm sure of it."

"You have nothing to apologise for, and thanks to Leo, I made it back in one piece."

"He told me that too," Ginger smiled at Leo, his cheeks flushed red, and he shifted the attention to the shiny new girotator held safely in Orix's hands.

"We got it. It's brand new apparently. The Deltas intercepted a Sovereign convoy last week, so it's like a treasure trove down there at the minute." Leo said excitedly

"Well, bring it inside so I can have a proper look then!"

25

DESCENT

Elias held the bokken overhead and brought it crashing down on Max's staff, he pushed back against Elias, and they both stubbornly refused to give up ground. Their faces contorted with effort as they grappled.

"You will beat me one day boy," Max taunted, shoving his staff into Elias's face.

Elias flowed with the movement and controlled his fall to the floor, in one fluid motion, he rolled back to his feet. He rushed towards Max, jumping into the air and catching him in the chest with a flurry of lightning-quick kicks before landing and quickly sweeping his legs. Elias used his powers to rip Max's staff from his hand before he hit the floor. He stepped over his fallen opponent and pinned him down with his own weapon. Max's lips curled up at the sides into a sinister smile, and his whiskers twitched as he lay prone on the ground.

"Good," Max shoved the staff out of his way and got back to his feet.

"Good?" Elias tossed the staff in Max's direction.

"Is that all?"

"Don't get cocky, you've still got a long way to go. But I'll give you your due, you can fight." Max said, casually catching the staff. "That's us done for today, I'll see you here again tomorrow. 0300 sharp."

Max didn't even look at him as he walked out. Elias slumped down to the floor, still breathing heavily. The sweat dripping off his brow. Nothing he ever did satisfied him. Despite Max's apathy, Elias felt he was finally making some real progress and had settled into a familiar routine. He trained with Max in the early mornings, cramming in a few hours of practice before heading over to the temple to meet Shimada. After that, it was straight to Bumble for more lectures on what was expected of him as humanity's saviour. Elias hated those sessions, he found them so unbelievably dull.

While Max gave him a hard time, he did enjoy the training and learning to use all of the Deltas equipment was a nice change to sword fighting. With Leo's help, he had gradually worked through the textbooks Bumble loaned him from the Grand Library, 'The Legend of the Earth Waker' and 'Five Elements: The Lifeblood of Gaia" by Sage Doran, 'The Elder Scrolls' by Grand Master Mutashi, and 'Defining Life' by First Master Trudelle. This was not an experience Elias enjoyed, it took him twice as long as it would anybody else to pick things up.

Leo once again tried to teach him how to read, but Elias found this the hardest skill of all to grasp, he still felt anxious every time Bumble gave him a new book. They seemed to be written in a different language, from a different time. He would stare at the pages, hoping somehow he would magically absorb their teachings without reading them. The words on the page would morph and transform into one big swirling mess before he slammed the books shut, trying to clear his head.

Thousands of years of history were captured within their pages, Elias thought it might take him that long to finish them. Luckily, Leo was so fast at reading, it gave him hope the end was almost in sight. His brother devoured every one of the books he brought home. They worked out a system where Leo would read the books before sitting down with him to explain the key concepts. That way, he could at least pretend he understood them. In truth, he thought this was a waste of time. What good would learning about the past do in their fight against the Sovereign? Leo was astounded by some of the things he read in the books, they would stay up late at night discussing all the weird and wonderful things he had learnt. Like the prophecies predicted by the first Sages of the Nihon, monks who dedicated their lives to studying the ways of the Nihon through the ages.

Over a thousand years ago, the Sages foretold the coming of Voltaire; predicting an age of destruction when a Nihon would betray Gaia and use her power to drive humanity to the brink of extinction. It was known as the final conflict. Sometimes the weight of all the history overwhelmed him, and he would think back to his days in the Jungle; when life seemed simpler. Just him and Leo, against the world, the way he liked it. But he tried his best to block out those concerns and focused on taking one day at a time, hoping eventually, everything would fall into place.

Elias pulled himself back to his feet, finished packing his things away and pulled a hoodie over his head. Something Leo read the night before had really stuck with him. 'Defining Life' claimed that the tradition of master and apprentice had only been established after the death of Golgordorf the Great's son.

He was destined to become the next Nihon but died in child-birth, forcing Golgordorf to seek out an apprentice. Elias wanted to discuss this passage with Bumble before he headed over to the temple.

He swung his rucksack over his shoulder and set off for the monastery. When he arrived, he noticed the giant front doors where ajar so he quietly let himself in and walked along the dimly lit corridors. As he reached the entrance to the Great Hall, he overheard a conversation taking place inside. Elias's curious side got the better of him, and he quietly snuck up to the door, pressing his ear against it. Instantly his hearing sharpened, honing in on the sounds coming from the room. The tick of the clock, the flickering of the lights, the footsteps of those pacing around inside and, most importantly of all, every word of the conversation.

"He is not ready, I don't care what you say," a voice said, Elias recognised it straight away, Max.

"He isn't progressing as we hoped, he has yet to learn even the most basic of Nihon skills." Another voice added, Bumble.

"That's an understatement, the boy can fight alright. He has a warrior soul, but as a Nihon, he is nowhere near ready. He tries his best, but we expect too much of him. At his age, he should have been training for over fifteen years by now. He is too far behind." Max grumbled, Elias had not heard him talk like this before, he sounded genuinely worried about him.

"I know, I know, but we need him to be ready." A third voice spoke, Tiberius.

The room fell silent for a few moments.

"Plans are afoot within the Sovereign to re-start Project Icarus. We need a Nihon now more than ever." Tiberius said gravely.

Elias pushed his ear closer to the door, his mind racing.

Bumble's voice cut through the silence. "I fear if we place too much pressure on him, he too could stray from the path. The boy has a temper, Max can testify to that, having been on the receiving end of it on several occasions." Bumble said flatly.

"He is powerful, there is no doubting that. He's hit me with some strong blows since we started, but he can't manage his emotions. The mana overwhelms him, and he lashes out like a child."

"I don't think Operation Lightning can succeed without him," Tiberius said.

"Then we must postpone, he is simply not ready", Bumble added.

"I disagree, I say we go ahead. If we can convince Mako to let Orix join us, then we don't need the boy." Max said. "Give me a spec ops robot over a Nihon any day of the week."

"Postponement is not an option," Tiberius said, "The Sovereign must not be allowed to complete Project Icarus, there is no time to waste, we must strike first."

Project Icarus, Operation Lightning, what on Earth were they talking about and why was he not ready to be involved in it. Dozens of questions were buzzing around his head when suddenly he lost concentration, and his rucksack slipped from his shoulder, hitting the stone floor with a loud thump.

Elias heard footsteps inside the room as somebody reached for the door. He grabbed his rucksack and bolted, making a racket as he raced down the corridors. Tiberius yanked open the door and scanned the dark hallway, but Elias was nowhere to be seen. He didn't look back, running as fast as he could to the grounds of the temple. When he staggered to a stop at the bottom of the Juniper Falls, his head was spinning. How could they talk about him like that, he was trying his best, but his best was not good enough.

His hands started to tingle, and he clenched his fists together, trying to force some feeling back into them, but it was useless, the numbness was overwhelming. The sensation started to spread up his arms, consuming his entire body. A quiet rage, grew inside of him as his head started to throb. The tingling became stronger and stronger, forcing Elias to his knees. Writhing in pain, he let out a shriek as he began to overheat, sweat pouring down his face. His hands were burning up and started to turn a violent shade of red. He thought he was about to explode with anger.

Elias watched in horror as his hands were set ablaze, he waved them in the air frantically trying to put them out the flames, but it was hopeless, the fire only grew in size. He opened his mind to the darkness he was struggling to hold back, using his fear to feed the rage, pouring fuel onto the fire burning within, as he did, the flames grew more voracious. He slowly rose back to his feet as his body started to acclimatise to the strange sensation and he realised he was in control of the blaze.

Elias toyed with the flames in his hands watching in astonishment as they curved around his forearm, creating a fiery cuff that reached all the way to his elbow. After a few moments staring into the inferno, he thrust out his hands and unleashed an immense stream of fire. He played with the flames for several minutes, shooting blazing fireballs off in all directions. Elias sensed the power of his element surging inside of him like a volcano waiting to erupt.

"Not ready. You'll see..." Elias muttered to himself as his face twisted into a smile, his eyes focussed on the fire raging in his palm.

26

THE DARKNESS

Elias rolled over in his bed and stared at the crimson display of his clock.

23.30.

Sleep was all but impossible these days, he had been getting less and less each night, but this set a new low. Every time he closed his eyes, his mind flooded with images he couldn't stop. Moving at a blistering pace, one after the other, like a whistle-stop tour through somebody else's nightmare. He couldn't tell what was happening, so instead he focussed on the sounds; screams, thousands of them, all crying out at once in a collective howl of despair.

He awoke in a cold sweat and lay there watching the minutes pass by, forcing himself to stay in bed for a little while longer, trying to drift off to sleep, but it was hopeless. Meditation seemed to be the only thing that gave him any respite from these pervasive visions, distracting him for long enough to block them from entering his head. He sat up and rubbed his swollen, puffy eyes, trying to wake himself up. He waved his hand, and his wardrobe opened, his clothes shook them-selves off their hangers and floated over to him. He wearily stood up, barely opening his eyes as the clothes started to dress him as if controlled by an invisible hand.

Elias stumbled through the apartment, grabbed his ruck-sack and bokken before heading out. He pulled up his hood, avoiding the wandering eyes of any passerby's as he briskly walked to the training ground. By the time Max joined him, he had been practising for nearly three hours.

"Let's not waste time, you warmed up?" Max shouted as he sauntered across the room.

"Yep," Elias replied curtly.

"Good." Max kicked up a staff from the ground and charged at Elias who calmly stood still, unarmed.

Elias ducked out the way at the last second as Max viciously swung his weapon at him. Again and again, Elias dodged and swerved out of the way. Max's strikes became more wild and uncontrolled as he grew frustrated from missing his target. Elias rolled to his side as another of Max's savage strikes flew past, he grabbed the staff in his hands, stopping it instantly. Elias and Max glared at each other. Max opened his jaws and let out a thunderous roar, trying to yank the staff out of Elias's grasp. Elias held firm and set it ablaze, engulfing the staff in a ferocious fire. Max let out a whimper as he broke his hold and backed away, holding his scorched hands.

Elias pulled the now flaming staff back and started to flip it around his body, causing it to glow a deep shade of red. Max looked incredulous as Elias launched the staff, hurling the fiery javelin towards his wounded foe. Max raised his hands trying to protect himself, but as the staff reached him, Elias unleashed a burst of fire from his hands and burnt it to a cinder. Max gently opened his eyes and shook the ashes out of his mane, he glanced down at his blackened hands and then stared at Elias with astonishment.

"Again!" Elias shouted as he summoned his bokken to his hand and rushed towards Max.

Tiberius gazed out from his balcony, watching the glowing embers of Albion's street lamps below. His thoughts drifted to Elias again, the boys' perseverance had impressed him since his arrival. He had thrown himself into his new role, spending nearly every waking hour training with either Shimada or Max. He still had much to learn, but with his attitude, there was no reason why he wouldn't reach his potential.

Tiberius wondered to himself whether Elias was prepared for the challenges ahead. The path of the Nihon was not an easy one, and with his newfound gifts came a burden of responsibility that many before him had struggled to cope with. The Council were right; to place the fate of the free world in the hands of an eighteen-year-old boy was a reckless and irresponsible thing to do, but what other choice was there. The resistance was in disarray, and with every passing day, the Sovereign's grip on the Citadel grew stronger.

Tiberius breathed a heavy sigh, and turned away from the balcony, he glimpsed at his reflection in the glass door. The mantle of leadership had taken an enormous toll on him. Where once stood a firm, youthful, full-bodied man with a head full of lush brown hair. He was now greeted by a grizzled and bearded grey face, his hair an ashen shade of grey and his once-prominent shoulders, sunk into his frame. Dark, tired eyes stared back at him.

As Tiberius placed his shaking hand on the glass door

leading to his apartment, he noticed Leo sitting in his favourite armchair. Tiberius took a deep breath, straightened his back and slid open the door.

"Why young Leo, how lovely to see you," Tiberius's face broke out into a beaming smile.

"I hope you don't mind me popping by, Ginger let me in," Leo said, getting up from his chair.

"Please, please sit down, it is always a pleasure to share your company. Is there anything, in particular, you wanted to discuss? Am I safe to assume my daughter hasn't been getting you into any more trouble?" He asked with a wry smile.

"Oh no, we learnt our lesson the first time," Leo added as he sat back down, the synthetic leather chair squeaked awkwardly as he saddled into it.

"Excellent, then how may I help? I sense something is troubling you?" Tiberius's expression dropped into a concerned frown as he took the seat next to Leo.

"Its..." Leo hesitated. "I'm not sure if I should be telling anyone this, but..." Leo anxiously scanned the room, making sure no one else overheard them.

"Please, Leo, everything you reveal to me shall stay between these four walls. I can assure you."

"It's...Elias. I'm worried about him," the words exploded out of Leo's mouth.

"I see. The pressure your brother is under must seem insurmountable at the moment, and all the attention that comes with fulfilling the role of a Nihon in Ronin culture can hardly help. Especially with one as unfamiliar with their customs as your brother."

"I don't think he minds the attention." Leo lied. "It makes a nice change to how we were treated in the Jungle. He loves the training though, he spends all night practising in our room..." Leo trailed off as Tiberius looked unconvinced.

"Its...just...er..." Leo struggled to find the right words.

"Please go on," Tiberius smiled kindly.

"His dreams have started again," Leo blurted out as he finally made eye contact with him.

"And I take it they are more ominous of late,"

"How did you know?"

"If I reveal something to you, you must vow to keep it secret."

"Of course" Leo added quickly.

"You can not discuss this with anyone, not your brother, not my daughter, nobody within Albion, do you understand?" Tiberius's voice hardened.

Leo gulped, he had never heard Tiberius talk like this before. He was now a lot more concerned than when he arrived.

"Okay."

"Your brother is beginning to experience what is referred to in the ancient language of the Nihon as 'Giri'." Tiberius hung his head.

"Giri?" Leo repeated the unfamiliar word.

"It translates loosely in our modern language to 'the burden hardest to bear', and it refers to an unending, internal struggle every Nihon must go through to overcome the darkness."

"The darkness...I don't understand."

"A Nihon is interconnected to everything on the planet, every person, every creature, every mineral, every fibre. All of Gaia's creations have a symbiotic relationship with Elias, it is this connection that grants your brother such incredible gifts. Because of the Nihon's unique ability to communicate with the world around them, they can use this link to manipulate everything we see before us." Tiberius explained.

"But what is the darkness, and why is it causing his nightmares?"

"Telekinesis, Telepathy, neuro-electronic interfacing, mind control, this has been called many things throughout history. In time, and with the right guidance your brother will be able to use this gift to delve into the minds of those around him and if he so wishes, to influence their thoughts and actions, just like he is learning to direct the elements."

Leo's eyes widened.

"But unfortunately, Elias's link to Gaia's creations is two-way, to be able to control it, he must first be able to communicate. Therefore as his power grows, he will become more and more connected to his environment. Unless Elias learns to regulate this connection, the suffering of the world will overwhelm him."

"So that is why he is having the dreams again?" Leo muttered.

"Yes, but these are not dreams Leonidas. Much like the visions that foretold of Elias's encounter with the Great Tree, these are not figments of his imagination. Rather they are the deepest depths of Gaia, a window into the pain her children are enduring." Tiberius's tone became urgent.

"Elias's mind will literally be flooded with the screams of the world around him, he will share the pain and anguish of those who feel it, every last person will reach out to him. That is why this immense burden is known as 'the darkness' by the Nihon who have battled it. A place very few ever have to enter, and those that do are never truly the same afterwards." Tiberius paused and hung his head.

"It can be an all-consuming void of desolation and misery

if not tamed. Elias, like all the Nihon before him, must discover how to shut the door, silence the voices. The despair that will ring out in his dreams will permeate to his very core if he allows it. You must help him fight his way through the shadows." Tiberius said gravely as he raised his head and rested his hand gently on Leo's knee.

"Does…does he know?" Leo asked quietly, fighting to hold back his tears.

"Yes, we've spoken about it. Elias is at a tremendous disadvantage to those that went before him, without the guiding hand of a master I fear his journey will be…" Tiberius took in a deep breath as he sat back in his armchair. "perilous."

"When Voltaire betrayed the Ronin and joined the Sovereign, he shattered an aeon old tradition of passing knowledge from master to apprentice. Handing over the keys to the world and sharing all the hard-fought lessons the Nihon have discovered through the ages."

Questions bounced around Leo's head, but he didn't want to interrupt Tiberius, he'd never spoken to him like this before.

"This was one of the pillars of Ronin society. The apprentice would be guided by his master as the power in their relationship gradually shifted, and in time the student would become the master and seek out his own apprentice. So the journey would begin again." Tiberius continued.

"Without a master, Elias has been cast out into the wilderness. He must learn what he can from the precious few in Albion who still remember the Nihon and from the remaining sacred texts Voltaire didn't destroy before he left." Tiberius stood up and walked around the room.

Leo dried his eyes with his shirt sleeve, he didn't want Tiberius to see him crying. As he watched Tiberius pace in front of him, he noticed his body appeared to have shrunk, as if a crushing weight had suddenly come crashing down upon him. He had come to rely on Tiberius as the man who always had an answer, but in an instant, he saw Tiberius for what he really was. Not just as a leader, but as a man and a father, struggling to grapple with the uncertainty that lay ahead.

"What can I do to help?" Leo asked solemnly.

"You are already doing so much, it is not fair to place such a grave responsibility on one as young as yourself,"

"Please, I want to help my brother," Leo shot up off his chair. "And I'm not that young. I turn eleven next week!"

"Alas, you are correct. I think it is only those who view the world through the eyes of a child, with an incorruptible innocence and virtuous heart that can ever guide someone through their darkest hour. I know that only too well. If it were not for young Ginger, I certainly would not have had the strength to continue fighting when all hope appeared lost." Tiberius walked over to Leo and knelt in front of him, clasping his hand firmly.

"You must never…never, never give up on your brother. No matter where he goes or what he does. Elias will need you in ways you can not imagine. He must face a battle like no other, and he must do it alone. But you can be the star that lights his way, even when he can not see beyond the darkness. You will be the light that guides him home." Tiberius's voice began to break.

"You must study the ancient texts. Use your insatiable thirst for knowledge and your assiduous nature to study the traditions of the Nihon. Understand that which he can not and be by his side when he is most alone." Tiberius's eyes welled up, his once-reliable smile began to waver.

"I will, I promise you I won't let him down," Leo placed his spare hand over the top of Tiberius's.

"I know you won't," Tiberius said as he pulled Leo into his chest.

"Now, I have kept you too long. Ginger told me you've got to re-buff Orix this afternoon after your latest escapades in Albion?" Tiberius's smile returned as he rose to his feet.

Leo smiled nervously "Yeah, we ran into a bit of trouble, and he got a bit banged up. Nothing too serious, though."

"Orix is lucky to have found two such diligent friends, he'll be as good as new in no time. I'm sure of it. Now please don't let me keep you any longer." Tiberius escorted Leo to the door.

"Alright," as Leo reached the door, he turned back to Tiberius and gave him another hug, squeezing him tightly.

"Don't worry, everything is going to be okay. I know it."

Tiberius ruffled his hair. "I wish I had your confidence".

Leo released his hold and opened up the door.

"As soon as I've finished with Orix I'm going to the monastery to see if Bumble will lend me some books," Leo declared, and with that, he was gone.

Tiberius carefully closed the door, and his smile dropped instantly, as the lock clicked shut he slumped down on to the floor, closed his eyes and let out a heavy sigh.

27

THE BRIEFING

"Everyone, you know the drill. Grab a seat, command will be here in five." Sanchez shouted as she stood by a giant screen at the front of the Shadows briefing room.

Elias and Leo were sat at the back of the amphitheatre, almost every seat taken with a member of the resistance. Orix hunkered down beside them on a staircase running through the centre. Leo spotted Diaz down on the main stage standing beside Sanchez, he casually saluted towards Leo who waved back at him enthusiastically.

"You any idea what this is all about?" Leo whispered, still watching Diaz.

"It's something called Operation Lightning I think, I overheard Tiberius and Max talking about it the other night," Elias replied.

"Lightning? Orix, any ideas?"

"I am afraid not, but if I can be of any assistance, I am here to help."

The chatter in the room died away the instant Colonel

Mako, and Max entered. Leo noticed Max's hands and fore-arms were bandaged up in thick white gauze. The lights in the room dimmed as the screen behind Sanchez came to life, she and Diaz saluted Mako before heading off the stage and taking a seat on the front row. Max followed them shortly after and sat down in the empty seat beside Sanchez, leaving Mako alone in the spotlight.

"Briefing for Operation Lightning commences at fourteen hundred, so synchronise watches now," Mako said sternly as she took her place behind the lectern. She spoke in short, sharp bursts. "I'll cut to the chase, our objective is to destroy or denigrate the SYCO facility."

The room fell silent as Mako flashed up an image of the gigantic power station on the screen behind her. Leo cast a worried glance at Elias, who seemed enthralled by the presentation.

"I'm sure you will all be familiar with it; it's been a target of ours for years. Recently acquired intelligence identified two potential structural weaknesses we will seek to exploit before they can be redressed." Mako flicked to another slide, this time to a schematic of the power station.

"Images A & B seen here are our objectives. Two omega class manifolds that are responsible for maintaining the core temperature across the site. Without these, the site will be unable to operate properly, if we are successful in destroying both of them, the Sovereign will have two options." Everyone in the room was transfixed on Mako's every word.

"One; continue to run the facility in its damaged state and risk a full-scale meltdown or two; conduct a complete shut down to repair the damaged manifolds." Mako pointed to a high-resolution photograph of the manifolds, they looked like massive electrical pylons with a cluster of lights around them.

"Our engineers estimate a full-scale repair would require a system shut down for up to six months. Our latest assessment indicated the Sovereign only has enough energy reserves to run for the city for a month at best without the SYCO's output. If we succeed, we will grind the Citadel to a halt."

The amphitheatre burst into life as everybody talked amongst themselves. Leo looked around and saw Diaz laughing as he spoke to some soldiers in the row behind him. He overheard someone mutter that they had never seen an operation on this scale before. He noticed Elias had a big grin on his face.

"What do you think?" Leo asked Orix.

"If the Colonel's assessment is correct then strategically, this could be catastrophic for the Citadel. The Sovereign must know this as well, they would likely have a sufficient contingency plan in place. The facility will be heavily fortified as well, so the Council must have absolute faith in that intelligence to even consider launching such a dangerous mission in enemy territory. There may also be a time-critical reason why we must undertake this mission now that they are not revealing."

"This will be a surgical strike. We will be going in light, I'll detail now which of your units will be involved." Noise erupted again as everyone looked around in confusion.

"Soldiers, quiet please," Mako said and the noise dissipated in an instant.

"This will be a black op, so numbers will be kept to an absolute minimum. Flint, Diaz, you will head up our two, six-man fire teams, call sign Ghost and Hammer, you will advance on Objective A & B simultaneously. Benson, you will head up the quick reaction force and will be on standby should anything go wrong and our boys need reinforcements. I want all our gunships ready to be at SYCO within five minutes of an SOS signal coming in."

Leo glanced over at Elias, he was leant forward and appeared in deep concentration, studying the Colonel's every word. His brow furrowed as he waited for the inevitable news of his involvement.

"Munro, I want your Intel guys running support out of the Ops room. The rest of you expect a busy night, you'll all be pulling double shifts on city watch to cover the slack. I don't think I need to overestimate how important this is for us. If we can pull this off, it might be the beginning of the end for the Sovereign." Mako boomed as she clapped her hands together.

She quickly snapped to attention and gave the audience a firm salute before marching out. Every soldier promptly rose to their feet and returned the salute, holding it firmly in place until she had disappeared from view. All around Leo, the soldiers started to make their way out, Diaz and Flint bumped fists with each other as they shared a joke. Leo noticed Tiberius at the front of the room, talking to Max. Leo tugged at Elias's arm, he still hadn't moved from his seat, sitting motionless, staring at the empty stage.

"Come on Eli, we better go. Doesn't look like we can help with this one." Leo whispered.

Elias ignored him. Leo waited a few moments before trying again.

"Eli, come on man we gotta go," said Leo.

"WELL GO THEN!" Elias exploded, he jumped out of his seat and shoved Leo out of the way. Orix rose to his feet defensively.

"Elias," Orix's voice hardened.

"Leave me alone." Elias muttered as he stormed out.

After searching for Elias around the base, he eventually found him in the training ground. Leo quietly closed the door behind him and watched in awe as Elias launched streams of fire across the room.

"Wow, when did you learn that?" Leo said, watching a massive burst of flames shoot out in front of his face.

Elias carried on shooting streams of blazing fire in all directions until he was exhausted and collapsed down to the floor, panting heavily.

"Eli, it's okay. You will have plenty of chances to help the Shadows." Leo said as he sat down next to Elias.

"Oh nice," Leo laughed as he sat down, the heat from Elias's display had warmed the floor around him. "It's like a heated seat."

Elias let out a laugh "Sorry about earlier." Elias said as he stretched his arm around Leo and pulled him in close.

"Don't worry about it. You've got a lot going on at the minute."

"I shouldn't have reacted like that though, it's not your fault. Or Orix's…it's just sometimes everything gets a bit…erm…much." Elias said as he pulled Leo further into him, ruffling his hair as he did. "Anyway check this out,"

Leo's jaw dropped as Elias stood up and shot out a series of fireballs from his hands. The bright orange glow blinding Leo as they exploded in front of him, one narrowly missed Max who had to duck down as he came marching into the training ground looking for Elias.

"Elias. Tiberius wants to see you back in the briefing room. Now. Leonidas, he wants to speak to you and Orix as well." Max shouted as he walked out.

Elias and Leo shared a confused look before jumping to their feet and following Max. When they arrived, they saw Orix was already there, deep in conversation with Tiberius.

"Boys, thank you so much for joining us," Tiberius said, turning to face them.

"I thought I owed you all an explanation as to why you weren't included," his eyes lingered on Elias.

"Since I stood down from the Council, the Colonel has very kindly sought my advice on military operations in an unofficial capacity. I want you all to understand that it was me who advised against including you both in this operation. Elias, Orix, I thought long and hard about whether or not the Colonel should include you two in the fire teams, and I tell you, it wasn't an easy decision to make."

Tiberius paced in front of the trio, his hands held behind his back.

"There is no margin for error with this one. This could be the tipping point for the resistance. Six months without power will cause turmoil in the Citadel. The Sovereign will have to switch off the grid and divert power to support the critical infrastructure. Without their twenty-four-hour propaganda machine running, we may finally be able to break their hold over the city." Tiberius said as he stopped pacing. "That's why I couldn't include either of you. The Deltas have trained together for years and know each other inside out. If anyone can pull this off without a hitch, its Diaz and Flint. However, I want you both to be on standby as part of the quick reaction force."

Elias tried to hide his smile.

"Now I want you to understand, this is no guarantee you will be deployed. Hopefully, everything will go to plan, and there will be no need for the QRF at all. But, if we need to adapt our plan, then we need our best assets ready to respond, and that includes you two." Tiberius said, his face breaking into a broad smile.

"Really?" Elias asked excitedly.

"Really. Operation Lightning starts at zero two hundred so I want you prepped and ready in the Ops Room at midnight. Now go get some rest." Tiberius saluted the three of them before leaving. Elias draped his arm over Leo's shoulder as they headed out.

"Wow, so you two are going to be part of this after all?" Leo said, trying to hide the concern in his voice.

"As Tiberius said, the whole thing should be completed without our involvement," Orix said reassuringly.

"Yeah, but if we are called upon, we'll nail it!" Elias squeezed Leo's shoulders.

"This is it, Leo, this is what I've been waiting for."

Leo tried to smile as he stared up at his brother and his guardian, but he couldn't. The thought of losing them both was too much for him.

As they made their way down the corridor, Leo spotted an unusual looking man waiting by the main entrance. He was wearing the same old-fashioned clothing Elias wore when training. The man looked unfazed as scores of soldiers dressed in camouflage fatigues, buzzed around him.

"Hidetoshi", Elias said with concern as he bowed.

"Elias," Shimada said softly as he returned the bow. "Leonidas, Orix. It is a pleasure to meet you both." He bowed again to each of them. "May I have a quick word with your brother?"

"Yeah, no problem," said Leo.

"Of course," said Orix as he ushered Leo away.

"Is everything okay?"

"Please take a seat," Shimada gestured to a small bench behind them, Elias sat down and noticed Shimada was carrying a large holdall which he placed delicately on the floor.

"This is something I wanted to do in more salubrious surroundings, but alas, time has betrayed us," Shimada said as he bent down and opened up the holdall. He pulled out a long rectangular object, wrapped in several layers of embroidered cloths.

Elias's eyes widened as he realised what was inside.

"This my student is your katana." Shimada unfurled the fabrics to reveal a large sword hidden inside a black lacquered scabbard. The hilt was braided in black silk, woven around an elaborate pattern of red diamonds. Elias couldn't take his eyes off it as Shimada carefully lifted it up by either end.

"In times long since passed, a Nihon would forge his own sword, creating a mystical bond between man and his weapon. But the last of the great sword-smiths have long since perished, and a new tradition has been established; the passing of the last great sword from master to student." Shimada said, gently placing it in Elias's hands.

It was lighter than he expected, weighing slightly less than his bokken.

"May I?"

"Of course, it belongs to you now." Shimada nodded encouragingly.

Elias cautiously stood to his feet, he held on to the scabbard tightly and with his other hand, gripped the hilt, its smooth silk wrapping felt soft against his skin. His grip tightened as he released the katana from its sheath and held it aloft. He inspected it carefully, the blade did not gleam like the swords hung in the temple. Instead, it was dark and grey with an almost granite appearance. It was just over half a metre in length and had a gentle curve to its edge. A beautiful undulating pattern of waves ran along the surface, like the rings of a tree. Elias wielded the katana in front of him, twirling it over his wrist before practising a few strikes.

"It's..." Elias sliced through the air in front of him again. "beautiful."

"Indeed." Shimada smiled and took a deep breath.

"Elias. Your people need you now more than ever, your journey will not be an easy one, but it is one I know you are capable of taking."

"Thank you." Elias had never heard Shimada speak so openly before. "I can't believe you came to Albion."

"Indeed, it has been quite the experience. But my time in exile is over, we have a new Nihon now."

Without saying another word, he pushed himself to his feet and walked away, leaving Elias standing in the corridor alone, sword in hand.

28

OPERATION LIGHTNING

"Ghost, come in. this is Overwatch." The radio crackled.

"Ghost here. We are about three clicks out. Approaching checkpoint whiskey." Diaz spoke back through his two-way earpiece.

"Okay, Ghost. We've got eyes on you and Hammer now, cameras are live." The radio spoke again.

Diaz stood up and played with the microscopic camera attached to his tactical vest, zooming it on Max's scarred face, his beard had been plaited into a tidy knot that dangled off his chin.

"All clear?" Diaz asked.

"Crystal. Thanks. GPS signals are strong. The QRF is on standby should you need it."

"I don't think that will be necessary. You can tell QRF it'll be a quiet night for them tonight." Diaz laughed.

"You can tell them yourselves when you get back."

Diaz walked through the cabin, checking over each of his soldiers, patting them on the shoulders as he worked down the line. Five Deltas, all dressed in matching state of the art, black battle armour stared back at him. Their chest rig's bursting with a vast array of grenades and enough ammunition to fight a small war. As Diaz nodded to each of them, they slid their helmets down over their faces, three green eyes lit up the darkened cabin as they activated the distinctive trifocal night-vision goggles incorporated into their masks.

"Look sharp boys. Be ready to go in five," Diaz said as he slid open the door of the cabin and perched on the edge, his legs dangling over the bottom of the aircraft. The lights of the Citadel glowed ominously on the horizon.

The Osprey shot through the city, racing in and out of the heavy grey clouds entombing the Citadel. High enough to avoid the cities air defences, but still hidden away from any citizens gazing up at the Iron Lung. Visibility was poor, but the pilots spent years studying mapping data to enable them to navigate from Albion to anywhere in the Citadel at ease. The glowing red light above Diaz indicated they had yet to reach their destination. He looked out and spotted the second Osprey, carrying Flint and fire-team Hammer, flying alongside them. It veered off, heading for checkpoint Yankee.

"You can tell them yourselves when you get back." Colonel Mako said as she stood over the microphone, studying the three enormous digital screens in front of her. They showed a birds-eye view of the SYCO facility, a live stream from Diaz's body-borne camera and a map tracking the progress of the Ospreys.

Mako stood in the centre of the Operations Room, the hub of the Shadows clandestine activities. Three semi-circular banks of desks surrounded her, each housed an intelligence officer, responsible for ensuring Mako had all the information she required.

"How is our access to the SYCO systems looking? I want a live feed of the CCTV cameras on screen 2 now," Mako demanded.

"Yes ma'am, we've had access to their systems for the last month and have been monitoring troop movements in the area intensively all week. I'll patch in a view from camera 227 now." The officer responded swiftly, and in a few clicks of his keyboard, a CCTV feed covering the central platform of the SYCO facility came onto the screen.

"This place is incredible," Elias gushed.

"Indeed, the operations centre is truly the jewel in our crown. Without it, we would not be able to carry out the types of daring raids that the Shadows have become known for." Tiberius said as he lent back into his chair, placing his legs on the desk in front of him.

Tiberius had secured Elias and Leo a place at the back of the Ops Room in an unused bank of desks. Orix was too big to fit inside, so Tiberius arranged for all the communications to be piped directly to him while he awaited further orders in the hanger with the rest of the QRF. As Elias watched Diaz walk through the cabin inspecting the Deltas one by one, he finally understood why the resistance was known as the Army of Shadows. Dressed all in black and with the ominous green glow of their optics, the Deltas had a demonic appearance. Elias could only imagine the fear that would grip anybody who came up against them, they were a terrifying sight to behold.

"So how long should this take?" Leo asked.

"It's hard to tell, but if all goes to plan, they should be back within the hour," said Tiberius

"Looks like are they preparing to land now," Elias pointed to the screens.

"Overwatch we're above checkpoint Whiskey now," said Diaz.

"Insertion authorised." Mako's voice rang out from the radio.

"Understood," Diaz replied.

"Right boys, we are cleared to engage. Stay on my six." Diaz pulled down his mask and gave a casual salute to his squad as the Osprey swooped out of the clouds and descended rapidly down on their target, hovering above an enormous circular turbine.

Diaz threw three thick black ropes out of the Osprey, he attached himself to one of them and jumped out, sliding down to the rooftop of the turbine below. He landed with a thud on the metal roof, five Deltas followed swiftly behind him. The Osprey took off at pace, disappearing back into the Iron Lung. Diaz pulled up his customised Volk V12 and gave a hand gesture indicating the others were to follow his lead. Five sets of green eyes peered over their rifles and nodded in unison. He guided them down a spiralling staircase snaking around the turbine to a wide-open platform that connected to several gangways, each leading off in a different direction.

"Objective Alpha is to the west," Diaz instructed through his earpiece as he approached a towering stairwell opposite them which they used to climb up to another level. At the end of a long gangway, they saw it; a vast metallic chamber, with spiralling exhaust outlets coiled around itself. The manifold.

"Max, you take up a vantage point to the south and give us cover, on my call, I want them dropped." Diaz pointed to two

Sovereign guards stationed high above the manifold in an observation post. Max nodded as he climbed up on the roof of a small outbuilding and hunkered down over his sniper rifle.

Diaz silently guided the Deltas across the platform, ducking for cover behind several walls as they progressed steadily towards their objective. The area was lightly guarded, and their insertion had apparently gone unnoticed. Everything was going as planned so far.

"Now," Diaz said, and in a flash the two guards collapsed, their limp bodies spilling out over the walls of their observation posts.

"Down." Max's gruff voice grunted through their earpieces.

Diaz paused for a split second as he smoothly pulled his weapon closer into his chest and fired at two guards who were patrolling up ahead. The silencer attached to the end of his rifle muffled the sound of the shots, letting out a deadly whisper. The bullets struck the soldiers in the back of the head, and their bodies crumpled to the ground with a dull thud. Diaz turned sharply to the right still holding his rifle in front of him and made his way along the gangway. As he did so, two of his squad broke away and took up defensive positions either side of the staircase.

Diaz swung his rifle around his back and raced to the manifold. He had practised this part of the operation a dozen times in the VR simulator back at Albion, so when he reached the control panel, he would know exactly what to do. Diaz slid his hands over the panel, twisted the handle and lifted up the lid, revealing the inner circuits of the system. He opened up a pouch on the front of his webbing and removed a small explosive charge which he had already prepared with a remote detonator. Diaz carefully placed it inside, activated it and then closed the lid. He placed several more charges at strategic points around the bottom of the structure.

"Charge A is set, heading to exfil now," Diaz said as he reached around for his weapon and headed back, collecting the two stationary Deltas who joined seamlessly behind him as he passed by.

"Charge B is set," said Flint through his earpiece.

Diaz led the way back across the central platform to their exfiltration point atop the turbine.

"Excellent stuff boys," Mako said into the mouthpiece "Get yourselves to the extraction point and await exfil."

Mako paced up and down the room as she watched their progress on the screen, they had dispatched a drone to fly overhead which was providing them with thermal imagery of the site. She tracked the red dots of the Ghost and Hammer squads scurrying across the site in real-time.

The Ops Room watched in silence as Diaz directed his men across the facility, collecting Max en-route before making their way back up the spiralling staircase to the top of the turbine. Flint's team mirrored their every step on the opposite side of the map as they approached their own exfil site.

"Overwatch. This is Ghost we are at checkpoint Whiskey and ready to execute. Are we clear to proceed?" Diaz's familiar voice boomed out from the speakers.

"Exfil is inbound. Light the place up." Mako smiled.

She turned to face the intel officer at the first computer, "Tell those Ospreys to bring my boys home. That place is about to go up in smoke," Mako nodded at Tiberius, who was still sitting at the back of the room with Elias and Leo.

The room let out a collective gasp as everyone watched the live CCTV feeds. One of the manifolds exploded in a massive blast of bright orange flame, debris flying everywhere. The remains of the mangled manifold disappeared behind a vast plume of smoke. A few cheers erupted until one by one, everyone's attention shifted to the second manifold. It was still very much intact.

Mako's face dropped, and she dashed over the Intel officer's desk.

"HAMMER! This is Overwatch! Come in! What the hell just happened down there? Why is Objective Beta still standing?" She screamed into the mouthpiece before slamming it down on the desk.

She stood in silence with her hands on her hips, eyes fixated on the screens ahead.

"Damn it," Diaz spat as he lifted his mask in frustration to inspect the manifold with his own eyes.

He saw that their target had been completely destroyed, a voracious fire had broken out, melting the gangway and everything else in its path. But the second manifold was untouched, Hammer's charge hadn't detonated.

"HAMMER!" Mako screeched through his earpiece again.

"Overwatch this is Hammer. I can confirm Objective Alpha has been destroyed, Objective Beta remains live. Requesting permission to re-engage?" Flint responded.

"Ghost requesting permission to assist with Objective Beta?" Diaz chipped in quickly, sliding his mask back over his face.

The radio went silent for a few minutes as Diaz and his men hunched over the safety railings watching the destruction unfold below. The fire had spread rapidly, consuming the central platform as dozens of guards flooded out, trying to fight back the roaring flames.

"The mission is over. Ospreys are inbound. Exfil as planned." Mako barked, Diaz heard Ghost let out a collective groan as they crouched down behind him.

"Overwatch. Are you sure? We have tactical options on the ground." Diaz asked, sensing the mood of his Deltas.

"That is a negative Ghost. Come home." Mako said sternly, the disappointment evident in her voice.

"Mission is over boys." Diaz grunted. "Osprey's are inbound. We are to evac immediately." Diaz said as his men burst out into a series of complaints. Their dissenting voices were soon drowned out by the sound of the Osprey as it came swooping down out of the Iron Lung and hovered over their position.

Max stood out like a solitary figure on the side of the turbine, watching the carnage through his sniper scope. His whiskers twitched and his nose scrunched up tightly as he picked up the faintest whiff of a familiar smell.

"Diaz!" He roared, "I've got a bad feeling about this."

Diaz ran over to Max and gestured to borrow his sniper rifle, he quickly glanced through the scope and caught a glimpse of a golden flash followed by a flare of smoke streaking in their direction.

"Incoming!" Diaz roared, dropping the sniper rifle as he dragged Max to the floor.

A missile streamed past them and slammed into the side of Osprey. A vicious explosion ripped through the hull of the aircraft as it burst into flames. Twirling uncontrollably, it tumbled out of the sky and crashed into some of the houses on the outskirts of the facility. Before Diaz had time to comprehend what was happening a hail of gunfire hammered their position.

"We need to get off this rooftop now," Diaz said as he readied his rifle and began firing down on the enemy.

The rest of his squad groggily got back to their feet and quickly made their way down the spiral staircase dashing behind cover as they descended.

"We need to hold up here and regroup with Hammer while we try to regain comms with Overwatch," Diaz shouted as he pointed to different areas of the platform. "We need arcs of fire here, here, and here. Max, I need you giving sniper support over there. We need to keep the enemy at a distance, or they'll overrun us in no time."

Without saying a word, the Deltas scrambled to their positions and readied their weapons. Diaz took his place behind a small wall and slowly peered over the top as hundreds of Sovereign troops rushed towards them.

***

Everyone in the Ops Room turned to face Mako who was pacing up and down at the back of the room with her hands clasped tightly behind her back. It was silent except for the static of the radio as one by one, the screens lost their feed and turned black

"Ma'am, what do you want us to do?" the Intel officer asked again.

Mako continued to pace back and forth without saying a word.

"I want the QRF dispatched now," Mako thundered so the whole room could hear. "Patch me through to Orix."

"Yes, Ma'am," The Intel officer sprung back to life as he tapped a few buttons on his keyboard, in an instant, the screens displayed an image of Orix, his blazing sapphire eyes were looking deep into the camera.

"Orix, it is time," Mako said facing the screen. "Are you up to date on the situation."

"Yes, Ma'am," Orix said. "I have been monitoring the progress of the mission."

"Excellent so you know what I am asking of you," Mako said cooly.

"Yes, Ma'am" Orix replied instantly.

Mako turned to face Elias, Leo and Tiberius.

"Elias. You are not a soldier, so I can not command you to go. The choice is your own. But if we could ever do with some of your Nihon magic, it's now." She said, staring Elias straight in the eye.

Elias gulped. He was so angry when he had been passed over for Operation Lightning, but watching the horror play out on screen brought the reality of war home to him. But this was what he had been training for, this was his moment, his chance to show everyone they were right to put their faith in him. To show them, he was the Nihon they had been waiting for.

"I'll go with Orix," Elias said without hesitation.

Leo shared a worried glance with Tiberius as he grabbed his brother's arm.

"Eli, are you sure you want to do this?" Leo asked.

"I have to go, I can't let Orix do into this alone," Elias said as he hugged his brother.

"I'll take you down now," Tiberius said sorrowfully. "Come, time is of the essence."

"Go bring our boys home," Mako said proudly as Elias, Leo and Tiberius walked out.

The buzz of the Ops Room started up again as soon as they left. No one said a word as they walked down to the hanger. When they arrived, it was alive with activity, dozens of heavily armed soldiers hurriedly gathered their gear and rushed on board two Osprey's preparing to take off. Leo spotted Orix standing, rifle in hand, on the ramp of a third, empty Osprey.

"I'm sorry, I can't do this!" Leo cried as he burst out into tears and ran off across the hanger.

"LEO!" Elias screamed as he lost sight of his brother who disappeared off behind a Mech as it attached a turret to the side of their Osprey.

"Leo, please!"

Orix's eyes flickered and dimmed, he nodded at Tiberius then ducked down and boarded the Osprey.

"Elias..." Tiberius said as he placed a hand on his shoulder. "This is a lot for your brother to cope with. He is contemplating losing the two people he cares most about in this world."

"Tell him..." Elias paused as he started to feel himself well up, he stared up at the ceiling and took a deep breath.

"Tell him I love him," he added quickly, trying to fight back the tears.

"I will," Tiberius said as he pulled Elias into a tight embrace.

The whir of the Osprey's engines drowned out their voices as the two gunships hovered off the ground before blasting off at pace, disappearing from view in an instant.

"You are a Nihon Elias, never forget that. Have faith in Gaia, and she will guide you home."

"Promise me you'll look after Leo," Elias shouted as he pushed away from Tiberius and stepped on to the boarding ramp.

"You can look after him yourself when you get back," Tiberius yelled back.

"Promise me!" Elias called out again.

"I will watch over him as if he was my own son. I promise." Tiberius shouted as the Osprey rose off the ground and started to turn away out of the hanger.

"May Gaia guide them," Tiberius said, watching them fly off into the distance.

29

Q.R.F

The journey to the Citadel did not take long, without the need to make a covert entrance into the city the Osprey travelled at breakneck speed. Elias was pinned back into his seat, clutching his safety harness tightly to his chest as they thundered through the clouds.

"We are here," Orix said calmly, sliding open the cabin door as they slowed down and began a rapid descent to the SYCO facility.

Elias studied the firefight raging below. Diaz and his squad were pinned down on the far side of the central platform as dozens of Sovereign soldiers swarmed on their position.

"Where are our gunships?" Orix said to the pilot.

"Down there," The pilot pointed to a smouldering crash site up ahead. "They got hit almost as soon as they arrived, looks like Munro's intel was way off. This place is a fortress, they've got air defences we didn't even know about, something's been firing missiles at our guys since we hit their air space. You two are all that's left of the QRF."

"You need to get us on the ground now," Orix replied.

"Roger," The pilot said weaving from side to side as he nosedived at the facility, Elias clenched his fists as his stomach flipped again.

"Right, I'll have to drop you off here." The pilot's voice screeched through the radio as he brought the Osprey to an abrupt stop. "I can't get any closer, but I'll provide air support for as long as I can."

Elias hurriedly unbuckled his harness, grabbed his sword from the storage unit under his feet and attached it his back using a magnetic scabbard.

"Are you ready?" Orix stared down at Elias as he stood beside him.

"As I'll ever be," Elias said, taking another deep breath.

"Then let us begin," Orix leapt from the Osprey, dropping on to the far edge of the SYCO facility with a tremendous thud.

He immediately reached for his weapon and charged at the enemy forces. Elias followed closely behind him, landing nimbly on his arches and sprinting as fast as he could to keep up with Orix, drawing his sword as he ran.

Orix readied his cannon and began firing massive projectiles across the central platform. The rounds smashed into the backs of the armoured Mech's closing in on Diaz, a burst of sparks spewed out as they lost power and crashed to the ground. Elias split away from Orix and watched in astonishment as the robot cut a path straight through the battlefield to finish off the flailing Mech's. He deposited his cannon in the cavity of his back and in a seamless motion pulled out the two large blades concealed within his armour. He swung them at the Mech, chopping straight through its thick steel armour and detaching its arm in one vicious blow. Orix hacked at the surviving Mech's until they all crumpled into a smouldering heap on the floor.

Elias sheltered behind a steel railing and began launching fireballs at the soldiers as they turned their weapons on Orix. A twirling, golden ball of fire flew across the battlefield and engulfed a group of soldiers who fell to the ground trying to escape the ravenous flames. Elias and Orix steadily fought their way forward, and the Sovereign soldiers started to retreat, Elias's incessant fireballs forcing them to fall back from their positions. Orix launched several more explosive projectiles into the clusters of withdrawing troops, sending them soaring in all directions.

Elias charged at three soldiers hunkered behind the charred remains of a burnt-out wall. As he approached, he drew his sword and ignited it, setting the blade ablaze. One of the soldiers reached for his knife and slashed at Elias, he bent backwards and avoided the tip of the blade which narrowly missed his face. Snapping back to his feet, Elias struck the soldier's knee with the heel of his foot, causing him to fall awkwardly over his leg. He struck the soldier in the face with the hilt of his sword before swiftly dispatching the remaining two with a flurry of flaming sword strikes. The fire danced around the edge of his blade as he twisted it around his body.

The remaining Osprey zoomed overhead, guns blazing as it bore down on the Sovereign soldiers who scattered in a blind panic trying to reach the nearest safe haven. A hail of bullets spewed out from the Osprey's dual-mounted cannons, obliterating them as they raced for cover. Elias and Orix turned to each other and nodded as they scanned the now deserted platform. Suddenly an explosion rocked the area, Elias looked on in horror as a missile slammed into the side of the Osprey causing it to spiral uncontrollably under a veil of smoke, tumbling at speed to the ground.

A distinctive black aircraft dropped out of the clouds and fired several more missiles which narrowly missed the Osprey as it spun out of control. The aircraft was unlike anything Elias had ever seen, a sleek black jet with a distinctive chine leading to the twin engines housed within its triangular wings.

"Elias, regroup with Diaz. I'll try to save the Osprey!"

Orix rushed towards the falling aircraft as it spiralled downward, leaving a dense plume of black smoke trailing behind it. Elias ran over to Diaz and the others who were crouched behind the remnants of the mangled manifold.

Orix raced alongside the Osprey as he tried to track its descent, he took up a position at the point of impact and braced himself. Catching the Osprey's weight as it crashed into him, forcing him backwards. He lost his footing and fell to one knee as he tried to slow its momentum, sparks spewing out viciously as they ground to a halt. The pilot jumped out and surveyed the damage. The left-wing still smouldering, he rushed to put out the flames with a handheld fire extinguisher.

"Thanks. I owe you one," The pilot said as he finished extinguishing the fire.

"What's the damage?" Orix asked quickly "Can you repair it?"

"I think so, but it'll take some time. I'll grab my tools now." The pilot said, pulling open the main cabin door. "What in Gaia's name are you doing here? Orix, you need to see this!"

"What is it?" Orix bent down and peered inside.

"Leonidas." He whispered to himself as he spotted Leo, bloodied and battered but alive as he emerged from a storage compartment.

"I'm...sorry...I...snuck on board. I couldn't let you go on

your own," Leo stammered apologetically as he crawled out from behind an upturned crate of ammunition.

"You idiot. You almost got yourself killed and now what are we supposed to do with you!" The pilot shrieked as he pointed off to the roaring fires in the distance. "This place is a war zone."

"The boy stays with me," Orix boomed as he helped Leo out. "Are you okay?"

"Yeah...I think so" Leo said as he hobbled forward, wincing with every step. His whole body ached, but he couldn't bring himself to admit it to Orix.

"Can you walk?"

"Yeah," Leo said groggily as he rubbed the blood off his head.

"Stay with me, we need to regroup with the others, their position is more defensible than ours. It is too dangerous for you to stay here." Orix turned to face the pilot.

"You stay here and repair the engine, I will escort the boy to safety. Signal us when the aircraft is operational again."

"Got it. Just get that kid outta here!" He yelled as he pulled a toolbox out of his cockpit.

"Leo, we must go now!"

A wildfire now raged across the entire facility as smoke filled the air. Leo hobbled behind his guardian, who continued to fire from the hip as he escorted Leo. The black aircraft was circling above them, a mysterious figure wearing a long white cloak stood on the rear ramp, studying the carnage from above.

"Who is that?" Leo mumbled.

"I do not know little one, but I fear we are about to be overrun," Orix replied, firing off a few rounds at the aircraft as it hovered overhead.

The mysterious figure raised a hand as Orix's projectiles flew towards the aircraft, the rounds appeared to swerve abruptly just before the point of impact, veering off course and exploding into the night sky. Orix and Leo ran over to the others, sliding in beside Diaz.

"Glad to have you with us big guy," Diaz said.

"LEO!" Diaz gasped, catching a glimpse of a bloodied figure emerging from Orix's shadow. Elias turned at the sound of his brother's name.

"What in the name of..." Elias said, spotting his brother limping painfully behind Orix.

"We need to escort the boy to safety," Orix said urging Leo over to Elias. "The pilot is repairing the Osprey, but it will be some time before it is operational again."

"Okay, well that gives us enough time to try and take down the last manifold before we hightail it out of here," Diaz said.

"Gather your men. Time is of the essence." Orix said as they scurried over to the second manifold.

Orix stopped in his tracks and watched as the black aircraft lowered its wings and began to descend, landing on the far side of the facility where the retreating Sovereign soldiers had regrouped. A long ramp lowered from its rear, and an entire company of heavily armoured Sovereign troops came rushing out.

"Diaz you need to see this," Orix said with a flicker of concern in his voice.

Diaz stopped and looked up as over two hundred heavily armed Sovereign soldiers filed out.

"What the..." Diaz said to himself.

"Shock Troops," Max muttered underneath his breath as the troopers marched out in formation, rapidly filtering out across the flaming platform and taking up defensive positions.

They wore glossy black armour, shielded behind a chunky exoskeleton, each carried a large carbine rifle and had a small jump pack strapped to their backs. Several more colossal Mech's followed, their reinforced armour making the machines Orix destroyed earlier look like a child's plaything.

"That's the Sovereign's elite guard," Sanchez said to Elias as she nodded over to the small army gathering opposite them.

A final figure made his way down the ramp, shrouded in a thin veil of mist. A monster of a man, standing over seven feet tall with a solid muscular frame. He wore pristine white battle armour and a matching cloak that draped along the floor behind him. His head was bald and covered in horrible burn scars, his pale skin, almost translucent in colour as if the life had been sapped from him. A chunky mechanical respirator sat over his mouth and nose, behind it, two glowing red eyes, raging like an inferno.

"It can't be..." Diaz said recognising the distinctive battle amour, he stood motionless and stared out in disbelief.

"Voltaire..." Max growled under his breath.

30

THERE IS ANOTHER

Diaz peered over the crumbling wall, it was peppered with bullet holes and covered in deep scorch marks. The SYCO facility was a war zone. Bodies were strewn across the ground, casualties from both sides. Bullet shells piled all around them, a noxious mix of sulphur, cordite and burning flesh filled the air. Voltaire's forces had closed off their exfiltration route and enveloped them against the remaining manifold. Their last line of communications with the Ops Centre went down when the Osprey carrying Orix and Elias crash-landed. It was hopeless, there was no way out.

Diaz pulled his rifle on top of the ruined wall and peered through the scope, aiming at the mass of enemy soldiers gathering around them. He couldn't understand how the Sovereign managed to mobilise a full company so quickly. The same thought kept creeping into his head; they knew we were coming.

"Why aren't they attacking?" Max grunted.

"They're waiting."

"For what?" Max asked.

"For him," Diaz said.

Voltaire stood motionless on the far side of the platform, his chin high in the air as he surveyed the carnage before him. Watching as his troops fanned out and encircled the Deltas. He calmly unfastened his cloak and let it drop to the ground before taking a deep breath and walking towards them.

"What are we going to do?" Elias asked as he crouched beside Diaz.

"Let him have it!" Diaz yelled as the combined force of Alpha and Beta squad opened fire.

Voltaire appeared unconcerned as a hail of bullets raced towards him. He nonchalantly waved his hand, and the shots veered off course, striking a nearby wall.

"Again!" Diaz roared as he slammed another magazine into his rifle.

Voltaire marched through a continuous barrage of gunfire. As the bullets neared the point of impact he lifted his arms, and the metal floor panels beneath him ripped up, creating a barrier. Hundreds of rounds pinged off the makeshift shield as Voltaire stood behind it.

"Elias now!" Diaz shouted as he ducked back behind the wall.

Elias pushed himself up and used every ounce of strength he had left to conjure up an immense fireball. He held the raging inferno in his hands before hurling it at Voltaire. The fireball exploded against the shield, and the whole thing went up in flames, consuming Voltaire in a ferocious fire.

"You did it!" Sanchez gasped as she patted Elias on the shoulder, for a moment he relaxed.

Maybe we might make it home after all, he thought.

"Look…" Max snarled, pulling Elias's focus back to the blazing fire.

The panels started to wobble in their place, shaking violently before being torn in two by Voltaire who stood unharmed.

"That's impossible," Flint muttered as he started to back away.

Voltaire stared at them, his eyes focussed on Elias, they ignited as he threw his arm forward and launched the smouldering panel at Elias. It hurtled towards them, travelling at a breathtaking speed.

"Move!" Sanchez cried as she scrambled to her feet and shoved Elias out of the way. But it was too late, the metal projectile smashed through the wall and impaled Sanchez to the floor, killing her in an instant.

Elias crashed to the ground with a thud, he looked on in shock, staring at Sanchez's lifeless body.

"Fall back!" Diaz shouted as he grabbed Elias by the scruff of the neck and hauled him to his feet.

Elias fixated on Sanchez's corpse before glancing back at Voltaire as he continued his relentless advance.

Max scurried alongside them, clutching his sniper rifle under his arm. With his spare hand, he opened up the webbing belt around his chest and retrieved a pulse grenade, tossing it over his shoulder. It rolled towards Voltaire and exploded in a blast of purple light. Voltaire reacted instantly and contained the detonation within an invisible sphere of energy before launching it at a cluster of Deltas trying to escape.

The explosion engulfed them, morphing into a vortex that pulled everything in its path towards it. A Delta clawed at the ground as he and two others were dragged towards its core. In a flash of blinding light, the vortex erupted, blasting them across the facility and out of view. The remaining Deltas fell back, hunkering behind another series of battered steel walls, damaged during their earlier encounter with the Sovereign. Orix shielded Leo under his arm, trying to hide him from the devastation unfolding around them.

Leo wriggled away from Orix and dashed over to Elias.

"Eli, I'm scared," Leo said as he collapsed into his brother's arms.

Elias didn't know what to say, so he just held his little brother and stroked his hair. This was it - the place where their story ends. In a world of war, there was no happy ending.

Elias looked out at what remained of the Operation Lightning task force; three bloodied and battered Deltas, faces coated with soot and grime, their ammunition spent, their spirits beaten down but not yet broken. A robot who had already taken way more damage than he was designed for and a traumatised little boy. His thoughts dwelled on his little brother, and he started to well up.

"I'm sorry for dragging you into this, Leo." He whispered as he kissed the top of his head.

Before Leo could speak, the wall they were hiding behind was ripped away and shredded into hundreds of tiny pieces. Voltaire towered overhead, for the first time within striking distance, a twisted smile hidden behind his respirator as he loomed down on the brothers.

Max instinctively jumped to his feet and reached for the tomahawk axe on his back. His face scrunched up into a furious snarl as he charged at Voltaire, angrily swinging his axe at him. But time and time again, Max missed his target. Voltaire dodged the blows without even taking a step back. After evading Max's onslaught, Voltaire seized his wrist, blocking the strike. Max let out a thunderous roar as Voltaire squeezed his forearm and the axe fell from his grip. In one fluid motion, Voltaire caught the axe with his spare hand and brought it down in a vicious strike that cut deep into Max's shoulder. Max wailed as Voltaire released him from his grasp, and punched him in the chest, sending him soaring across the platform.

While Voltaire grappled with Max, Diaz stood up and readied his rifle, before he was able to fire a shot Voltaire clenched his fist, and the weapon was ripped away from his grasp. Diaz quickly reached for his sidearm and managed to fire a single round, before it too was snatched away from him. The weapons dropped to the ground with a metallic clunk as Voltaire thrust his hand at Diaz, an unseen force took him off his feet and drove him into a nearby railing.

"Go, Go, GO!" Flint cried as he dragged Elias and Leo to their feet, shoving them back towards Orix. He tried to raise his rifle, but Voltaire hurled Max's tomahawk at him, downing him with one deadly blow.

"It is time little one," Orix said as he ushered Elias and Leo behind him.

"No, no, please don't do this," Leo sobbed as he clutched hold of Orix's finger.

"I am sorry Leonidas, there is no other way. Voltaire must be stopped." Orix said, his eyes dimming as he stared down at Leo.

"Elias, you need to hide, get inside the manifold and do not let them find you. There is still hope. Others will come." Orix said firmly before turning and pulling away from Leo.

"But...I..." The tears streamed down Leo's cheeks as he looked back and forth between Orix and his brother.

"Go NOW!" Orix shouted as he extended his hidden wrist

blades. Elias took Leo by the hand and turned to face the manifold. Leo's eyes remained fixated on his guardian.

Orix positioned himself in between Voltaire and the brothers, he took up a fighting stance with both blades in front of his torso. Voltaire reached over his shoulder and grabbed hold of a hilt hidden in his armour, he pulled out a gleaming silver katana and held it aloft. Voltaire flexed his hand around the hilt, and the blade buzzed with a ripple of electricity. The metal shimmered and hummed with a life of its own as if wrapped in lightning.

Orix charged at Voltaire, chopping down with both of his blades. But Voltaire was too fast. Despite his hulking frame, he moved swiftly and easily dodged Orix's attacks. The robot pursued Voltaire with one wild swing after another. In the blink of an eye, Voltaire attacked, he ducked under Orix's strike and sliced his blade cleanly through the robot's shoulder joint, detaching Orix's arm from his body. Voltaire danced around the flailing robot before severing Orix's remaining arm at the elbow with another clinical strike. He teetered forward, and Voltaire kicked his knee, crushing the joint and forcing him to collapse.

Voltaire turned away and headed for the brothers.

"No!" Orix groaned, staggering forward on his crumpled leg.

Voltaire turned back and raised his hand to the sky, an incredible fork of lighting broke through the thick clouds and landed in Voltaire's hand. He studied the current flowing along his fingertips before unleashing it on Orix. The barrage of electrical energy pummelled him in the chest, and his body shuddered as his circuits were overloaded. His sapphire eyes flickered uncontrollably before fading to grey as his charred remains fell to the ground.

"No!" Leo screamed.

At the sound of Leo's voice, Voltaire turned and glowered at them. Elias carefully manoeuvred his brother behind him as he approached.

"Run," Elias said as he stepped away from his brother, not even turning to face him.

"Eli, No!" Leo pleaded as he clutched at Elias's sleeve. "Please, please, don't do this."

Elias gritted his teeth as he shoved his brother away, Leo staggered backwards and fell over his feet.

"It's me he wants, find somewhere safe and hide."

"But…you…you can't beat him!" Leo shrieked.

Elias stepped forward to face Voltaire, he drew his sword again and ignited it. He launched himself forward, flying through the air with a series of kicks that caught Voltaire on the chest. Elias landed nimbly on his feet, spun the sword over his wrist and swung viciously at Voltaire's head. Voltaire leaned backwards as the blade narrowly missed his face. He bounced back to his feet and sidestepped away from several strikes as Elias pursued him.

Voltaire held his lightning sword in a one-handed stance, easily deflecting Elias's strikes. Every time their blades clashed, Voltaire's weapon let out a hiss of sparks that caused Elias to flinch. He could hear Voltaire sniggering under his respirator every time he repelled another one of his attacks. He felt the rage starting to build up inside of him again, and as it did the flames from his blade began to spread down the hilt, covering his hands.

"Good," Voltaire spoke, his voice strained and mechanical. "Feed the hate."

"Argh!" Elias roared as he lifted his weapon high above his head and chopped down at his enemy.

Voltaire moved at the last second and caught hold of Elias's flaming sword in his hand, stopping the blade instantly. Elias stared into Voltaire's blazing red eyes, and a sense of dread crept over him. He looked down at his sword and the flames started to flicker, desperately fighting to stay alight as Elias tried to wrestle his weapon from Voltaire. Then with a puff, the fire was extinguished. A thin waft of smoke drifting away from the edge of the blade.

"That's enough my apprentice," Voltaire said as he forced him to lower his weapon.

Elias struggled to fight back, his arms started to tremble as he battled to wrench the sword from Voltaire's grasp. But Voltaire's power was overwhelming. Leo jumped up to his feet and rushed over to them.

"Stop it!" Leo cried as he tried to shove Voltaire away from his brother, but he was pushing against a dead weight.

"Leave him alone!" Leo screamed, clawing at the giant, frantically trying to push him away.

"I..." Elias muttered as his face turned red with anguish.

Voltaire gazed down at Leo with a bemused expression on his face.

"am..." The sword started to rise again, somehow having Leo close by strengthened his resolve. Voltaire furrowed his brow and stared deep into Elias's eyes.

"...not your apprentice." Elias declared as the sword broke free and instantly reignited.

Voltaire's eyes widened as Elias swung the sword at his head with a backhanded strike. Voltaire leaned away, and the blade skimmed across the tubing of his respirator.

"ENOUGH!" Voltaire boomed as he stepped forward and struck Elias in the neck with the side of his hand. Elias dropped to his knees, clutching his throat, gasping for air. The flaming sword fell to the ground, and the fire faded out.

"NO!" Leo wailed as he stared at Voltaire and shoved him again.

This time Voltaire moved.

As Leo's hands thumped against his armour, a shockwave reverberated between them that sent Voltaire flying. He hurtled back across the platform and crashed into his shuttle, causing a massive dent in the metalwork.

"The boy! Kill the boy!" Voltaire ordered as he crawled forward on all fours, his damaged respirator hanging loosely off his face. He staggered back to his feet, grasping at the ramp of his shuttle for support.

The Shock Troopers moved at speed, using their jump packs to take giant strides across the platform, manoeuvring together in perfect symmetry as they advanced. Leo slumped on the floor beside his brother as he struggled to breathe. He sat, staring dead ahead, his eyes overwhelmed by everything unfolding around him.

He wasn't sure how long he sat beside Elias, consumed by the horror. When he finally rose to his feet, time appeared to stand still. Silence surrounded him. He saw the battlefield clearly now. Diaz crawling on his knees, trying to reach his rifle. Max fighting to stem the flow of blood from his shoulder. Sanchez's lifeless body pinned to the floor under an enormous steel spike and Orix's charred remains. He glanced down at his brother, writhing in pain, clawing at his throat.

No longer afraid Leo began to walk towards the legion of Shock Troopers as they opened fire. He studied the sea of bullets slowly approaching, taking an age to reach him, as if travelling through water. He held out his hand, and in an instant, they stopped, hanging in the air like floating raindrops.

He stood perfectly still, one hand raised, surrounded by the swarm of tungsten tipped rounds hovering in front him.

Elias dragged himself to his knees and looked on, astonished by the sight before his eyes.

Leo clenched his fist, and the bullets dropped to the ground one after the other, creating a crescendo of metallic dings. The sound of gunfire stopped as the Shock Troopers looked on in confusion. Leo turned his back on them and made his way to the manifold. He stopped by Orix's smouldering corpse, staring up at the monstrous structure in front of him. A mesh of twisting metal and chrome wires, looped around a monumental dome. Leo glanced down at his fallen guardian, his eyes lingered on Orix's scorched chest plate, the fatal blow.

A sense of despair flooded over him, and something surged through his veins, a sensation he had never encountered before. He let out a primal scream and fell to his knees. As he sank to the ground, an enormous wave of energy exploded out from underneath him. It spread outwards and crashed into the manifold, causing it to tremble and groan as its foundations started to collapse, buckling under the immense weight.

Leo pushed himself back to his feet, his eyes glazed over with a white shroud as the twisted remains of the manifold tumbled down in front of him. Moments before the ruins hit the ground, Leo thrust out both of his hands, and the falling rubble stopped dead, hovering like a destructive cloud. He brought his hands over his head, and as he did so, the floating debris followed, with a final cry, he flung his arms forward. The wreckage flew overhead towards the stunned Shock Troopers.

Elias stared up at the colossal shadow of the manifolds remnants, the darkness covering him for a few fleeting seconds as it passed by above. The panicked Shock Troopers threw down their weapons, scattering off in all directions as they desperately tried to escape. The wreckage hit the ground with an earsplitting crash, decimating everything in its path. The entire central platform was destroyed beyond all recognition; a mess of mangled steel, blood and bone. Every enemy soldier wiped out, their shuttle obliterated.

Only one figure remained.

Voltaire stood out like a solitary star in the night sky, standing in the centre of the newly created wasteland, untouched by the devastation around him. His pristine white armour, now blackened and torn to shreds. He lifted his head, holding his respirator in place, his glowing red eyes locked on the brothers.

Leo stood on the far side of the facility, staring at his hands in a trance-like state. He raised his head and took a few tentative steps forward, unsteady on his feet, then without warning, he collapsed into a heap on the floor.

The battle was over.

31

———

BLINK

Elias heard the familiar sound above, hidden amongst the ash-like clouds, an Osprey was approaching. He rolled to his side and dragged himself to his feet, still clutching at his throat. He looked around at the carnage surrounding him, the facility was as a wasteland, bodies everywhere. He spotted his brother laid on the floor and rushed over, skidding to his knee's alongside him.

"Leo, Leo!" Elias shouted, trying to rouse him. "Talk to me!" He held Leo's limp head in his hands.

Hands trembling, Elias shook Leo more vigorously, and as he did, Leo's eyelids began to flutter.

"That's it bro, come back to me," Elias said as he stroked his brother's face.

"Eli," Leo said weakly as he drowsily opened his eyes.

Elias's heart leapt, he was alive. He held his brother tightly to his chest as he knelt beside him.

"What...happened?" Leo's eyes opened wider.

Before Elias could respond, he saw an Osprey break through the clouds and land on the far side of the facility where the manifold had previously been located. He watched as Diaz heaved Flint on his shoulder, and a severely wounded Max dragged Orix's charred remains towards it.

"There's no time Leo, we have to get out of here. Can you walk?" Elias asked as he heaved Leo back to his feet.

"Yeah I think so," he said, hobbling forward painfully.

Elias looped Leo's arm over his shoulder for support as he guided him over to the Osprey. Their legs buckled as they felt the ground tremble, causing them to stagger forwards. Elias crashed to the floor, and Leo fell to his side as a huge crack tore open the platform in half between them.

Elias scrambled on all fours and looked up as Voltaire stood before them, his arms held aloft as he ripped the facility apart.

"LEO!" Elias screamed as his brother was driven further away from him. He could hear the sound of the Osprey as it ignited its engines and returned to the air, hovering overhead. Max and Diaz stood on the opened ramp, urging Elias over.

"Elias! Quickly!" Diaz screamed.

"I can't leave Leo!" Elias shouted as he looked back at Diaz.

"There's no time for this," Max roared as he jumped off the Osprey and grabbed hold of Elias, with one hand he threw him by the scruff of his neck onto the ramp. The Osprey swerved as Voltaire launched a jagged piece of metal at it, Elias, Max and Diaz all tumbled over as the Osprey manoeuvred around the facility towards Leo.

"Leo!" Elias screamed as he staggered back to his feet. "You'll have to jump!"

The Osprey narrowly avoided another projectile as the pilot's voice came screeching through the radio. "We haven't got much time, we need to get out of here before he hits us. This is the last Osprey in our fleet, if we go down ain't nobody coming for us!"

"Give us one more pass, we aren't leaving that boy behind!" Diaz roared into the radio as he slammed the handset back into place.

Voltaire marched towards Leo as the facility collapsed around them, creating a vast chasm between Leo and the Osprey.

"You need to jump!" Elias screamed as he leaned off the ramp, hanging from one of the landing legs, extending his free hand.

"We need to go now!" The pilot screamed again as the Osprey started to tilt away from the platform.

"Leo, jump! NOW!" Elias pleaded.

Leo took one last look at Voltaire before breaking out into a sprint, running as fast as he could and flinging himself off the edge of the platform. Elias leaned out even further, reaching out with his fingertips, desperately trying to reach his brother. Time seemed to stand still as Leo frantically kicked out at the air, trying to cover the distance between them. The air around him buzzed with static, shimmering with a radiant purple glow, appearing to bend and refract, before erupting into a flash of dazzling light.

Elias was momentarily blinded and turned his head away for a split second. When he looked back, Leo was nowhere to be seen. The Osprey banked away from the facility and raced up towards the sky. The last thing Elias saw before he disappeared into the Iron Lung, was Voltaire's blazing red eyes, glowing like burning coals. He slumped back onto the ramp as it jerkily closed in front of him. He sat, mouth open, aghast. His eyes not believing what they had just seen.

Leo. His brother. Was gone.

32

____

THE WAY

Elias slowly opened his eyes and stared up at the cold, grey interior of the Osprey. The lights of the city flashed by as they flew across the Citadel. He looked to his right and spotted Orix, his shattered and broken body burnt beyond recognition. A mess of warped metal and tangled wires. But his eyes still flickered, the unmistakable blue shimmer remained. He was alive.

"Argh," Elias groaned as he tried to sit up, every part of his body ached.

"Easy, easy," Diaz bent forward out of the seat in front of him. He gently guided Elias back down to the makeshift bed. His dreadlocks were matted with dried blood and grit, he was wearing a thickly padded bandage over one of his eyes.

"What...what happened?" Elias flinched as he spoke, even talking hurt.

Diaz shook his head, struggling to find the right words.

"Man, I don't even know where to begin..."

"Leo - where is he?" Elias asked urgently.

"He's... he's gone."

"What!" Elias screamed as he shot up out of bed, craning his neck to search the cabin. "What happened? Where is he?"

"I...I don't know Eli, he...just disappeared."

With Diaz's words, the memories of his final moments at the SYCO facility came flooding back to him. His brother...saved them. Somehow, he destroyed everything around him, and Voltaire, even Voltaire couldn't stop him. Then he just…vanished.

Elias didn't know what to say. "What...what happened?"

"Your brother is a Nihon Elias," Max said as he rested one of his giant paws of Elias's shoulders.

"But... that's impossible," said Elias.

"I know, but it is also true. You saw as well as I did, the raw power in your brother's hands. I have never seen anything like it, he decimated an entire company of Shock Troopers like they were nothing."

Elias sat in stunned silence. None of this made any sense. His eyes started to well up as he stared down at the rows of black body bags lined up neatly together on the floor; the remains of their fallen comrades. On the far side of the Osprey, he noticed Flint, his bloodied and battered body lying prone in a medical pod.

His mind was racing. This wasn't the way their story was supposed to end.

"Do..." Elias couldn't bring himself to ask the question. "Do you think he is still alive?"

Max took a deep breath. "I know he is."

"If he's out there we'll find him, I promise," said Diaz. "But first of all, we've gotta figure out what the hell is going on. Try and get some rest Eli, its gonna be a while before we get back to Albion."

Elias shuffled back down onto his bed and stared blankly out of the open cabin door, watching as the city lights faded into the distance. Diaz, aided by Max hobbled over and sat down on the edge of the open door, his legs dangling over the side of the Osprey.

"You fought well today Diaz..." Max paused before grunting "for a human."

"I'll take that as a compliment, Max. How you holding up?" Diaz asked as he looked up at the bloodstained bandage covering Max's torso.

"I'll live."

"What do you make of all this? Is Leo really a Nihon?"

"Without a doubt, and a powerful one at that. You saw what he did to Voltaire and his troopers, he slaughtered them without raising a sweat."

Diaz shook his head. "How can that be possible, master and apprentice, that is the way it has always been."

"I know, that is the way. But not anymore, there are three Nihon now."

"I still can't believe Voltaire is back, I thought we'd seen the last of that monster. How is he still alive?"

"I don't know, he looked as much machine as man now. The Autarch has a lot of resources at his disposal."

"But not even he could have survived the blast at Icarus, the fires still rage there to this day."

"Anything is possible when a Nihon is involved, and Voltaire was the most powerful Nihon in history. Well, until today." Max said, looking out over the desert, the wind blowing through his long blond mane and ruffling his whiskers.

"They knew we were coming, Max."

The words hung in the air as the pair exchanged a worried glance.

"I know," said Max "this can mean only one thing..."

They paused and looked around at the survivors; a broken Elias, a barely functioning Orix and Flint, severely wounded and fighting for his life.

"There is a spy amongst us," Max added.

"My concern is if they knew we were coming, then they know about Albion," said Diaz.

Max grunted in agreement. "All I know for sure, is the only people we can trust right now are on this Osprey."

Elias knelt over his rucksack and shoved in the last of his kit. He grabbed his sword and attached it to his back. At the sounds of footsteps entering the hanger, he swiftly turned and reached over his shoulder for the hilt.

"So you are really going to do this?" Tiberius asked as he approached.

Elias's grip on his sword relaxed as he heard the familiar sound of Tiberius's voice.

"I don't have a choice. He's my brother. I have to find him."

"I know Eli, we all want Leo back home with us. We've had our men scouring every intelligence channel for any sign of him. But we've heard nothing."

"I know, that's why I need to go."

"But go where? We have no idea where he is."

"That's not going to stop me finding him,"

Tiberius shook his head in disappointment. "But your wounds haven't healed yet, you must rest. The resistance needs you now more than ever."

"I didn't want any of this Orion. I'd give up all of my

power in a heartbeat to have him back next to me. Leo is the only thing that matters to me and, I will never stop searching for him."

"I understand Elias and I promise you, we will use every resource at our disposal to find him."

"You already promised me that you would look after him, and here we are."

Tiberius looked crestfallen at Elias's remark, he sighed and gently nodded his head.

"Okay, I won't try to talk you around again. But please take this." Tiberius handed Elias a small device that looked like a metallic cigar.

"What is it?"

"A one-way communicator, when you find your brother. Activate it, and I will send every last man we have to bring you both home."

Elias took the device and slipped it into his pocket, forcing a small smile as he did. Tiberius patted him on the shoulder and grimaced.

"May Gaia guide you."

Elias picked up his rucksack and swung it over his shoulder before stepping onto the ramp of the resistance's last remaining Osprey.

"Thanks for doing this," Elias shouted through the cabin.

"No problem," the pilot replied, leaning out from the cockpit.

"Well, I won't forget it. Just get me out of Albion, and I'll head out on my own."

"I don't think so, soldier," said Diaz.

Elias looked down and watched as Diaz hobbled up the ramp, dressed in desert battle armour, rifle in hand, his eye still heavily bandaged.

"I can do this on my own,"

"I know you can, but we stand together," said Diaz.

Max marched past Diaz and up the ramp, stowed his equipment in the overhead lockers and sat down next to Elias without saying a word.

"Thank you,"

Max strained a smile and nodded his head.

"There's one more who wanted to join us," said Diaz as he turned back and welcomed another person onto the Osprey. He was dressed in a long trench coat, and Elias recognised his face instantly.

"Dash," Elias said, rushing over to greet him.

"You don't have to do this, you should be with your family,"

"I know, but I can't let you guys do this on your own." Dash held Elias at arm's length, measuring him up.

"You've come a long way, son. Now, let's go find that brother of yours."

33

ABYSS

Leo awoke with a jolt, his body shuddering as he sat trembling in the corner. He pushed himself up against the wall and stumbled forward, clutching his hands tightly to his chest. His vision was still blurry, slowly coming back to him with every step. He looked up and saw that he was in a grimy bathroom. He didn't recognise it as anywhere he had been before. It wasn't Albion, and it definitely wasn't the Jungle.

He noticed some light peering underneath the door. He staggered towards it, using one of his hands to steady himself against the wall. Running his fingers across the broken and chipped tiles. The ringing in his ears eased off, and he picked up the sound of music playing up ahead, a thunderous electronic bass line.

Leo pushed open the door and was instantly bathed in the bright glow of a green neon light. He raised his hand to shield his eyes, and somebody barged into him, pushing him into a dank, humid room. He was surrounded by people, jumping and dancing to the synthetic music, their bodies slick with sweat. He fought against the crowd, trying to push his way through the sea of bodies.

It was dark inside, and Leo couldn't make out what was going on, he glimpsed the lasers shining overhead. Every few seconds, the neon glow illuminated those around him. Augs, hundreds of them, huddled together tightly as they danced.

"Hey little dude," an aug said as he lifted his pink shutter shades and stared at Leo with his ocular implants.

The aug rested his metallic hand on Leo's shoulder and swayed him back and forth to the rhythm of the music. As the aug's hand rested on his shoulder, Leo had a sudden flashback to SYCO, Voltaire's' blazing red eyes burning down on him. He suddenly came back to his senses and shoved off the aug's hand. Pushing himself through the crowd as he frantically tried to find a way out. The sound was deafening, the thumping bass lines reverberated through his chest as he raised his hands to his ears. He crouched down and started to scream, but no one heard him.

He perched in a corner, rocking back and forth when suddenly the music stopped. The lasers went off, and the entire room was plunged into pitch-black darkness. Leo released the grip around his ears and heard the crowd starting to chant excitedly, anticipating a sudden return of the beat. Leo heard a loud whump as one by one, the distinctive green glow of the exit signs illuminated all around them. The crowd let out a collective groan of disappointment and started to grumble amongst themselves, others continued dancing on their own, oblivious to what was happening. Figures, hidden behind bright LED torchlights came bursting through the exits.

"Right every one out!" A voice shouted from behind the light.

Leo had no idea what was going on, but he stood up and started to follow the lines of people heading for the exits.

"What's going?" Someone asked.

"Quick hide the noops," another whispered.

"We gonna get our money back or what?" an angry aug asked the man holding the flashlight.

"Yeah, yeah, just get up the stairs. The cashier will sort out refunds." The man said, flashing the torch up a steep staircase.

Each step had an emergency light on it, outlining the path ahead. Leo was carried along by the swarm of people, all begrudgingly making their way outside. They spilt out onto a side street, and he felt the cold air hit his face.

"What the..." a voice muttered.

"What happened to the lights?"

"Blackout!" an aug shouted as he grabbed two neon green glow sticks from his pocket and started dancing to his own beat.

Leo drifted away from the augs and wandered along the street. After the deafening noise of the club, it was eerily quiet. Streetlamps flickered overhead, struggling to stay alight. He carried on walking until he stepped out on to a vast city square, teeming with people. He swivelled on the spot, taking in his new surroundings. Shops, hundreds of them, for as far as he could see, selling every kind of tech imaginable. Next-generation cybernetics he didn't even know existed. But every shop appeared closed, their interior lights and over-head signs all turned off. Leo noticed people being ushered out of the shops and into the square. They all looked confused and slightly bewildered by what was happening.

He looked up, and his jaw dropped, up ahead was the biggest cityscape he had ever seen. Thousands of glass panelled, high-rise towers, all covered in massive digital advertising screens reached up to the sky. All of the screens were blank, except one, situated in the centre of the tallest building, a vast skyscraper penetrating the clouds above. He stood rooted to the spot as those around slowly joined him. Everyone stood together as they watched Autarch Vicentine address the city.

"Children of the Citadel, it is with deep regret that I must inform you that tonight, we have been the victim of a callous terrorist attack. One of our city's main power stations, the SYCO facility, which I know many of your loved ones work at, has been destroyed by the Army of Shadows."

Leo's eyes widened as he listened to Vicentine's words.

"My men are working tirelessly to restore power to the city, but how long this will take, I am unable to say. We are focussing our efforts on returning power to our hospitals and emergency services. Thousands of brave utility workers and soldiers have died as a result of this cowardly attack, and many more will die before this crisis is over."

Leo couldn't believe what he was hearing. Was it true? Had they really killed all those people?

"These terrorists will not succeed, we will not be cowed by them, divided and forced into changing our way of life. We will defeat this scourge. Today marks the turning point in our war with the Army of Shadows. I will not rest until every last one of them has been wiped from the face of the Earth." Vicentine slowly shook his head.

The screen split in two as a grainy CCTV image flashed up next to Vicentine's video stream.

"This is not a child, this is the terrorist responsible for the devastation at the SYCO facility. He may still be in our city. We must find him." Vicentine roared as the video stream cut to black and was replaced by a wanted notice, containing information about the alleged attacker and details of a generous reward for his capture.

Leo gazed up at the giant screen in disbelief, staring at his own reflection. Unable to comprehend what had just happened. He pulled up his hood and stepped back from the people who had gathered around him to watch the announcement. Slowly navigating his way through the crowd as he felt the eyes of the Citadel bearing down upon him.

ABOUT THE AUTHOR

Cole Martyn spent his childhood lost in the magical worlds of Tolkien, Herbert and Lucas. He discovered the joy of writing at an early age but took over twenty years before finally sitting down to write the science fiction series he had always wanted to read.

He lives in the UK, with his wife, young children, and an ever growing collection of Star Wars memorabilia.

God in the Machine is his debut novel.

www.godinthemachine.co.uk

Printed in Great Britain
by Amazon

1cd3380b-a51c-4198-959c-c86846810cdeR01